IN HER PLACE

Replaced
Book 2

NOLON KING
LAUREN STREET

STERLING & STONE

Chapter One

DENISE WAS the first one to see her sister Laura's ultrasound. "Look at those feet," she said. "He's a Grady for sure."

"Mom always said we had Flintstone feet," Laura said with a laugh. She ran a hand over her baby bump. "I'll love him just the same, Flintstone feet and all."

"I love him already. And just for the record, I plan on spoiling him until he graduates college. I'll be his favorite aunt."

"You're his only aunt," Laura corrected.

"Semantics."

Once they were done cooing over Denise's nephew and the doctor dismissed them, they headed out to the parking lot to Denise's SUV. Denise climbed behind the wheel and started the engine while Laura fiddled with her seatbelt. "Do you need an extension?"

"Smart ass. I'm not *that* big."

"Yet!" Denise added with a grin. "If those feet of his get any bigger, you'll need a C-section. Or two."

"Ha ha."

"Seriously," Denise said. "You look adorable. And that thing they say about pregnant women glowing? If your glow was any brighter, I'd need to wear sunscreen."

Laura ran her fingers over the pearls around her neck. They went well with the yellow sundress she wore. But Laura always looked gorgeous. She had that quality that made men want to have her and women want to be her best friend. She smiled that *Madonna* smile, as Denise called it — the one where her lips turned up, but her gaze turned inward, as if already looking into the future of the child growing inside her.

"Don't get too attached to those pearls," Denise said. "They'll be mine in a few months."

"Pearls before swine," Laura said. An old joke, but one that made them both smile.

Denise could almost see her mother beaming at the two of them, the ever-present pearls around her neck. When their mother had passed, Denise and Laura both wanted the pearls to remember their mother, so they came up with a plan. Their birthdays were six months apart, so at every birthday, they exchanged the pearls and wore them for six months until the next birthday arrived.

Laura blinked away tears. "Mom would have loved becoming a grandmother."

"Yes, and she'd have been a fabulous grandmother." Once they were both buckled in, Denise pulled out of the doctor's parking lot. "Want to stop for coffee?" she asked.

"Not today. I can't wait to go home and show Connor the ultrasound pictures. He'll be so excited — he was hoping for a boy."

Denise tamped down a burst of irritation. "I'm surprised he didn't come with you today."

"He had to work. You know how it is."

Denise nodded. It was a subject she wasn't willing to get into, not today of all days. Laura was so happy, so—

Jesus!

The semi came out of nowhere, filling her vision as it veered directly into her lane. Denise jerked on the wheel and the car lurched sideways in what seemed like slow motion. She hit the brakes, but nothing happened.

Then the back wheels went into a skid and the car slid into a half turn.

She wanted to scream, but she couldn't breathe.

Denise grabbed her sister's hand as the truck barreled toward them, heading straight for Laura on the passenger side. NO!

Denise hit the brakes harder, but her foot went straight to the floor without resistance and the car didn't even slow down.

What the hell was wrong with the brakes?

She'd barely finished the thought when the truck slammed into them fast and hard. The impact was explosive, metal squealing, glass shattering. Denise was jerked sideways, her head smashing against the driver's side window as Laura's hand went limp in hers.

"No, no, *NO!*" she screamed.

DENISE JERKED UPWARDS, still screaming, but excruciating pain in her hips stopped her from sitting up. A hand reached out and grasped her shoulder, pressing her back down to the pillow. She heard someone calling for a nurse, but in her mind all she could see was blood, so much blood. The last thing she remembered hearing was her sister gasping for breath. Then silence, an eerie, horrible silence.

"No. Laura, no!"

She pulled at the tubes that tangled around her wrist, then clawed at the tape on her arm holding the needle in, wanting to run. To where? Where was Laura?

And the baby. Oh my God, the baby.

A nurse rushed in and hurried to her bedside, then grabbed Denise's wrist and said, "Hold still."

"My sister," she cried out, but the nurse held her still while she adjusted the tubes and needles. "Where is my sister?"

"Calm down," the nurse said, switching the IV bag beside the bed, then injecting something into the line. "The doctor will be right in to talk to you. But you need to calm down."

"Please, I need to see her," Denise begged as the nurse jotted notes in her chart.

But then she left Denise alone.

No, not alone. Someone had called the nurse.

She turned her head in slow motion, suddenly dizzy. Connor stood on the other side of the bed. His usually tanned skin looked pale, like he'd spent the last month under fluorescent lights, and the dark circles under his eyes made him look almost gaunt.

What was he doing here when he should be with Laura?

The dizziness intensified as a wave of lethargy floated over her. Denise suspected the nurse had added something to the IV to force her to relax. She lay back, resting her head against the pillow, suddenly too tired to think. A tear slid slowly down her cheek.

Connor stepped toward the bed and rested a hand on her arm. His eyes, which used to sparkle with mirth, seemed veiled in sadness. "I thought we were going to lose you, too," he said.

Too? Denise squeezed her eyes shut, unwilling to believe the import of that word.

She struggled to remember what had happened, but her head felt like it was filled with lead. The truck. The brakes. She'd hit the brakes. Or had she? They'd been talking about Connor and she'd been annoyed with him, but she couldn't remember why.

The truck had seemed to come from nowhere. Had she not been paying attention?

Was the accident her fault?

When she opened her eyes again, Connor was still looking at her with that sad, defeated expression.

Except that he seemed so far away in the cold light of the too-bright overhead lights that made her eyes sting.

"Laura?" Denise croaked.

He shook his head. And then the tears she'd been trying to hold back erupted in a torrent of agony. "Oh God, it's my fault, I was driving. The baby. Connor, the baby."

"It was an accident," he said.

And then he joined her, resting his face in his hands as sobs racked his body.

They cried together for the lives lost forever.

Laura was gone. The baby was gone. And she'd been driving. Denise knew she'd never forgive herself.

"When is the funeral?" she asked when she couldn't cry anymore.

Connor looked away. "It … it was two weeks ago."

"What?" Denise shook her head trying to understand.

"You've been in a coma," Connor said. "We weren't sure if you'd come out of it or not. I had to…" He stopped and swallowed hard. "I had to make the arrangements."

She'd missed the funeral. She wasn't even going to get to say goodbye to them.

I don't deserve to. My fault.

"How long have I been in a coma?"

"Nearly a month now."

Someone knocked on the open door, and Denise could barely find the energy to turn her head to see a doctor approach. Speaking calmly, he confirmed what Connor had told her. Not only had she been in a coma for nearly a month, but she'd suffered a concussion, a broken leg, a fractured pelvis, and uterine bleeding, along with many bruises and contusions. While she was comatose, they'd had to do surgery to repair the pelvic fracture and remove her damaged uterus. But she was alive, and that was more than could be said for Laura and her unborn child.

Denise thought of the gifts she'd already bought in anticipation of her nephew's birth. The stuffed bear he'd never hold, the layette outfits he'd never wear, and the rattles that would remain silent. Forever. All because of her.

"I wish it had been me," she murmured.

Connor turned away, neither agreeing nor disagreeing. It would have been easier if he had agreed, if he'd raged at her, if he'd demanded that she somehow make it up to him for stealing his family.

Somehow his quiet acceptance of his loss — and her part in it — was worse.

Connor cleared his throat. "I've put her things in storage. I just couldn't bear to be around them. The memories hurt too much."

Denise nodded. She couldn't imagine what the last month had been like for him. Burying his wife and unborn child. Walking like a ghost through his own house with nothing but memories assaulting him at every corner. Her heart broke for both of them.

She felt Laura's absence as a hollowness in her world. How could her happy, smiling, exuberant sister be gone?

She had so much to live for, so much to look forward to. It wasn't possible that her essence no longer existed.

Then, in a wave of selfishness, Denise wondered how she'd go on without her sister's love, without her advice and companionship. Their parents had both been only children, so she had no aunts, uncles, or cousins. When their parents died, Laura was the only family she'd had left, and now Laura was gone as well.

Stop it, she chided herself. *Laura's life was cut short, and all you can think of is how it will affect you? Selfish, selfish, selfish.*

Connor sniffled and wiped the tears from his eyes, then turned back to face Denise. "If there's any of Laura's things you want from the storage unit, just let me know."

Denise shook her head. There was nothing she wanted. She simply wanted her sister back.

Then she remembered.

"Oh, there is one thing," she said. "My mother's pearls."

Connor cocked his head, a frown wrinkling his brow. "Pearls?"

"Yes, the pearls that belonged to my mother. Laura and I traded them on each of our birthdays, remember?"

Connor shook his head. "I guess I never paid attention. I'll look for them."

"Laura wore them to her doctor's appointment." She vividly remembered Laura tugging on the strand in the car. "We even joked about them."

"They weren't with her belongings when they..." He swallowed hard.

"I'm sorry. It's just, I know she was wearing them in the car. Where could they have gone?"

"I have no idea." He looked equally puzzled by the mystery.

Her heart thumped in her chest and sweat broke out

on her forehead. Suddenly, finding the pearls was the most important thing in the world. They were the one thing she had to remember not only her mother, but now her sister as well. "Can you check with the police? The funeral home?" She reached out and grasped Connor's hand. "We have to find them, Connor. We have to find them."

The look on his face made her feel like the most selfish person in the world. He'd just buried his wife and child. A string of pearls was nothing compared to what he'd lost. How could she bother him with something so trivial?

But he didn't reproach her for panicking over a necklace.

"It's okay," he said. "I'll see what I can do. If you say she was wearing them in the car, then they have to be somewhere. I'll check with the police."

She broke down and cried, as if her tears were a bottomless well that would never dry.

"Thank you," she sobbed. "Thank you."

He patted her hand, then turned to leave. "I have to go now, but I'll be back later tonight, okay?"

Denise nodded, grateful to have someone she could count on. With Laura gone, Connor was the closest thing she had to family.

TRUE TO HIS WORD, Connor showed up that evening carrying a large takeout cup. "I brought you a malted milkshake. Your favorite."

Denise pushed aside the half-eaten tray of hospital food to make room for the malted milk. Connor was right. It was her favorite. It had been Laura's favorite as well, a leftover from their childhood. There was only one place across town that still made them, which meant that Connor had gone out of his way to get it for her.

"Thank you," she said, touched by his thoughtfulness. There was no question Connor could be charming and likable, but there was the other side too. He could be moody and controlling. Laura had left him once, appearing on Denise's doorstep on a Tuesday night in tears, claiming that she'd had enough of his jealousy — apparently Laura couldn't work late without him suspecting her of flirting with one of managers. In a show of sisterly support, Denise had provided gallons of Chunky Monkey ice cream and called Connor every name in the book, which she regretted the following week when they reconciled. But the experience had left a bitter taste in her mouth. She'd never badmouthed him again, but she'd also refused to be pulled in by Connor's charms.

But this felt different. He seemed so lost and alone. She sipped on her malt and watched him pull up a chair to the side of her hospital bed.

"How are you feeling?" he asked.

Not great, but that felt trivial when she should be on her knees thanking everything in the universe for the fact that she was alive. She'd had time to catalog her injuries, the most serious of which was a broken leg. Still, the cast was uncomfortable and heavy. She felt weaker than she ever had in her life - every time she tried to move, it was like she was pushing against extra gravity. And while the drugs dampened the pain, it was still there hovering in the distance, waiting to pounce as soon as they wore off. But then again, she was alive, wasn't she?

"No complaints. Anxious to go home." She frowned. "Assuming I still have a home to go back to."

"You do. I took care of the rent on your apartment."

That was a surprise. He'd found the time in mourning

to pay her bills? She had a hard time imagining him doing that without Laura to suggest it.

She felt guilty and ungrateful for even thinking that.

"Thank you."

It wasn't the first time she'd thanked him since waking up, and she was sure it wouldn't be the last.

He shrugged. "It was the least I could do. Laura would have wanted me to take care of things for you until you were better." He stopped and took a deep breath. "However, I'm not so sure you should go back there alone. You still need time to heal and recover. It won't be easy going up and down the stairs of your apartment, or getting groceries, or cooking and cleaning."

Denise was about to argue, then realized he was right. With her right leg in a cast, she'd struggle to do anything and she'd be trapped inside, since her old apartment building had no elevator. But what were her options?

"I think you should move in with me," Connor said, as if answering her unspoken question. He held up a hand to ward off any concerns she may have. "Just for a little while. I can take you to physical therapy and doctor's appointments. I'm going to have to eat anyway, so it's just as easy to bring home food for two." He looked away, then back again. "You'd be doing me a favor. The house is lonely without Laura."

That was what finally convinced her. She was lonely too. Maybe they'd be a little less lonely together.

Even though it would be strange to live with her sister's husband. To have him care for her the way he would've cared for Laura. And the baby.

She pushed that thought away quickly, before the guilt overwhelmed her again.

Denise told herself that Laura would've wanted her to keep Connor company until he was through the worst of his grief. He would be taking care of her, but maybe she would be taking care of him too.

"Okay," she agreed. "But only until I get my strength back."

IT WAS another week before she was able to leave the hospital. Another week getting used to the idea that her sister was gone for good. And Connor was there every night, making sure she was comfortable, bringing her little treats he knew she'd enjoy. They'd grown closer in the last week than the two years he was married to her sister.

Still, it had been surreal when he'd wheeled her from the car to the front door of the house he'd shared with Laura, knowing that she would be staying here with him, but without her sister.

Once inside, it got even more surreal.

Even though Connor had told her he'd put all of Laura's things in storage, it was still strange being in the house without any signs of her sister. Her clothes were gone, her jewelry, the little knickknacks she sprinkled around the house. The lion figurine she'd bought during a trip to Hong Kong. Her cheer squad trophy from senior year. The crystal vase that had once been their grandmother's, one that Laura used to fill with flowers once a week without fail.

The only reminder of Laura in the entire house was Connor and Laura's wedding picture. Denise remembered the day clearly. Laura was so beautiful in her vintage wedding dress, wearing an art déco emerald wedding band in rose gold that Denise had helped Connor pick out. They'd gone to half a dozen upscale jewelers and argued at each one before she'd convinced him that Laura wouldn't want a huge, gaudy diamond. She'd been right, although it had been hard to stay quiet when Laura showed the emerald off at the engagement party while Connor crowed about how he'd known it was her ring the moment he laid eyes on it. But Laura's thousand-watt smile was worth it.

Seeing that beautiful smile in their wedding picture made Denise realize once again how much she'd lost.

Her gaze kept returning to the wedding picture, transporting. Not a cloud in the blue, blue sky. A picture-perfect wedding day. Laura beamed, the most beautiful bride in the world. The only thing marring the day was the fact that they had no family in attendance. It didn't seem to matter, though. They had each other.

Tears blurred her vision. Would she ever be able to remember her sister without grieving? Would she ever smile at an odd memory or remember her voice without tearing up?

She didn't realize Connor was there until she felt his hand rest on her shoulder. "I miss her too." His touch was comforting. "It was a beautiful day, wasn't it?"

He took the picture from her hands. "It sure was."

Connor helped her settle on the couch with her laptop and moved an ottoman so she could prop her broken leg up on it. "Can I get you anything else before I swing by the office?"

"I'm comfortable, thanks." Denise sighed as she leaned back. "Please don't let me keep you from doing whatever you need to do."

"I'll be back in a few hours with dinner."

Once he was gone, she logged into her Etsy shop and found several orders she'd missed while she was in the hospital: two hand-dyed macrame wall-hangings, a hanging potholder, and a table runner. Luckily, she had enough inventory to get through the next few months. She hated to ask Connor to drop by her apartment and bring the items here, along with shipping supplies. Maybe she could find someone online to help her haul her entire inventory here, including materials for making more. Since she would be couch-bound while her broken leg finished healing, she could at least keep her hands busy.

Her Etsy store was her only means of support, unless she wanted to sell some of her shares in the family business.

Maybe she should. It didn't seem fair to ask Connor to support her for months, but the doctor had said it could be that long before she was walking again.

Chapter Two

As HER BODY SLOWLY HEALED, Connor did everything he could to make her comfortable. Before she even realized she was hungry, he brought her food. When she ran out of medication, he picked more up for her. When she so much as sighed, he offered her a pillow or suggested something to watch or refilled her cup with tea.

And when she cried for her sister and her unborn nephew, he held her and told her it wasn't her fault and promised her it was going to be okay. She hated herself for wanting to believe him, but that didn't stop her from turning to him every time the grief overwhelmed her.

Soon comfort in mourning became a snuggle on the couch while they watched Laura's favorite movie together. Then he kissed her tenderly as they sat in the porch swing on the back patio, watching the sun set. He held her hand at the doctor's office when he took her in for appointments, and he brought her flowers just to cheer her up.

This was a side of him that Denise had never seen - sweet, thoughtful, always tending to her comfort. Laura had complained about him over Chunky Monkey when he'd made her angry, but she'd kept the intimate parts of their marriage to herself. Now Denise understood why Laura had gone back to him. Why she hurried home to him, even when he missed their first child's ultrasound.

If Denise had known then, she would've felt jealous. Now she felt guilty for slipping so easily into her dead sister's life. She'd fully intended to move back into her apartment as soon as she could navigate the stairs on crutches. But Connor made it so easy to like him, it was hard to say no to him.

She'd been living with him for four months when he'd proposed, taking her to dinner at her favorite restaurant, The Upper Crust, where he'd gotten down on one knee in front of a packed crowd of Dallas elite and asked her to make him the happiest man on Earth as he offered up a velvet-clad box.

As she stared at the diamond-encrusted engagement ring inside — almost identical to the one he'd wanted to buy Laura — a petty part of her wondered if he'd picked it because he'd wanted to finally win that argument. She immediately felt ashamed. Most brides would be ecstatic to show off a three-carat diamond as proof of their fiancé's love.

As he waited for her to answer, looking like a man deeply in love, her mouth went dry and her heart began to pound. She should have expected to see friends and colleagues here, because the majority of Dallas's wealthy had earned their money in the oil business. But the fact that Connor had chosen this particular restaurant for his proposal, knowing that they'd be seen by people who knew them, felt less like thoughtfulness and more like pressure.

And the little speech he'd given felt so practiced, it was hard not to wonder if he'd used those same words when he'd asked Laura to marry him.

All these thoughts made her feel like the most ungrateful person who'd ever lived.

Because he made it so easy to say yes. But it felt wrong that it would be so easy to agree to spend the rest of her life with him. After everything they'd been through, how could she know how she truly felt about him?

He'd comforted and cared for her, been there for her like no other man had ever been. But did she love him for that? Or did she feel obligated to return his feelings because she owed him, not just for the care, but for the loss of his sister and his child? How much of their connection was shared grief rather than true affection?

What if they were mistaking loneliness for love?

She felt a flash of anger. He was forcing her to commit — or to crush him — while some of the most influential people they knew watched and waited. If she said no, it would be her reputation that would suffer for rejecting her sister's husband.

But when she tore her eyes away from the ring and saw the hopeful, vulnerable expression on her face, that anger melted away. Whatever the origin of their feelings, she believed that he had grown to care for her.

After everything he'd been through, didn't he deserve to be happy?

Didn't they both?

"Yes," she said, and the entire restaurant erupted in cheers and applause. Connor beamed as he took the ring from its box — that obnoxiously gaudy ring that would've made Laura roll her eyes in pure contempt — and he slipped it onto her finger, then stood and pulled her to her feet so he could kiss her before presenting her to the still-applauding crowd of their peers.

"My fiancée," he said proudly as he slipped his arm

around her waist and hugged her closer. Then he whispered, "The real celebration will happen at home."

Their waiter brought champagne on ice and the most decadent chocolate dessert Denise had ever seen. It was exactly the kind of confectionary monstrosity that Laura would have loved.

Denise hated that she loved it too.

Later than night, while Connor slept, Denise paced in front of Laura's wedding photo, unable to calm the roil of emotions that gripped her.

"Is this wrong?" she asked her sister's image. "Am I a terrible person? I wish you were here to tell me what to do."

But if Laura was here, none of this would be happening. Denise would still be going to work every day, doing macrame and making jewelry in the evenings, and helping Laura shop for baby things on the weekends. She'd be getting ready to be an aunt, reading baby books so she'd know every milestone they needed to celebrate. Checking in to make sure Laura remembered her prenatals and singing songs to her sister's belly as her little nephew grew.

She couldn't decide if she was honoring her sister's memory or cheapening it.

All she knew was that if she was going to marry Connor, she couldn't do it in front of everyone. She'd felt like such a hypocrite tonight as friends and colleagues had stopped by the table to congratulate them. The more witnesses, the more humiliating it would be to discover that she'd married Connor for the wrong reasons. How could she look their family and friends in the eye and swear to them that she loved Connor? How could she walk down the aisle wondering if they thought she was a terrible person for getting her sister killed and marrying her brother-in-law?

What if they refused to come at all?

So, when he came down the next morning to find her staring dully into the cup of coffee she'd made after a sleepless night, she asked if he'd mind eloping.

"You don't want a wedding?" He seemed more curious than offended. "Are you sure?"

"We can fill out a marriage application online, then make an appointment with the county clerk."

"Why don't you want a wedding?"

"I…" She couldn't explain without insulting him. "If that's a problem—"

He smiled gently and cupped her cheek in his palm. "I don't care where we get married, as long as I can be with you."

Denise exhaled, practically giddy with relief. "And can we not tell people right away?"

"Are you embarrassed to be seen with me?" he teased.

"I want the ceremony to be just for us."

That earned her a quick kiss. "Let's fill out the application right now." Then he paused. "Please tell me there's more coffee in the pot."

She poured him a cup while he fetched her laptop, then they applied for a marriage license together.

Three days later, a county clerk declared them husband and wife.

Denise told herself that Laura would be happy for them.

Chapter Three

It HAD BEEN six months since she'd moved in with Connor, and she still hadn't gone back to her own apartment. Her body had healed, but the guilt and shame remained. No matter how many times she replayed the accident in her mind, it always ended the same. The terror as the truck swerved, heading straight for them. The frozen feeling as she floored the brakes and nothing happened. The sickening lurch as the car began to skid. The bone-shattering impact of the truck slamming into Laura's door, crumpling metal as Denise was thrown sideways, her head smashing into the window. Laura's hand going limp as pain exploded in Denise's head and her leg. Laura's limp hand in hers as the darkness took her.

Laura dead. The baby dead.

Her fault.

She couldn't bring her sister back, and she could never forgive herself.

Sitting cross-legged on the checkered picnic blanket outside the cabin that their parents had left to her and Laura, Denise stared out at the mountains. She felt dwarfed in their presence, the same way she'd felt lost in her sister's shadow.

And then there was Connor.

She'd grown used to Connor's care, and despite her earlier qualms, she'd fallen for his charm. When he'd asked her to marry him, she wasn't sure if it was because he'd fallen in love with her or because she reminded him of Laura.

And what about her own feelings? Did she love Connor, or was she simply grateful that he represented safety and security in a world that was empty of both? They were tangled together in a tidepool of grief, love, and loneliness.

A cool breeze touched her cheek, and she closed her eyes, took a deep breath, and let it out slowly, the way her therapist had told her to do when she felt stressed or anxious. She stayed that way until she felt Connor's touch on her arm.

She turned to him and smiled. Ever since Laura's death, his hair had slowly turned gray, streaks of silver at first, making him look dashing, then more and more as the months passed. Was it the stress of losing his wife and unborn child that caused his hair to turn gray, or would it have happened naturally? Now it was almost completely gray, and somehow that made him seem less like Laura's husband and more like her own. At least this version of Connor belonged to her.

Sometimes she wondered if he ever compared her to Laura, and if so, whether he found her wanting. But she did her best to push that unworthy thought away whenever it popped up to spoil an otherwise-wonderful moment with him.

She noticed he'd poured the rest of the wine into her

glass. He broke off a piece of baguette and handed it to her.

"I'm thinking of selling the house," he said. "How do you feel about that?"

She played with the bread, breaking it into crumbs that fell onto her lap. She thought it was a good decision. It was the home he and Laura had built together, where they made their memories. *Where they'd made love.* But she couldn't say that. She didn't even want to think about that.

Guilt cut through her as she considered her answer. Encouraging him to sell felt selfish. Was it fair to tell him she would never feel at home in the house he'd shared with her sister? Would it seem like jealousy?

She wondered for the millionth time what Laura would think about their engagement. She wanted to believe that her sister would be happy that they'd taken comfort in each other, but what if that was just more selfishness?

"It's your home."

He pulled her close. "It's your home too."

She shook her head. "Not really. There are too many memories here. I feel like a ghost wandering around my sister's house."

"It will never be your sister's house again," Connor said softly. "It's our decision now."

That just made her feel worse, because that was her fault. She'd never intended to take Laura's house from her, or her husband, but somehow it had happened, anyway.

But she couldn't say that to him either. He'd just feel bad for making her feel bad, and he didn't deserve that. Not when he'd been so kind these past six months.

"Maybe a fresh start would be easier," she said.

He smiled and brushed a hand through her hair. "I'll put the house on the market, and we can start looking for a place. A place we can call our own."

That sounded perfect. A place of their own. Maybe she wouldn't feel like a second choice, a pale imitation of his first love. She wished she could give him a child to replace the one she'd stolen from him in the accident, but that hope had been stolen from her at the same time.

He picked up the remnants of their picnic. She'd barely touched any of the food, only picking at a few grapes. Her appetite had disappeared, and she'd grown thin over the last few months, almost as if she was trying to disappear. She brushed the crumbs from her lap and stood up, helping Connor put away the uneaten food.

It had been his idea to get away for the day, unusual since he'd always been such a workaholic. Maybe Laura's death had taught him the value of living in the moment instead of spending all his time at work. The picnic at the cabin was his idea as well.

"Have you thought about selling this place too?" he asked.

"The cabin?" The thought took her by surprise. The cabin had been in her family for years. Unlike Connor and Laura's house, the cabin contained all of her happiest memories. Memories of her mother and father. Memories of summers at the lake with cookouts and fishing and s'mores around the campfire. This was before their mother became ill and everything changed.

Maybe she didn't deserve the cabin, but she didn't want to give it up.

"It's up to you," he said. "It's all yours now."

He'd probably meant it to sound supportive, but it made her feel guilty for clinging to it when he was trying so hard to move forward, and to help her move forward too.

Connor picked up the basket and they headed toward the car. With each step, Denise felt her heart speed up as her chest constricted, making it harder to inhale. Her body stiffened, and she started to limp, even though the doctor had assured her that the break in her leg was completely healed.

She wondered if she'd ever be comfortable getting in a car again. It was a long drive to Dallas, one she knew would strain her nerves. But she was determined to get over her fear. She stopped before getting in the car, one hand resting on the door handle.

Connor glanced over and tilted his head. "Do you need a little support?"

A little support. That was their code for the pills the doctor prescribed for her nerves. Just a mild relaxer to get her through the rough patches. There were a lot of rough patches.

Connor handed her a bottle of water and shook a pill into her palm. She threw her head back and swallowed. One little pill. That was all she needed. She didn't even stop to wonder if taking it was a good idea on top of two glasses of wine. Surely Connor wouldn't have suggested it if it were.

She climbed in the car and pulled her seat belt on, then closed her eyes and took three deep breaths, waiting for her heartbeat to calm. Connor sat behind the wheel. He rested his hand on her leg. "Let me know when you're ready."

He was so patient with her. Another man would have given up by now.

"Ready?"

She nodded. But her fingers clenched, digging into the leather seat. She forced herself to breathe deeply. Inhale to the count of four, then hold, then exhale to the count of four. She had to get herself back in control for the drive home.

When Connor turned the key in the ignition, a shiver

ran down her spine. Would she ever feel comfortable in a car again? Let alone driving by herself?

She focused on the trees and the mountains in the distance, anything but looking at the road ahead. When a car passed by, her shoulders tensed and she gripped the seat harder. When they approached the scene of the accident, Denise clenched her eyes shut. In her mind she could hear the screams and see the blood, her sister's neck bent at a sharp angle and the veil of death cloaking her eyes. Denise choked out a sob.

Connor pulled the car over and took her face in his hands. "You have to stop blaming yourself," he said. "It wasn't your fault. The insurance company claimed it was mechanical failure."

"I can't help it. I was the one driving. I keep going back, wondering if I could have somehow avoided it. Maybe if we'd left a few minutes sooner. Or taken a different route."

"Don't torture yourself, babe. There's nothing you could have done differently. It was an accident."

"I know, but I can't help but wonder if there was some way to avoid it. And why…" She stopped and swallowed a sob. "Why her and not me? She had so much more to live for."

Connor. The baby. The company that she loved to run, with Connor at her side.

"Stop it." Connor's voice became stern. "Remember what your therapist said. *Survivor's guilt.* It's normal."

"There's nothing normal about this," Denise said. Not just the accident itself, but the fact that she was now married to her sister's husband. And now she and Connor were considering selling the house, the last thing left that belonged to Laura — her home and all the memories it contained. A few minutes ago, it had seemed like a good idea, but now...

Connor tapped her leg, and she opened her eyes, aware of the fact that they'd passed the site of the accident. "One day you'll be able to make the drive with your eyes wide open."

Denise nodded. "If we move, I won't have to pass this way ever again."

Even so, she knew the guilt would remain.

"Maybe not," he said. "But avoidance is only a short-term fix."

She knew he was right. She could avoid driving past the site of the accident, but the guilt would always be with her.

THAT EVENING, the two of them scrolled through internet sites. They narrowed their search down to half a dozen developments. Denise told herself it was what he wanted, and it would be wrong of her to hold him back when he was ready to move on.

"I really like this one," Connor said. He scrolled through pictures of model homes. "It's under development. But if we get in on the ground floor, we can get one of the bigger models at a reasonable price."

"Hackberry Haven? It sounds like a cartoon village." She laughed. "Or a place where fairytale characters live."

Connor made a muscle man pose. "Gaston at your service."

Denise curtsied and mimed fanning herself. "Oh Gaston. I'm honored, but my heart belongs to the Beast."

Connor feigned shock. "But I'm so handsome! What does the Beast have that I don't?"

Denise blinked her eyes in what she hoped was a coquettish gesture. "Books," she said. "The Beast has a library full of books."

"I have a book," Connor said. "Hold on." He turned and rushed through the door. A few minutes later he came back holding a book: *The Every Man's Guide to Success in the Business World.*

Denise shook her head. "That's not a book. That's a manual. A real book has romance, action, adventure!"

"You want romance?" He flexed an imaginary muscle, then swooped her up in his arms. "How's this for romance?"

Denise giggled and allowed herself to be swept off her feet.

It wasn't the first time Connor had carried her. When her leg was healing, he'd insist on carrying her up to the bedroom at night and downstairs in the morning. She was surprised at how effortlessly he lifted her. No one would confuse Connor with a gym rat, but he had muscles under his tailored business suits and carried her as if she was no lighter than a feather.

She wondered if he'd carried Laura upstairs like this too. It was hard not to feel like she was living her sister's life.

She forced herself to shove the comparison aside, for Connor's sake. It didn't matter what he'd done with Laura. It only mattered that they were moving on. Together.

Chapter Four

"WHAT DO YOU MEAN, you bought a house?" Denise stared at Connor in disbelief. "We haven't even started looking."

His expression said he'd been expecting another reaction altogether.

"I walked through it after you said you liked the floor plan, and I agreed with your choice."

"That wasn't a choice. I thought we were just fantasizing while we looked at the website."

Connor moved closer and cupped her cheek with his palm. "Is that so bad, that I want to make my wife's fantasy come true?"

He meant it to be romantic, but Denise had to resist the urge to jerk away at his touch. He'd bought one of the bigger models in Hackberry Haven, without even looking at it, without giving *her* a chance to look at it.

This was the Connor that had sent Laura to Denise's door for late-night ice cream, sure that whatever he wanted, everyone else would want too, and if they didn't, he could convince them. Denise had called him controlling then, but Laura had later insisted that she loved his confidence.

Maybe he just can't wait to move on with you.

"Connor, should we talk about—"

"How much I love you?" Connor bent closer, like he was leaning in for a kiss. "How I would do anything to make you happy, even surprise you with your fantasy house?"

When he said it that way, she felt so ungrateful. After everything he'd done for her, to help her heal both physically and emotionally, why was her first impulse always to resist?

Because you don't deserve it. You don't deserve him.

"Say something," he urged, "before I start to think I've made a terrible mistake."

Maybe there was something wrong with her, that she heard a threat when he begged her to approve of his gift.

"I'm sorry, I was so surprised, I didn't know what to say," she apologized, tipping her head back in acquiescence. "You take such wonderful care of me."

"If you don't like it—"

"I'm sure I'll love it." Now she felt even more ungrateful. "It's my fantasy house, remember?"

He'd kissed her then. She swallowed her guilt and kissed him back.

Maybe this was for the best. If he was ready to move on, she should be too.

But she couldn't help but wonder what Laura would think.

ONLY THREE WEEKS LATER, the old house was sold, and Connor had insisted on handling all the arrangements, including having movers pack all their things — except for the suitcase of clothes and toiletries she'd brought with her in the car. Tonight they'd be spending their first night in the new house.

A sign at the entrance of Hackberry Haven proclaimed it was a new housing development with lots selling fast. Not selling fast enough, Denise realized as they drove through the development. It was like driving through a ghost town. "Where is everyone?"

"Well, sales have been slow, from what I understand. But they're anticipating full occupancy by the end of the year." Connor rushed forward as if she needed convincing. "And because of that, we got in on the ground floor at a rate that's practically a steal. In this booming market, we'll make double our money back if we choose to sell in a few years."

They wound their way through the development, but the community that had seemed enticing on the website felt depressingly boring in real life. All the houses looked the same — two-story single-family homes painted in varying shades of beige. The models were mirror images, but other than that, it was nearly impossible to tell them apart.

"How will we know which house is ours?"

Connor shrugged. "Once we move in, we can personalize our house. Paint the door red or something."

"Or turquoise."

"Whatever you'd like." Connor pulled into the driveway of a house impossible to distinguish from any of the others, if not for the numbers over the door. 202 Oakmont Drive. It was at the end of the development on a quiet cul-de-sac.

"We're lucky to have neighbors on each side," Connor said. "So you won't feel so alone here when I'm at work."

They walked into a fully furnished house.

"This was one of the model homes," Connor said. "I bought it furnished, so we didn't have to deal with moving costs. Besides, you said you wanted all new things."

She did, but she would have liked to be able to pick out the furniture and decorations herself. Although it was beautiful, it wasn't exactly her style. She couldn't complain, though. She knew Connor was simply trying to make things easier for her, as he'd been doing since the accident.

This is what moving on looks like. And that was what she'd wanted, wasn't it?

So she hid her disappointment and smiled at him. "How did I end up with such a thoughtful husband?"

His smile told her that had been the right answer. "Let me give you the tour."

The tour started and ended in the bedroom, but after Connor had exhausted them both, she laid in bed, disquieted by the heavy silence and the generic perfection of the room, which had clearly been staged by a professional to be appealing without possessing a glimmer of personality that might offend a prospective buyer's personal sense of taste.

In a way, it was perfect for moving on, almost a blank canvas that she could start adding to, without a single reminder of Laura.

Except that the *absence* of Laura was also a *reminder* of Laura.

She would have to find a way to fill this place with her own things. Only happy things. Maybe a lamp from the cabin, and the quilt that they used to make a pillow fort during childhood summers. She could make a macrame hanging for the opposite wall, in robin's egg blue and soft gold to brighten up the pale beige paint.

Then some plants in the windows, in hand-painted

pots. Just the thought of starting a new project in this place cheered her. Having her own workspace. Finding a new rhythm in the home Connor had given her.

She would make this place hers. Then she would be able to move on.

When Connor went to work the next day, she puttered around the house, familiarizing herself with the layout. The kitchen had state-of-the-art appliances. She'd need a computer degree to figure out how to use them. A back-yard patio featured a grill and outdoor furniture, including a comfy loveseat glider she knew would quickly become her favorite place to sit with a book and a pitcher of lemonade.

But he hadn't had time to buy groceries yet, and the thought of riding in a car without Connor felt suffocating. Even with a little *support*, she might slip into panic and disintegrate in front of a total stranger. So she settled for leftover pizza, then spent the rest of the morning rear-ranging the room where she would work and measuring the space, then ordering a table that would be perfect for spreading out a project and a set of cubby shelves to store her supplies.

Now that she was Connor's wife, they shared a joint bank account, but her finger still hesitated over the Checkout button for a few moments as she reminded herself that she didn't have to ask permission, that Connor would be happy she was settling into their new home. This was the fresh start they both wanted.

It was ridiculous that she still felt like she was spending her sister's money.

To banish that thought, she went online to search for inspiration for the wall hanging she wanted to make for the bedroom. But no matter how hard she tried, she hated every design she sketched. By mid-afternoon, she was channel-surfing and checking the clock every few minutes, wishing that Connor would come home early so they could get out of the house together. Dinner, a movie, even a walk someplace other than this deserted neighborhood. She was surprised to discover that she missed the sounds of distant traffic, the neighbor's dog barking at the mail carrier, even those annoying wind chimes that clanged from across the street of their old house.

But the silence here was stifling. Worse than a grave-yard, where at least the wind might rustle the trees or the grass might soften the footsteps of visitors stopping by to remember a loved one.

Denise hobbled to the kitchen to swallow one of her support pills. Then she grabbed the TV remote and turned the volume up higher.

Over the next few days, a few neighbors moved in. Glen came first, taking the house next door. He seemed nice, but he was sixty shades of normal. The kind of guy who neighbors would tell journalists, "He seemed like such a nice guy." And he did. That alone was suspicious.

Helen and her husband Ronald lived on the other side. Helen had a stern face, which she jokingly called her *resting bitch face*, but when she smiled, her entire face lit up and drew you in. She moved with the grace of a dancer and exuded a confidence that Denise envied. Ronald was movie-star handsome, with effortlessly messy hair that fell in soft curls over his forehead and brilliant blue eyes that would make women swoon if he appeared on the big screen.

Then there were the Parkers, Sandra and Diego, who lived two doors down. Diego had skin the color of cappuc-cino and jet-black hair pulled straight back from his face. When he smiled, a gold tooth winked from inside his mouth. Sandra was taller than her husband, with hair a shade of red never seen in nature.

Still, they were at the end of a mostly empty neighborhood. She shouldn't have felt so lonely while Connor was at work, but half the time the neighbors were gone, whether at work or pursuing their own interests, and most of the time, Denise felt like the only person inhabiting the entire development.

But when she joked to Connor that sometimes she felt like the last woman on Earth, he frowned. "Can't you amuse yourself with all that yarn I carted over from your apartment?"

Denise blinked, surprised by his annoyance. "I wasn't complaining. I just miss talking to people."

"I know, you miss talking to me while I'm at work." He gave her a peck on the cheek, then scooped his keys off the kitchen counter and slid them in his pocket. "You can tell me everything tonight."

"I can hardly wait," she said, faking a smile until he left the kitchen.

But she really missed talking with Laura, who had been her best friend as well as her sister. Even though she'd been busy running the company, she always found time to text during breaks in her day. Or to have lunch once in a blue moon. Or run errands together on the weekends.

But now, all she had was Connor, who never texted from work unless it was to remind her to take her meds, or to ask what she wanted him to pick up on his way home.

He was doing his best, she told herself. Without Laura, he had sole responsibility for running the entire company. Of course he wouldn't have time to text her between meetings just to chat.

But knowing that didn't make her feel less lonely.

It did make her feel guilty when he came home that

night and announced that he'd arranged a weekend getaway to Austin at a bed-and-breakfast overlooking Canyon Lake. A road trip was the last thing she wanted right now, but how could she complain about that when he was being so thoughtful? She'd just have to make sure she had some extra support for the three-hour car ride.

But despite the pills, Denise was an exhausted bundle of nerves by the time they arrived. Connor had insisted on talking about work at first — nothing but interoffice politics among people she didn't know and moments from meetings out of context. She did her best to follow, but after she'd confused Sharon with Cherise for the third time, he sighed and said, "Be thankful you don't have to deal with any of this. It's going to be crazy until we're out of the danger zone."

"I wish there was something I could do to help."

He gave her a tired smile. "Don't worry about it. You've been out of the loop for months, and you were never invested in the way your sister was. I shouldn't have bothered you with any of it."

That stung, even though it was true. She spent the rest of the trip staring out the window, but it was hard to appreciate the beauty of the surroundings as the trees flashed by. Connor had never said anything like that before, and she wondered if he'd expected her to step up and take Laura's place at his side in the company as soon as her injuries had healed.

Would they have more to talk about if she had?

Or would she still feel just as lonely there as she did in their empty neighborhood?

As he pulled the car to a stop, she let out a small sigh, clenching her hands as they rested on her knees to stop their trembling.

Connor reached out to place a hand over hers. "I'm

sorry. I know the drive was hard on you. Would you like a little support?"

A little support. She'd been taking the pills more and more often these days, often at Connor's urging. They weren't helping as much as they used to. She felt a little spurt of panic at the possibility that they might stop working altogether. She could barely stand to be in a car when she took them. She'd be trapped at home for the rest of her life.

"Let's go inside," he said after she didn't reply. He grabbed their bags and unlocked the front door with the code the host had sent. Inside was warm wood and soft cushioned furniture.

"Cozy," she said, looking around. There was a full kitchen. Connor had packed drinks and snacks, but they'd have to run to the grocery store if they wanted to cook a meal.

Connor poured her a glass of water, then reached into his pocket and shook two pills into her palm. She swallowed them, grateful for the comfort they'd provide. Better to be a little sleepy than ruin the whole weekend.

"Hey, look at this," Connor said. He picked up a remote and hit a button, which turned on a fireplace. "It's like magic!"

Denise forced a giggle. "Magic fire. Too bad the kitchen doesn't cook a magic meal."

"Are you hungry?"

She shook her head. "No." Then, because he looked concerned, she added. "It's really lovely. Thank you for arranging this."

She was more surprised that he'd actually taken a weekend off. Lately, he worked all the time, late nights and weekends. Not that it was anything new. Connor had always been a bit of a workaholic. Even more so lately, however. And when he was home, he was either on the phone or whipping off business emails.

Denise felt guilty that he was taking on not only his own work at the company, but Laura's and hers as well. But she wasn't ready to go back to work. Not yet. She couldn't face everyone after what happened.

"Let's check out the rest of the place," Connor said. He took her hand, then they wandered through the house. Three bedrooms and two baths were standard fare, but the pearl in the oyster was the outdoor deck. It had a jacuzzi and a breathtaking view of the lake.

"I could live here," Denise said, leaning against the rail to admire the view.

"I think it's time to open that bottle of wine we brought."

Denise didn't say anything. She was already feeling a little wobbly from the pills she'd taken. Wine would only make her more sleepy. But she didn't want to spoil his sudden good mood.

Connor came out with two glasses of wine. "A toast," he said, handing her one of the glasses. "To new beginnings."

They clinked glasses. "New beginnings." It was as good a toast as any.

Connor stared out at the lake. "It really is a gorgeous view. Maybe one day we'll buy a vacation home on the lake."

"Yeah, when we hit the lottery."

Connor smiled as if he knew something she didn't. He brought the bottle of wine out and refilled both of their glasses. By now, Denise was feeling light-headed.

"What do you say we give the jacuzzi a try tonight?" Connor removed the cover and turned on the jets.

"I didn't bring a bathing suit."

Connor gestured to the wide-open space around them. "We're pretty secluded here. We don't need bathing suits." His grin was both sexy and challenging.

Maybe it was the wine, or the glint in his eyes, but Denise took the cue and began stripping out of her clothes. She tried to move seductively but ended up tripping on her dropped panties and nearly falling headfirst into the jacuzzi.

"Woah there," Connor said with a laugh. He reached for her, his hands sliding down her naked skin. "Beautiful," he whispered into her hair. Then he kissed her.

They never did make it into the jacuzzi.

DENISE WOKE NAKED AND ALONE. It was dark outside, so she'd slept several hours. She looked around, disoriented. Where was she? Then she remembered the vacation rental. And the jacuzzi. Warmth flooded her cheeks. She'd never acted so wantonly before. Anyone could have come by and seen them.

But it had made Connor happy. And she owed him for how hard he'd been working to make her happy.

The guilty voice in her head said she owed him for a lot more than that. But she shoved that thought aside.

"Connor?"

No answer.

She slid out of bed, searching for her clothes, but the overnight bag wasn't in the bedroom. She wrapped the bedsheet around her and went looking for him. The house was dark and unfamiliar. She hit light switches as she went along, but there was no sign of Connor. She did find her overnight bag by the door, so at least she was able to shed the bed sheet and put on clothes. She felt less vulnerable dressed.

While she was changing, she heard the front door open. "Connor?"

"Oh, you're awake."

She came out, fully dressed. "Where were you?"

He held out a grocery bag. "I went out to get us some food. Submarine sandwiches and potato salad for dinner, if you have an appetite."

She didn't, but since he'd gone through the trouble, she mustered as much enthusiasm as she could. While Connor unpacked the grocery bags, she opened the kitchen cabinets and pulled out dishes and silverware.

But when they sat down to eat, the food was tasteless, even the crunchy green onions in the potato salad. She wondered if that was a side effect of the pills.

"When I'm not in the car, I'm doing pretty well," she ventured. "I wonder if I should stop taking these pills."

Connor shook his head. "I don't think that's a good idea. Your therapist prescribed them for a reason."

She struggled to hide her frustration. "Since he's not my therapist anymore, maybe I should see what it's like not to be drugged and half asleep all the time."

"Or maybe we should find a new therapist. One who understands what you've gone through."

"Maybe." She pushed aside the half-eaten sandwich. "I'll wrap this up and eat it tomorrow. Unless you had other plans?"

"No, I just picked up a bunch of stuff we could throw together." He took out a jar of marinara sauce, pasta, and mixed salad greens. "I got your coffee, too," he said, holding up the Columbian blend she preferred.

Her earlier irritation dissolved in the face of his thoughtfulness. "Thanks," she said, forcing a smile.

That's how the entire weekend went. She vacillated between irritation and gratitude, even though Connor was clearly doing everything he could to make sure she was enjoying herself. She wondered again if it could be the pills — was she overdoing them? She was still within the maximum dosage on the bottle's label. And sometimes when Connor wasn't home, she didn't take them at all. So it didn't seem like she was addicted to them.

But why else would his kindness get on her nerves?

WHEN THEY ARRIVED BACK HOME, their next-door neighbor Glen was outside washing his car. He waved and called them over. Denise just wanted to go inside and lie down — the pills she'd taken to tolerate the drive home had made her feel doped up, but she still felt the tight thrum of panic beneath the surface of all that mental fog.

She didn't want to be rude, though, so she put on a smile and joined him.

"How was your trip?" Greg dropped a sponge into a nearby bucket of suds, then wiped his hand and held it out to shake Connor's hand.

"Great." Connor turned to Denise, who nodded but didn't add anything to the conversation. She didn't need strangers knowing about her emotional issues. Or anything else, for that matter.

"Did you hit a lot of traffic?"

A shiver ran down Denise's spine.

The truck, veering into her lane.

The shriek of tearing metal.

Pain in her head. Her hip.

Laura's hand going limp.

"Not too bad," Connor said, wrapping an arm around

Denise's shoulder and giving her a comforting squeeze, as if he knew that Greg's innocent question had triggered the flash of memory.

Fogged up as her head was, she was dying to take another pill and sleep for the rest of the day.

Maybe they were addictive after all. Or maybe she was just weak.

"So, I was meaning to ask … I'm planning a neighborhood barbecue." He glanced around and snorted. "For what little neighborhood there is."

Denise couldn't agree more. "When?"

"I was thinking maybe Friday night? I've got a rack of ribs and some bratwurst. I've already invited the Parkers, and they're bringing potato salad and chips."

"Sounds great," Connor said. "We can bring—"

Denise grabbed his arm. "Friday night is the Grady Oil party." She turned to Greg. "It's our company's 80th anniversary."

"Grady Oil is your company?"

"My family's business." Denise swallowed. It felt like lying to claim her role in running the company, given that she hadn't gone back for more than half a year, but she still had her shares, and theoretically, she had the right to walk back into the office tomorrow and start doing her old job again. "My parents founded it, and Connor's been running it while I've been healing."

Connor didn't challenge her statement, although she saw a flicker of displeasure on his face before he smiled again and shrugged. "Sorry, Greg, we have previous plans."

"No problem. We'll do the barbecue on Saturday instead. Would that work?"

Connor turned to Denise, eyebrows raised.

"Sure, Saturday will be fine," she said. "I'll make a dessert."

"Perfect." Greg reached in the bucket for his sponge and gave it a squeeze. "See you then."

Denise turned and walked toward their front door while Connor unloaded the overnight bags. She turned the key and stepped inside. It still felt like stepping into a show-room, with its generic furniture and pale beige everything.

The only thing that was familiar was Laura's and Connor's wedding picture on the mantel. Initially, Connor hadn't wanted it up there, but he'd humored her when she insisted they put it somewhere she could see it. It was the only reminder she had of happier times, and that was worth the twinge of guilt she felt every time she looked at it. Guilt that she deserved.

She ran her finger along the edge of the picture frame, then turned when she heard Connor enter. "Maybe now that we have a bigger place, we can get some of Laura's things out of storage."

"I don't know. I'm not sure either one of us is ready for that."

Denise sighed. Maybe he was right. She ran her finger over her sister's smile, afraid that the day might come when she wouldn't remember what her sister looked like or the sound of her voice. She was so beautiful in her wedding gown, carrying a bouquet of pink carnations. Denise frowned. Pink carnations? She thought the bouquet had been made of pink rosebuds. She shook her head, trying to remember exactly what flowers were in the bouquet, but the memory had faded. Maybe they were carnations. The entire day was a big blur.

"I miss you so much, Sis," she murmured, tears clouding her vision.

She turned and reached for her overnight bag. "I'm

going to take a shower," she called over her shoulder, then headed up the stairs. In the bathroom, she began unpacking her toiletries and pulled out a blue toothbrush.

But her toothbrush was yellow.

She looked at it, trying to figure out how it had gotten in her bag. Then she dug through the bag, looking for hers. Had she forgotten to pack it this morning? She didn't think so. She had a distinct memory of checking each room before they'd left. The bathroom counter had been clear.

"Connor? Have you seen my toothbrush?"

Connor poked his head in the bedroom. "It's in your hand, silly."

"No. This isn't mine. My toothbrush is yellow."

She rifled through the bag again, tossing things aside and getting more frantic by the moment. "Mine is yellow. This one must be yours."

He stepped closer. "Nope. Mine is red. Maybe you left yours at the vacation rental?"

Denise shook her head. "Where did this one come from, if it's not mine and not yours?"

Connor frowned and stared. "I'm pretty sure your toothbrush was blue, hon."

Denise threw up her hands. "Fine. I'll just get another one out of the cabinet." She marched to the bathroom cabinet and pulled out the package of toothbrushes. They were all blue. Every last one of them.

She held up the package and turned to face Connor. "This is not funny."

"What?"

"Where are the yellow ones? I know they were here." She stopped and frowned. "Do you think someone's been in the house?"

Connor laughed. "Yeah, they broke in and switched your toothbrushes but didn't take anything else." He lowered his voice, as if speaking to a child. "More likely you're just mistaken."

"Or maybe you bought these," she said. "Blue was Laura's favorite color."

"Yeah, maybe that's it."

But she could tell he was only humoring her. Besides, she distinctly remembered buying the value pack of YELLOW toothbrushes.

Or did she? Now she was starting to doubt herself. The pills made her foggy, and it was possible they were messing with her memory too. After all, she couldn't remember if the flowers in Laura's bouquet were roses or carnations, and she'd helped Laura choose everything. Could she have accidentally bought blue toothbrushes last time without realizing it, but remembered buying yellow ones the time before that?

She shrugged and took a toothbrush out of the package. What did it matter what color it was, as long as she could brush her teeth with it?

She finished unpacking her overnight bag, putting the matter out of her mind. There were more important things to worry about. Like the 80th anniversary of Grady Oil. She hadn't been back there since the accident. She couldn't bear the thought of walking in the door and seeing the pity in everyone's eyes. She and Laura had worked side by side at the family business for as long as she could remember. But she'd let things slide. Thank God for Connor. He was doing not only his own job but picking up her slack and Laura's responsibilities. No wonder he worked long into the night and weekend. And he never complained. She felt like a fool for making a big deal about something as silly as a toothbrush.

Once everything was put away, she joined Connor downstairs. They were both exhausted, so she made a light dinner of soup and salad. Glancing out the window, she noticed Glen's car was gone and his windows dark. The driveway was still wet where he'd washed the car.

"That's odd," she said, stepping away from the window.

"What's that?"

"Glen. He was just there washing his car, but now he's gone and the house is dark." It was no business of hers if he wanted to take his just-washed car out for a drive. But for some reason, his disappearance bothered her. "Just seems strange, is all. How much do you know about our neighbor?"

"Not much at all. We've run into each other on our way in or out. Waved, said good morning. That's about it. I guess we'll get to know him better at the barbecue."

"Yeah." She pulled out her planner and scheduled the barbecue for Saturday with a note to plan something for dessert. But it was the bright red circle around Friday that made her stomach drop. The 80th anniversary party for Grady Oil.

Tell the truth. You don't want to go back because you're afraid of what they all think of you for marrying your sister's husband.

As if reading her mind, Connor came up behind her and rubbed her shoulders. "It won't be the same without Laura."

Denise took a deep breath, wondering if he was aware of any rumors. "I'm not sure how I'll get through it."

"I'll be right by your side," he said. "We'll get through it together."

She leaned back into his embrace. The one thing she knew for sure was that she could count on Connor.

"Hey," he said. "Why don't you go shopping and buy something new to wear to the party?"

She smiled. If only it were that easy. But maybe she could find something online?

He kissed the side of her neck, clearly hoping to turn the moment into something more seductive, but she stiffened, and he released her. She wasn't in the mood. The anniversary party was still on her mind. The closer the time came, the less she wanted to attend.

"I'm sorry," she said, turning away.

The blue toothbrush was sitting on the edge of the sink. She picked it up, then put it down again. It just didn't feel right. Blue was Laura's favorite color. She always had to have the blue token when they played board games. When she picked out clothes, she invariably chose blue, not only because it was her favorite color, but people always told her it made her eyes stand out. It got so Denise didn't buy anything blue unless she was buying it for her sister, which made the blue toothbrush so out of place.

After completing her nighttime routine, she joined Connor in bed. He closed the book he'd been reading and set it on the nightstand. She glanced at the title, *Making Workspace Archetypes Work for You*. "How is it?"

"Good," he said. "You should read it when I'm done. I only have a few chapters left."

She nodded noncommittally. It sounded like the last book on earth she'd want to read. But she'd do it for him. Maybe it was his way of getting her interested in the company again.

Or maybe he just wanted her to come back to his world, instead of forcing him to visit hers.

They didn't have much in common anymore. The drive to Austin had shown her that. He never quite stopped working, even when he was at home, while she spent her days watching TV and knotting cords into elaborate designs and being suspicious of their neighbors. No wonder she'd felt so disconnected from him lately.

Maybe it was time to cut out the pills and start taking control of her life again.

Tomorrow.

Chapter Five

THE NEXT MORNING, Denise woke to sunshine streaming through the bedroom window. She heard the shower running and realized she'd overslept. She yawned and stretched lazily, then snuggled beneath the covers. She'd been sleeping later and later, almost as if she was avoiding the day ahead.

Connor stepped out of the bathroom. "Hey, sleepyhead." He leaned over and kissed her, smelling like soap and the spicy scent of his aftershave.

She stifled another yawn. "You're bright and chipper this morning."

"It's a beautiful day. What's on your agenda today?"

Agenda. The word felt so wrong for staying at home in this empty house, but he seemed oblivious. Or if he was teasing her, she couldn't tell.

Let's see. She could go for a run. Organize the pantry. Maybe go through the paint samples she'd picked up at the hardware store and choose what color to paint the front door. Anything but sit on the couch in this empty house, waiting for Connor to come home.

But none of that felt agenda-worthy.

"That depends." She sat up and stretched. "Will you be home for dinner?"

Connor tightened his tie, then glanced at his watch. "I'll do my best," he said, coming over to plant a kiss on her forehead. "Try not to overdo it."

Then he turned and dashed through the door. Sometimes Denise wished he was as excited to come home as he was to leave for the office.

Maybe he would be, if she wasn't so dopey all the time.

Time to take control of your life. Step one, no pills.

She rolled out of bed, slid her feet into bunny slippers, then shuffled into the kitchen, smiling when she saw Connor had left a full pot of coffee warming on the burner. She poured a cup and reached for a donut from the box he'd brought home yesterday. Not exactly healthy, but she'd burn off the calories on her run. But first, coffee.

Twenty minutes later, fully caffeinated and showered, she pulled her hair up in a high ponytail and laced up her running shoes. She stepped outside and stretched her hamstrings. Helen, her neighbor on the right, was leaving for work. Denise waved and Helen waved back, calling out a brisk good morning. They hadn't spoken much other than hello and goodbye, and Denise was determined to change that. Glen's barbecue would be a good opportunity to get to know not only Helen but her other neighbors a little better.

She set off at a slow pace, gradually increasing her speed until she felt that familiar burst of endorphins. Her feet pounded the pavement, and the wind cooled the sweat from her brow. Her heartbeat pounded in sync with her steps. She ran past empty houses, feeling somehow vulnerable. It was too quiet.

Before she knew it, she'd run into an area where most

of the homes were still under construction. They seemed sad, half built and forgotten. A cloud passed over the sun, and a chill ran down her spine.

She wiped sweat from her eyes, and when her vision cleared, she saw a shadow pass behind an open doorway. She blinked and slowed down. There was someone there. A man in a purple hoodie. He was staring right at her from the doorway of one of the empty houses, but his face was shadowed and she couldn't make out his features.

A tarp flapped in the breeze and the figure disappeared. Denise slowed to a stop. Had she really seen someone, or was it just the wind and an overactive imagination? Suddenly she felt exposed with no sign of anyone in the empty houses lining the street. If she screamed, no one would hear her.

Her instincts sent a warning, making her heart race and a cold sweat break out on her forehead. For a moment, she was frozen in fear. Then she turned and ran back home, afraid to look back. She felt an imminent sense of danger, sure someone or something was following her. But each time she looked back over her shoulder, straining for a glimpse of purple among the half-built structures, she saw nothing.

By the time her house came into view, her breath was coming in short, hard gasps and her leg, which she'd thought was completely healed, screamed in pain. She cursed herself for allowing herself to get so out of shape. Sweat dripped down the back of her neck and her cheeks burned. She was so grateful to be back, and only now wondered how the few people who actually lived in this ghost town happened to live on the same cul-de-sac as she and Connor. What were the chances that the only buyers had selected houses right next to one another?

But Connor had said something about getting a deal

on a model home that was already furnished. Maybe that was the case with all of their neighbors.

Inside she glanced at the wedding picture on the mantel. There was something different about it, but she wasn't going there again. Not for the first time, she wished she had a wedding picture of her own to frame. But she and Connor had been married quietly by a Justice of the Peace, and at the time, she hadn't wanted pictures to celebrate the occasion. She realized now that some part of her had felt ashamed to be marrying him. A picture would've felt like evidence of a crime.

All she wanted right now was a shower and to feel safe again. Safe. She turned and made sure the door was locked. She peeked out the window, but there was no sign that anyone had followed her.

Finally feeling secure, she stripped out of her sweaty clothes and stepped into the shower. The hot water eased her aching muscles, and the steam cleared her head. The more she thought about it, the more convinced she was that she'd simply let her imagination run away with her.

Clean and refreshed, she made her way to her craft room. Connor had helped her set up a macrame studio on the second floor.

During her recovery she'd returned to making macrame earrings, bracelets and hanging plant holders. Her fingers still remembered the techniques she'd learned from her mother. It had brought back happy memories of working at the kitchen table on her first project, an owl that had turned out lopsided because her inexperienced hands couldn't keep the tension consistent. Her mother had hung it up in the den anyway, and Denise had been so proud.

She'd felt happy turning her hobby into a business, discovering that there was a demand for the intricate wall hangings. Her Etsy really took off after she began posting on Instagram. Now she could barely keep up with the orders for some of her more unique designs.

Her office was filled with shelves holding with colored cords, findings, and beads. There was a wooden table with an adjustable ring light for her online videos where she demonstrated knotting techniques. Her subscribers had grown from a handful to thousands. No one was more surprised than she was.

It was a job she could handle, unlike Grady Oil. Denise couldn't bear the thought of going back to the office without Laura.

She printed out the new orders. One was for a large dreamcatcher she'd just reduced in price. It was one of her favorite pieces, and she hated to let it go. That was the hardest part of her job. She put so much love and attention into her original designs that it was like letting go of her own children when she sent the pieces off to a new owner. But she couldn't keep everything she made. They'd have to buy one of those empty houses in the development just to store it all.

She wrapped the dreamcatcher in tissue paper, added a handwritten thank-you note and a handmade macrame bookmark as a thank-you gift. She was convinced that the extra personal touch was the reason so many of her customers came back. She addressed the package and added it to the pile of outgoing orders. As much as she hated the thought of driving, she wanted to get the orders in the mail. Whenever a customer reviewed their order, they always commented about how quickly it had arrived. She took pride in that.

She carried the packages out of her craft room. Halfway down the stairs, she heard scratching at the front door. She stopped, tilted her head, and listened, but there was no further sound.

"Connor?"

No reply.

She walked downstairs slowly, still on the alert in case the sound started up again.

She knew what Connor would say. It was just the sound of a new house settling. Nothing to worry about. She made her way to the door and peeked out the side window. No one there. She opened the door and looked down to see if there were scratches on the door. Maybe an animal had been trying to get in. But there was nothing. She wasn't sure whether to be relieved or not.

Was she imagining things, or was it something worse?

It took a few minutes to work herself up to getting in the car. This time, she told herself, she'd be fine. She turned the ignition and her heartbeat quickened, pounding so loud that she could hear nothing else. She froze, unable to move or put the car in gear. Riding in a car was one thing, but being behind the wheel brought it all back. She hadn't been able to drive a car since the accident, although she had tried. Tried and failed, on more occasions than one.

Gasping for breath, she stepped out of the car and pulled out her phone. She had her Uber set up with her home address. She typed in the words "post office" for destination and hit the pick up button. Otherwise she'd have to depend on Connor to take her everywhere, and he was hardly ever home anymore. Her therapist promised the fear of driving was temporary and soon she'd be able to get behind the wheel without having a panic attack. She hoped that was the case, but feared that if it hadn't happened yet it may never happen at all.

When the Uber driver arrived, she climbed in the car and placed her packages on the seat beside her.

"Going to the post office?" the driver asked.

"Yeah, I'm not really sure where it is yet," she said, fumbling with her phone trying to get to her maps app.

"No problem. I know how to get there."

Relieved, Denise put her phone back in her bag. Eventually she'd know her way around, but for now she was relying on strangers to take her where she needed to go.

As the driver wound his way out of the development, she couldn't help watching for a flash of purple in each house they passed.

"I didn't think this place was open yet," the driver said.

"I guess they hit a snag," she replied. "Only a handful of the houses have been sold, so it's a bit of a ghost town."

The driver laughed. "You can say that again. I was sure I had the wrong address when I drove by all those unfinished houses."

Denise thought it was odd as well. Surely some more people should have moved in by now. Instead, the place had an abandoned look, sure to attract vagrants and thieves. It hadn't occurred to her before, but maybe the man in the hoodie hadn't been stalking her. Maybe he'd been looking for something to steal. Construction tools, or furnishings from some of the empty model houses. And didn't people also steal copper wiring?

The driver dropped Denise off at the post office in under fifteen minutes. As remote as the development felt, at least they weren't too far from civilization. In addition to the post office, Main Street offered a bustling coffee shop, two high-end boutiques, a bookstore, a mom-and-pop diner, and several small-business storefronts. There wasn't time to explore, however. The post office closed in thirty minutes, and she wanted to get these packages in the mail.

She nodded at a man who held the door open while she balanced packages against her chest. Luckily the line wasn't long and seemed to be moving quickly. Moments later, she felt a hand on her shoulder and turned.

"Denise? I thought that was you."

Raquel.

She'd been one of her best friends in high school. They'd grown apart afterward, keeping in touch with the occasional birthday card or text message. It's not as if they'd had a fight or anything. They'd just grown apart. Still, it was surprising that Raquel hadn't called or stopped by to see how she was doing. Denise clutched the packages to her chest, blocking Raquel's attempt to come in for a hug.

"How have you been?" Raquel chirped.

"How do you think I've been?"

Raquel looked away. "I'm sorry I haven't been in touch. I wanted to visit you in the hospital, but I'm just … I'm not good with hospitals and stuff."

"Funny, neither am I. But I was stuck there. It might have been nice to have a visitor every once in a while, though." Once she started, the words poured out. "It would have been really nice to have a friend around to talk to while I was recovering and mourning my sister." Her breath caught on a sob.

"I'm sorry."

"And it might have been nice to have a shoulder to cry on all of those months."

Raquel's eyes narrowed. "Well, from what I've heard, you had Laura's husband's shoulder to cry on. I guess that's all the 'friend' you needed, right?"

Denise turned away, tears blurring her vision. She'd worried that's what people would think, that she'd just slipped into her sister's place without a second thought. But hearing it out loud hurt even more than she'd thought it would. It wasn't like that. Connor had helped her get through the most difficult time of her life. He never judged or blamed her. She did enough blaming for both of them.

But she guessed she should start expecting the rest of the world to blame her too.

Before she could respond, it was her turn at the counter. The postal worker weighed her packages and tallied up the bill. She swiped her credit card and took the receipt, avoiding Raquel's eyes as she stormed out the door.

She slipped into the coffee shop next door, smiled at the barista, and ordered a caramel macchiato. From her vantage point, she watched Raquel leave the post office and climb into a cherry-red convertible. It looked sleek and sporty. When Connor had insisted on buying her a new car to replace the one destroyed in the accident, Denise had chosen it based on safety records and reliability. She'd yet to drive it.

For the first time, she wondered if he was disappointed about that.

Her phone vibrated in her pocket. She glanced at the text message from Connor. *I'll be home for dinner tonight. Don't bother cooking. I'll pick something up. Italian or Chinese?*

Italian, she texted back. *With an order of garlic bread.* She added a smiley emoji and a heart. She felt better already. The macchiato had done its job, and knowing Connor wouldn't be working late tonight was icing on the cake. Or in this case, froth on the coffee.

THE SMELL of tomato sauce and garlic greeted her when she opened the door, making her mouth water and her stomach grumble in anticipation.

Connor met her at the door. "I hope you're hungry."

"Mmmm…" She raised her lips to him, and he wrapped his arms around her, resting his hands on her lower back. He leaned forward and pressed his lips to hers, soft at first, then more urgent as he pulled her closer. She relaxed against him for a moment, then Raquel's words came back to her.

You had Laura's husband's shoulder to cry on.

She stiffened and pulled away. "Let's eat before dinner gets cold."

His smile turned chilly. "Sure, nothing worse than cold lasagna."

Well, she could think of a few things, but she kept a smile on her face and followed Connor into the dining room. On the way, she glanced at the wedding picture on the mantel. There was still something different about it, but she couldn't put her finger on it. She stopped and stared at it. Was it Laura's smile? Hadn't it been bigger before? More joyful? Less like a grimace?

"Connor?"

He turned and stared, tipping his head with a questioning gaze.

"Does this picture look different to you?"

He stepped closer and picked up the framed photograph. "No. Different how?"

Denise blinked, trying to bring it into focus. "Her smile looks different to me."

Connor stared at her, a frown on his face. "Are you sure you don't want me to put this into storage with the rest of Laura's things?"

"No, that's not it." Or was it? Could these perceived changes be a result of the guilt she still felt? And was she so reluctant to get rid of her sister's wedding photo because she felt she deserved the constant reminder of that guilt?

Connor shook his head, as if he was disappointed in her, or more likely, tired of her confusion.

She just needed a moment alone. "I'll be right back."

"But dinner—"

"I'll just be a minute."

She rushed upstairs. In the bathroom, she pressed a wet washcloth to her face and tried to clear her mind. This entire day was one big question after another, from the person she was sure she saw on her morning run, to her encounter with Raquel, and now thinking the picture looked different. She couldn't shake the feeling she was disappointing Connor, and if he didn't already know what people were thinking about them, it was probably better not to talk to him about her conversation with Raquel. She decided not to tell him about running into her.

She hung the washcloth up and noticed her toothbrush on the counter. Yellow. *What the…?*

She went to the cupboard. All yellow toothbrushes in the package. She was sure they were all blue before. She rubbed her eyes. Maybe she was going insane.

She wanted to blame it on the anti-anxiety pills, but she hadn't taken them for a couple of days.

Could she be going through some sort of withdrawal?

Or was this a sign that she should start taking them again?

Connor called upstairs. "Are you okay?"

"Fine," she lied.

"Come on down. Dinner's getting cold."

She put the toothbrushes away and went downstairs. Connor had set the table with Laura's good dishes. Laura had been an excellent cook, and Denise had enjoyed more wonderful meals on these dishes than she could count. She felt a flash of anger. When she'd suggested bringing some of Laura's things from storage, he'd nixed the idea, but then he went there to get her sister's dishes without asking her? He was the one who'd pushed hard for a fresh start from the beginning of their relationship. It was almost as if he was trying to make her feel bad. As if her weakness was the reason he couldn't have mementos of his dead wife.

Connor probably didn't even realize how many memories these dishes would bring up. Or maybe he didn't think she'd recognize them because it had been so long since she'd eaten from them. She'd had an unsettling day, possibly made worse by the fact that she'd stopped taking her pills, and she might be overreacting to something he didn't realize would bother her. He'd made a point to ask her what she wanted him to bring home for dinner, like he always did. If he was trying to make her feel bad, why would he do that?

She decided that she *was* overreacting, and that she should assume that the dishes were an innocent misstep. Maybe he had packed them up at the old house but never taken them to storage in the first place, and when the movers brought the box over, he'd unpacked them without even realizing they were Laura's. This was Connor, the most patient and caring man she'd ever met. How many men would devote themselves to nursing their sister-in-law back to health just weeks after losing their wife and child?

Connor poured her a glass of wine. She sipped it gratefully, then took a deep breath. She'd lost her appetite but made a good show of pushing lasagna around her dish and nibbling on the garlic bread. Connor seemed not to notice.

"How was your day?" he asked.

Denise shrugged. "Fine. I filled some orders and dropped them off at the post office. There's a cute little coffee shop downtown, and I spent some time there."

"Alone?"

"Yes, of course." What kind of question was that? He

knew she didn't have any friends here. No one she could call and express her concerns with. Did he expect her to have already made friends with their new neighbors?

He poured her another glass of wine. "You didn't eat much."

She normally stopped at one glass, but tonight she felt she needed the fortification.

"I'm not as hungry as I thought." She pushed her plate away and took another sip of wine. "How was your day?" she asked, changing the subject.

He rubbed his forehead, looking stressed. "I wasn't sure whether to tell you, but there've been rumblings around the office of a hostile takeover."

"What?" Denise shook her head. "What does that mean?"

"Basically it's when one company targets another company to acquire it against its will, despite objections from the board of directors."

Denise stood and carried her plate to the kitchen. She scraped it into the garbage, then turned back to Connor. "I don't understand. How can they take the company over against our will?"

Connor shrugged. "They can buy up shares from the stockholders, for one thing. That's how Kraft Foods took over Cadbury back in 2009."

She wondered if he'd read that in *Making Workspace Archetypes Work for You.*

"No one would've dared tried it while Laura and I were at the helm together," Connor added, and it was hard not to take that as a criticism. As if she was the weak link that someone might use to get to him.

Denise sank into her chair and lifted the glass of wine, which was magically full again. How many glasses did that make? Two? Three?

"Should I be worried?" she asked, noticing the slightest slur to her words.

"No," he said. "I have it under control. Besides, it's just a rumor."

"Usually if there's a rumor, there's some truth behind it."

"Maybe," he said, "but since you and I hold the controlling shares together, it wouldn't matter how many shares they acquired, it wouldn't be enough."

She shot him a worried glance. "Are you sure?"

He reached out and covered her hand with his, giving it a little squeeze. "I'm sure. Grady Oil has lasted eighty years, and it's going to last eighty more."

Denise drained the rest of her wine, then carried the empty glass to the sink before Connor could refill it again. She was already feeling light-headed. That's when she noticed the paper bag on the counter next to the takeout containers. "What's this?"

"Oh, I forgot." He opened the bag and pulled out a bottle of pills. "Ginkgo biloba," he explained. "Frieda, our new receptionist, recommended it. She says it's good for cognitive health or something. She implied that someone *my age* could benefit from taking it."

Denise laughed. "It's the gray hair."

He ran a hand through his hair. "Does it make me look that old?"

"It makes you look distinguished. Like a silver fox. Maybe I should be worried that Frieda is hitting on you?"

"Not a chance."

It was strange that the receptionist was able to talk him into taking a supplement so easily. So far, he'd avoided her own attempts to get him to improve his diet. He'd thumbed his nose at green juice, collagen extract, and ginger tablets.

Maybe he was turning a corner, and ginkgo biloba was the first tiny step in making a dietary change.

She picked up her phone, googled ginkgo biloba, and found it was also used as an aid in improving mental functions and treating anxiety.

"Maybe I should start taking it too," she said with a wry laugh. "Especially after the toothbrush incident."

"Toothbrush incident?"

"Yes, they're back to being yellow. This morning they were blue, remember?"

Connor shook his head. "No, this morning they were yellow, and you insisted they should be blue."

"No, I distinctly remember…" *Did she?* Now that he mentioned it, she wasn't so sure. More residual side effects from the pills she'd stopped taking? Maybe an all-natural approach to improving her memory would be a better idea than taking more medication. She wondered if ginkgo biloba would help with panic attacks too.

She checked the label on the bottle. *Take one on an empty stomach before bed.*

She shook her head. She'd already had too much wine. She didn't want to add anything else to the mix.

Together they loaded the dishwasher and put the rest of the leftovers in the refrigerator. Connor put on a movie, but Denise was too drowsy to pay attention. When the movie was over, she told Connor she was feeling sleepy and intended to read in bed.

"Go ahead," he said. "I'll be up after the news."

She kissed him on the forehead, then made her way upstairs to brush her teeth. Good, the toothbrush was still yellow. She wasn't going crazy. She changed and laid down in bed, but before she could even get a chapter into her new book, she drifted off to sleep.

Chapter Six

DENISE HAD a full day ahead of her. First the hairdresser, then the nail salon. When was the last time she'd pampered herself? Not since Laura's death. Pampering was her sister's thing, and she'd always dragged Denise along. They'd shop, have a massage, pick an outrageous nail color, and then go to lunch. It was their special time together. Now it just felt like a chore. But she needed to look her best for the gala tonight. Having inherited half of Laura's shares, Denise was the major shareholder and last surviving Grady of Grady Oil. She needed to look the part.

The hairdresser pulled her hair up into a fancy up-do, just right for the gala event. Denise barely recognized herself in the mirror. Once her hair and nails were done, she decided to take Connor's advice and shop for a new evening gown. She found herself walking with a bounce to her step. And when she glanced in the dressing room mirror, she was surprised to see a genuine smile on her face, not the fake smile she planted there for the public to see.

The dress she picked out was emerald green with a sweetheart neckline. She turned and posed in the mirror. She felt pretty. The dress was expensive, but a small price to pay for the way it made her feel. She only hoped Connor would like it as well.

HER HOPES WERE REWARDED when she stepped out of the bedroom that evening, all dressed and ready for the party. Connor's eyes widened. "Wow, you look gorgeous!"

Denise eyed him in his midnight blue suit. "You're looking pretty fabulous yourself."

He made a palms-up gesture. "This old thing?"

Denise laughed and slipped her arm into the crook of his elbow. "We make a good-looking pair, don't you say?"

Connor leaned over and kissed the top of her head. "We sure do."

But then Denise saw a shadow pass over his face. Was he thinking of Laura? Comparing her to her sister?

Just then there was a honk outside. Denise glanced out the window. Their ride was here. They went downstairs and Denise grabbed her clutch. It was covered in rhinestones, something she only used on special occasions. The purse was small enough to be unobtrusive, but big enough to hold her phone and a tube of lipstick.

Connor stared at the small purse. "Is that Laura's?"

"Huh? No, it's mine. I splurged on it back in high school to wear with my prom dress."

"Oh, okay." He nodded, but she could see he still looked suspicious.

Had she ever let Laura borrow it? Maybe that's when he'd seen it and assumed it belonged to her. But no, Denise didn't remember lending it out. She hadn't even seen it for years. She'd just dug it out of the back of her closet this week.

She stopped in the living room and glanced at the wedding picture. Connor had moved from the mantel, and it was now hanging on the wall. Did her sister's smile look different again? She stepped closer to study it.

"Now what?" Connor couldn't hide the exasperation in his voice.

"Nothing. It's nothing."

Another honk sounded, more forceful this time.

Connor took her hand. "Let's go," he said.

Denise didn't have time to admire the sleek limousine. She was ushered into the back, where they joined several others: Grady Oil CFO Allen and his wife Pamela, COO Barbara and her husband William, and HR Manager Kelly and her husband Charles.

Charles passed around champagne flutes and popped a bottle of champagne. Denise sipped on hers, afraid she'd get tipsy and start imagining things again.

Kelly leaned forward. "I love your dress. Where did you get it?"

Denise told her about the boutique she'd discovered downtown.

"Seriously," Pamela said. "You look amazing. Especially after…" She stopped and cleared her throat.

Denise looked away, her glow fading. She had a feeling the accident would be on everyone's minds today, and she hated the thought of being the center of attention. Connor looked over and gave her a wink, as if to say everything would be all right. She smiled back, grateful she'd have him by her side to face the onslaught of questions and concerns that would surely come her way this evening.

"So," Barbara said, "how do you like the new house?"

"It's gorgeous. I'm not used to living in such a big

house." She thought about the family cabin on Lake Lavon, hers alone now that Laura was gone. Connor was urging her to sell it, but the cabin held so many memories, she hated to let it go.

Charles leaned toward Connor. "What's with all the empty houses over there?"

Connor shrugged and downed some champagne. "I thought it would be filling up more by now. I called the construction company, and apparently there's an issue with some outstanding loans. The bank has put a lien on the construction company."

"Sucks," said Glen.

"Yeah. So nothing can be sold at the moment."

"You're pretty isolated out there."

"We have a few neighbors on the cul-de-sac who bought before the financial problems started."

Denise turned to Connor. "When did you find this out?"

He gave a short laugh. "I told you yesterday, remember?"

She shook her head. "No." She'd certainly remember if he'd told her the development might be empty for … *who knows how long*?

Connor frowned. "We had an entire conversation about it in the kitchen. Right after you told me about the man in the purple hoodie watching you from one of the empty houses."

Denise started to correct him. She hadn't told him about the man, had she?

He added, "After we talked about it, I called to see when construction would start up again because honestly, it was a bit unnerving. I worry about you."

Denise was confused. She had no memory of telling Connor about the man in purple, and she didn't remember a conversation about the developer's problems selling the empty homes. Her voice was strained. "I don't remember."

She could feel everyone's eyes on her as the conversation came to a stop. She looked from one to the other. This wasn't the image she wanted to project. She tried to laugh it off.

"I probably zoned out. Between the move and building up my strength again…" Her voice softened. "I guess I've been in a bit of a fog."

Connor reached out and squeezed her hand. It was meant to be comforting, but it felt more like a warning. Was she saying too much? Acting unstable? The last thing she wanted was to embarrass him tonight. While she stayed home, he had to face the rumors every day he went to work, and to lead despite what his employees might think.

She tried to regain her composure, brushing imaginary lint from her dress.

Pamela stared at her for a long moment, then looked away. And as suddenly as it stopped, conversation started up again. When Charles offered her more champagne, she shook her head no, then leaned back and let the conversation flow around her.

Chapter Seven

THE LIMO DRIVER dropped them off at one of the largest hotels in the city, an iconic tower with a five-star restaurant at the top, offering customers a 360-degree view of the city. It was one of Denise's favorite places to eat, so she was delighted that the company party was being held there.

When they entered the ballroom, they were greeted by a colorful banner congratulating Grady Oil on its 80th anniversary. Clients and employees filled the space, gathered in small, intimate groups. The room brimmed with conversation, along with the slow jazz by a band playing on the bandstand. The excitement was contagious, and Denise felt adrenaline rushing through her body. It was a bit overwhelming considering she'd practically been a hermit these past few months.

She forced herself to keep her chin up and her shoulders back, like Laura would if she were here tonight. She was still a Grady, and she wanted to make their parents proud. Surely she could maintain this façade for a few hours.

They strolled around the room, chatting with clients

and employees alike. There were a lot of pitying stares and questions about "how she was feeling." She felt pinned under a microscope. She heard whispering as she passed by groups of people and knew they were talking about her behind her back. She held tighter to Connor's arm, drawing strength from his presence. If he could ignore the gossip, so could she.

As the majority shareholders, they could afford to ignore it.

But right now, she would've given anything for a little extra *support*. She'd left the pills at home, not wanting to spend the evening in a fog, but now she wondered if that was a mistake.

Tuxedoed waiters strolled by with cocktails and champagne on silver platters. Denise grabbed a glass from a passing waiter. She'd need plenty of fortification to get through this night. By the time they were called to dinner, she was enveloped in a nice warm glow.

She and Connor were seated at the head table, along with the passengers from their limo. It was obvious that she wasn't the only one who'd imbibed a little more than usual. Pamela and Kelly were laughing and slurring their words, despite disapproving glances from each of their husbands.

The food was beautifully presented, but none of it tasted like she remembered. It didn't taste like anything at all, just like most of the food she'd eaten recently. More residual side effects from the pills?

Disappointed, she cut the chicken piccata into little pieces and pushed it from one side of her dish to the other while the dinner conversation swirled around her. Being around all of these familiar faces made her uncomfortable. Laura and Connor had been the ones who handled most of the work-related duties. Denise had always been more comfortable standing in the background. But as Connor's wife, she couldn't avoid being at the center of attention. She wondered how much of the attention was due to their respect for Connor and how much was sordid curiosity about Denise becoming her sister's replacement at his side, in all senses of the word.

She reached for her glass of wine and drained it, hating that she couldn't escape that thought.

After dinner, everyone gathered back in the ballroom, where the Master of Ceremonies took the stage. The MC glanced their way and looked directly at Denise. Her eyes widened, and she shook her head. *No, no, no.* There was no way she was going up on that stage with all eyes on her. It didn't matter that she held a controlling interest in the company. Connor was the spokesperson. She nudged him and he nodded, a gesture caught by the MC, who introduced Connor to the gathered crowd.

Applause filled the room as Connor made his way to the stage. "It's nice to see you all here celebrating Grady Oil's 80th anniversary," he said. "I know many of you were here on the day Laura and Denise's great-grandfather founded the company."

Laughter followed his remark. He mimed writing on a slip of paper. "I'm taking notes on who is here as well. There will be pink slips going out in the morning."

More laughter. Denise smiled. Connor excelled at this.

She felt a new wave of gratitude for him, especially for his willingness to shield her from the things she wasn't ready to handle yet. She wasn't sure what she would have done without him these last few months.

"I hope you enjoyed dinner. At sixty dollars a plate, you better have." He shouted out to the company's head of accounting, "We've got that covered, right, Teddy?"

Teddy made a point of shaking his head and shrugging his shoulders.

Then Connor grew more serious. "The future of the company was in doubt after Laura's death." His eyes glistened, and the room fell into solemn silence. Denise's throat tightened, and she fought back her own tears. "My late wife was the heart of Grady Oil, and when she came to work, she put everything she had into making sure things were done right. I learned something from her every day as I worked alongside her to make this company great."

Laura would be proud that Connor was working so hard to keep the family business running.

Denise dabbed at the corner of her eyes with her napkin, hating that she was crying in front of all these people who might have spent the last six months gossiping about her in her absence and were probably pitying her tonight. They had lost a boss in Laura, but she had lost a sister and a best friend.

And Connor had lost even more.

Connor raised his champagne glass in a toast. "To Laura," he said, his voice cracking.

Everyone in the room raised their glasses and joined in. "To Laura."

Denise started to raise her glass, but her arm trembled and her shoulders shook with suppressed sobs.

"Excuse me," she said, getting up from the table.

She rushed to the restroom and locked herself in one of the stalls, where she finally let go and sobbed. It hurt so much, being around employees that she and Laura had shared so much time with. She felt like an imposter without Laura by her side. She could never be the businesswoman Laura had been. Surely everyone could see that. No wonder they all whispered behind her back. She had no right even being here.

Maybe she'd confused their pity with contempt. Maybe they were happy she'd never come back.

It was foolish of her to think she could get through tonight without her pills. She hadn't been ready to come back. Maybe she never would be.

Finally getting herself under control, she wiped her eyes and was about to leave the stall when she heard the door open. She recognized the drunken giggling belonging to Pamela and Kelly. She could have joined them, but she knew her eyes were red and swollen from crying and didn't want to have to answer any questions. She'd wait until they were gone so she could put cold water on her face before rejoining the party.

Then she heard her name mentioned and her heart stuttered. "Denise didn't even wait until her sister's body was cold in the ground before snagging her husband."

They laughed at the vicious comment. "I think he married her out of pity. She doesn't hold a candle to Laura."

"Classic rebound," the other woman said. "Happens all the time. Someone swoops in and traps a grieving widower. Who knows, maybe she was after him all along."

"Yeah, maybe she fiddled with the brakes herself."

Pamela gasped.

Kelly laughed. "I know, I'm terrible."

"Well, you're just saying what everyone is thinking."

Denise stood frozen. Was that really what other people were thinking, or was it just drunken conjecture? The accusation was too hideous to contemplate. She wanted to throw up. But she wouldn't give them the satisfaction. She told herself that Kelly's statement said more about her character than Denise's.

But that didn't make it any easier to bear.

She waited while the women took turns in the stalls,

then washed their hands and left the room, freeing her to leave her own stall. She wet a paper towel and held it to her face, making herself look as presentable as possible. She straightened her shoulders, determined not to let them see her upset.

Outside the restroom, she walked right past Pamela and Kelly. Their eyes widened when they saw her emerge from the very room they'd just exited. They glanced at each other, shame reddening their cheeks.

"Excuse me," Denise said, strutting past them as if she wasn't devastated inside. Finding Connor talking to one of Grady Oil's clients, she reached for his arm.

He gave her a questioning glance. "Everything okay?"

She nodded. "I'm just not feeling well. Migraine. Would you mind if I left?"

"I'll go with you," he said.

"No. You stay. This is what you're good at, and one of us should be here."

He nodded, maybe giving in a little too easily. It wasn't as if she wanted him to leave with her, but he could have given up more of a fight.

Selfish. He'd kept this company going since the accident despite his own personal grief. He had every right to enjoy the respect and camaraderie of his employees, some of whom thought Denise was capable of killing her own sister.

Her nausea intensified, and Connor frowned in concern.

"Let me call you a driver," he said, taking out his phone. He finished the call and told her it would be about five minutes.

She thanked him, when what she really wanted to do was scream. Or faint. Or take every pill in her bottle the second she got home.

"I'll walk you outside," he said, taking her arm and leading her to the elevator.

Her cheeks burned as she passed Pamela and Kelly whispering and watching her. Kelly looked ashamed, but Pamela looked defiant, like she was hoping Denise would challenge them.

Of course, she didn't.

When the driver arrived, Connor gave her a hug and a kiss on the cheek. "Take something for that migraine. I'll see you when I get home."

"I will," she said. "Take your time. I'll probably be asleep when you get there." But she had a feeling sleep wasn't going to come easily. If she did fall asleep, Pamela and Kelly's words would be following her into her nightmares.

But the gossip was right about one thing — she paled in comparison to Laura, and she always would've been the first to admit it. She wasn't as pretty or charming or driven. While Laura was always on the honor roll, Denise was a solid "C" student.

When she thought about it from that perspective, she understood why Connor's marriage to her didn't make sense to people like Pamela and Kelly. To them, it probably looked like confident, successful Connor settled for her in the aftermath of mourning his family.

It didn't help that she'd needed him after the accident. Not financially — she could have sold some of her shares until she was fit to come back to the office — but physically and emotionally. But she hadn't come back, had she? She'd married him and settled into being his wife, as far as anyone else could tell.

And the way things were going, she wasn't sure if she'd ever go back to work. She'd never been passionate about her job to begin with. But she'd never tried to do anything else, because Laura was passionate about it, and she hadn't been able to imagine herself *not* working alongside her sister.

It was the same with Connor: she wasn't passionate about him either, but she'd been adrift, and he was the anchor she'd needed once she'd been unmoored from her sister. He was the closest thing she had left to family, and she couldn't bear the thought of being alone. She'd needed someone to grieve with her, and he'd needed the same.

She wanted to love him. He deserved that for his steadfast support and his kind care.

But she didn't.

Yet another way that she paled in comparison to Laura.

Chapter Eight

"Ma'am?"

Denise had been lost in thought and hadn't realized they'd reached her house. She shook her head. "Sorry."

She reached for her purse, but the driver shook her off. "Your husband already paid for the ride and the tip."

"Thank you," she said, stepping out of the car. She looked around and frowned. Both houses on either side of hers were dark. As the driver pulled away, she was overcome with a sense of isolation. She rushed to the door, went inside, and locked it behind her. Her tension eased as she turned on all the lights in the house. She checked the rest of the doors to make sure she was safely locked inside. Only then did she feel safe enough to kick off her shoes and coat.

She glanced at the picture on the wall. Laura's grin looked much wider, almost malevolent. She shook her head. Her mind was playing tricks on her. How much had she had to drink? She took down the picture and laid it face down on the coffee table. Maybe it wasn't such a good idea to have this reminder around.

She thought about taking one pill, just to take the edge off and ease her into sleep. But she worried about it interacting with all the drinks she'd had to get through the anniversary event. Problem was, the alcohol wasn't making her sleepy, either, just making it harder not to cycle through the same depressing thoughts.

It was only 11:00 pm, and she was wide awake. No sense going to bed only to lie there staring at the ceiling. She turned on the TV and flipped through her favorite stations, but nothing appealed to her. She checked her phone to see if there was a message from Connor, but nothing.

Evidently, he was having a great time without her.

Wasn't that what she wanted him to do?

Still, she felt alone and abandoned.

She picked up a book to read, but it was too dark and depressing. She needed something upbeat with a happy ending to get her out of this funk. She picked up her Kindle and scrolled through the books she'd loaded. Finally she found a sweet romance with a Christmas theme. That should do the trick.

A dozen chapters into the book, she looked up at the time. Midnight. Connor still wasn't home. Her eyes were tired from reading. She yawned, ready for bed.

Upstairs, she stripped out of her dress. The evening gown, which had felt so glamorous when she put it on, now felt like a weight on her shoulders. She doubted she'd ever wear it again. It would forever remind her of Kelly's accusation, and the way Pamela laughed and said it was what everyone was thinking.

Denise couldn't imagine going back to her old job now, looking each person in the face and wondering if they thought she had murdered her sister.

As annoying as Connor could be sometimes, at least he

knew her better than that. He might be the only person in the world who truly knew her, now that Laura was dead.

She put on a sports bra and linen shorts, her typical sleepwear. She still didn't feel comfortable sleeping naked beside Connor. Not yet, anyway.

Despite the fact that she'd lied about having a migraine, she thought it might be smart to take something to help her sleep. She went into the bathroom and got the sleeping pills out of the medicine chest, but the label warned her about taking these with alcohol too. As she contemplated risking it anyway, she noticed the blue toothbrush sitting on the sink. She rushed to the closet to check the pack. All blue.

What the…?

She chucked the entire package in the garbage. So much for that. She'd buy new toothbrushes in the morning.

She took half a sleeping pill before climbing into bed, and apparently it did its job, because she only woke up when she heard Connor come into the bedroom. Her head felt as if it was stuffed with cotton, and her mouth tasted foul. Connor leaned in for a kiss, but she turned her head away.

"How are you feeling?" he asked.

She blinked. "Not great."

She sat up and reached for the bottle of water on her nightstand and took a long swallow.

"Is it because of my speech?" he asked. "Was it too much?"

"No. I liked it. I think it was appropriate to acknowledge Laura's contribution to the company. Especially on our 80th anniversary." She frowned. "It just makes me sad hearing her spoken of in the past tense. I'm not sure I'll ever get used to the fact that she's gone. That I just can't pick up the phone and talk to her or meet her for coffee."

"I know," he said gently. "It still doesn't seem possible. A beautiful light has gone out of the world."

Yes, Denise thought. That was exactly how it felt. Connor understood, even if no one else did.

He stripped out of his clothes and crawled into bed. His body was warm and comforting beside her.

She snuggled close, spooning against his strong, hard chest. "How do you think she'd feel about this? Us?"

"Hmm. I think she'd be happy that the two people she loved most in the world have each other to lean on for support and comfort."

Denise wanted to believe that too. "Have you ever had second thoughts? You know, about us getting married?"

"No." His arms tightened around her. "Have you?"

Denise hesitated. Should she tell him what she'd overheard? "Just stuff people are saying," she said without going into specifics.

His voice hardened. "Don't pay any attention to gossip. People have no idea the hell we've been through. If we've found love in our grief, then that's all that matters."

Denise wasn't ready to say she'd found love. She'd found comfort and stability. And she was grateful to Connor for being there when she needed him most. What would she have done without him? Maybe it would grow into love at some point. But she knew she'd never be Connor's first love. That place was forever reserved for Laura.

Connor's hand slid up her side and cupped her breast, his thumb caressing her nipple in slow, languorous circles. He was giving her time to stop him if she wanted. All she had to do was turn away. But she needed the comfort as much as he did, whether it was an expression of love or simply two people who needed to feel a connection instead of the emptiness of loss.

Finding no resistance, he explored further, touching her in all the places that pushed negative thoughts out of her mind. She felt him hard against her bottom and knew the time for changing her mind had passed.

She turned and pressed her lips to his for a slow, lingering kiss. In case there was any question left in his mind, she raised her hips and stroked the length of his erection. With a soft groan, he reached down and slid her shorts off, pressing himself against her warmth. Before long, she no longer had to pretend to feel passion, as their natural instincts took over. There were no tender words of love, only thrusts and groans and quickening pace until they were both spent with release. Only then did Denise finally fall into a deep and dreamless sleep.

Chapter Nine

THE NEXT MORNING, Denise yawned and stretched, surprised at how deeply she'd slept. The sun was streaming in the window. She felt refreshed and more alive than she'd felt in a long time. *Good sex will do that for you*, she thought with a smile.

Downstairs, she joined Connor, who was eating cereal at the kitchen counter.

"You can at least sit at the table," she joked.

"Why dirty two surfaces?" He slung an arm around her waist. "How are you feeling this morning?"

"Mmmm…"

"That's what I thought," he said with a bit of male cockiness.

"Pretty sure of yourself, aren't you?"

He grinned. "No complaints so far."

Maybe it didn't matter if she loved Connor, as long as she could make him happy.

She turned to the cabinet and grabbed a bowl, then poured herself some cereal. It was cozy, sharing breakfast together. She hadn't realized before how nice it was to have someone to eat with, to watch television with, or to cuddle with in bed.

"What are your plans for today?" he asked.

"Don't know. Probably working on some of my outstanding orders. What about you?"

"I'm going into the office for a bit."

"On Saturday?"

He shrugged. "I just need to tie up a few loose ends. I'll be back in time for the barbecue."

"Oh, that's tonight, right?"

"Uh huh. You said you'd make dessert."

"That's right. I guess I know what I'll be doing today."

He finished his cereal, then rinsed his bowl out and placed it in the dishwasher. She followed him to the door and noticed the picture was hanging back on the wall.

"I took this down," she said, pointing to the picture.

"Oh? I thought maybe you had put it on the coffee table because it fell. Do you want me to take it down?"

She stared at the picture. It was back to normal. She was starting to wonder how much damage she'd done to her head in the accident. Or maybe the anti-anxiety pills had been helping? A lot of the memory problems seemed to have started after she stopped taking them.

"No," she said. "I don't know. It's fine."

He kissed her cheek and headed out the door. She watched him leave, a frown on her face. The doctor had told her that her concussion had healed, but maybe it had messed up her head more than she thought. What if she had brain damage and they'd missed it?

But she wasn't having any of the other symptoms that they'd told her to watch for, like headaches or missing time or difficulty doing everyday things. It was just her confusion about very specific things, like the wedding pictures and the toothbrushes.

Things related to Laura.

Maybe she *was* going crazy. Guilt could do that to a person, couldn't it?

She rinsed out her bowl and placed it in the dishwasher, then went upstairs. Toothbrush. Yellow. She squinted her eyes. Maybe the toothbrush wasn't changing colors, but her vision was tricking her. Like those Facebook pictures of dresses that could look gray one way and green the other. She blinked her eyes, then held them closed to the count of five.

When she opened them again, the toothbrush was still yellow. She put it in the drawer. Closed it. Opened it. Yellow. Closed it. Opened it again. Still yellow.

She shook her head. She must have imagined the blue one. There was no other explanation.

She glanced at her reflection in the mirror. "You are losing your ever-loving mind."

Maybe Connor was right about her needing to find another therapist.

With a deep breath, she turned away and walked into her craft room, where she printed out some shipping labels. At least here in her studio, everything was normal and predictable. No pictures that changed or toothbrushes that switched colors. She packed up her orders to take to the post office. She'd have to go to the grocery store when she was out to buy ingredients for the dessert she was going to make for the barbecue that night. Until then, she'd spend some time restocking her supply of planter hangers.

Working on an elaborate new design took her mind off of her worries. Before she knew it, hours had passed. It felt good to be working with her hands and doing what she loved best.

She stood and stretched the kinks out of her back. A sound downstairs caught her attention. She stopped and tilted her head to listen. Was that a door closing? She leaned out of the doorway and called down. "Connor?"

Nothing.

She tiptoed downstairs, listening intently, but no further sounds broke the silence. In the living room, she peeked out the front door. Connor's car wasn't in the driveway.

Then she checked the garage, but his car wasn't there either. She chewed on her thumb and listened, her senses on high alert. Was it just her imagination, or was someone hiding in the house?

She walked past the picture and started. What the hell? Laura's face had changed again, now looking even more malevolent than before, her eyes narrowed as if in fury.

How? Had someone come in and changed it somehow?

No, that was crazy.

She ran outside and spotted Helen unloading groceries from the trunk of her car. Helen looked over. "What's wrong?"

Denise rushed over. "Did you see anyone coming out of my house?"

"Someone was in your house?"

"I don't know." Now she was unsure of what she'd heard. "I was upstairs, and I thought I heard the door slam closed. And then things seemed to have changed."

"Changed? How so?"

Now Denise felt silly. "Maybe it was just my imagination."

"Wait here," Helen said. She went into her garage and came back out holding a golf club. "Come on. Let's check it out.

Helen led the way, holding the golf club on her

shoulder like a baseball bat. Together they searched the house from top to bottom. In the bathroom, Denise opened the drawer to find her toothbrush right where she'd left it. Still yellow.

She slammed the drawer shut, not trusting her own eyes anymore.

"All clear," Helen said, letting the golf club fall to her side. "Are you sure you heard someone?"

"I thought so. Maybe it was just my imagination." Seemed as if she was saying that a lot lately.

"It's easy to be spooked. I blame the construction company for leaving the neighborhood empty. It's an open invitation to thieves and criminals and all kinds of mischief makers. I don't blame you at all for being suspicious. Keep your door locked from now on, okay?"

Denise nodded. "Helen?"

"Hmm?"

"What do you think of that picture there?" Would she comment that Laura looked angry rather than joyous?

Helen walked closer to inspect it. "It's a beautiful picture. That's your sister, right?"

"Yes, that's Laura."

"She's lovely." Helen's voice softened. "The question is, how do you feel about having their wedding picture on display?"

Denise took a deep breath. She wanted to confide in someone, but she was afraid of looking foolish. "It's not the picture that bothers me. It's just … it seems to change. One day the bouquet is the way I remembered, and the next day it's not. Sometimes Laura is smiling, and sometimes she has an expression on her face that's almost vicious."

Helen gave her a questioning look. "Has anyone else noticed these differences?"

She had a vivid memory of one of the earliest signs of her mother's mental problems. There was a picture of the Last Supper on the wall. Denise's mother was convinced that Jesus was staring at her, his eyes following her around the room. The more they tried to convince her the eyes in the painting weren't following her and were in fact closed, the more agitated she became. Was it a coincidence — or proof that she was following in her mother's footsteps?

"No." Denise shook her head. "I'm starting to think I'm losing my mind."

Helen went over and gave her a hug. "Oh honey. You've been through a lot. Don't be so hard on yourself. I'm sure there's a reasonable explanation."

"Like someone breaking in and changing the picture while I was upstairs?" It sounded ridiculous when she said it aloud, but the only other explanation was that she was losing her mind. Why would someone mess with her like that?

"Do you want me to stay with you until Connor comes home?"

"No, I'll be fine. I promise to lock the doors and try not to be so skittish in the future."

"Okay, but I'll be right next door if you need me." Helen walked out the door, calling over her shoulder. "See you at the barbecue tonight."

"Yes, see you tonight." That reminded Denise that she'd promised to make a dessert for the barbecue. There was still time to get the ingredients.

She went to her recipe file and chose a strawberry shortcake. It was one of her specialties, made with vanilla cake mix in a 9x12 pan, covered with a sweet strawberry glaze. It made enough to feed a small crowd with plenty left over.

She made a list of ingredients, then called Connor. "Will you be coming home soon?"

"I'm afraid not for a few more hours. Still have some loose ends to tie up here. Why? Everything all right?"

"Yeah." She didn't want to tell him that she had *imagined* an intruder, or that the photo had mysteriously changed again. "I was hoping you'd be able to run me to the grocery store."

"Oh," he replied. "It's really not so far. Are you sure you can't drive there by yourself?"

She bristled. He knew she wasn't ready to get behind the wheel yet. But another part of herself was angry that she couldn't just do it. He already worked so hard for them both, and she still expected him to do drive her everywhere.

But there was no way she could drive herself to the store. She wouldn't make it out of the driveway.

"Look, if you want me to come home to take you to the store, I will." But she could tell by the sound of his voice he was only being conciliatory, and it made her feel childish.

"No, you take care of whatever it is you have to. I'll figure something out."

"Really, Denise, if you just put your mind to it, there's no reason you can't just drive. Mind over matter."

"Okay." She kept her voice level, but anger pooled in her belly. It wasn't as easy as mind over matter. Why couldn't he understand how hard it was for her to get behind the wheel of a car after what happened? "Bye."

He would be annoyed with her tonight for hanging up on him, but she couldn't help herself.

She considered asking Helen to drive her to the store, but she already felt foolish for having confided about hallucinating the intruder and the changes to Laura's picture.

She would feel even worse asking the neighbor she barely knew to be her chauffeur because she couldn't handle simple tasks that any adult should be able to do.

Bad enough that Connor knew how pathetic she was. She didn't want her neighbors to see her that way too.

Chapter Ten

SHE TRIED, she really did. It wasn't as if she didn't *want* to drive. Her logical mind told her she was being irrational. But as soon as she got behind the wheel, her heartbeat accelerated and she broke out in a cold sweat. A feeling of impending doom tightened her throat. The panic attack had control of her, not the other way around. She would be a danger on the road if she tried to push through it and drive anyway.

She gave up and called a rideshare.

She chastised herself while she waited for the panic to subside. By the time the driver arrived, she had her emotions under control. She climbed in the back and instructed the driver to take her to the nearest grocery store.

As Denise shopped for the ingredients she'd need for her strawberry shortcake — strawberries, cake mix, graham crackers, and whipped cream — she was starting to feel better. Baking would help, giving her something to do that she knew she could accomplish. And impressing Helen and the other neighbors with the dessert would make them more likely to accept her. She felt so lonely all the time. Just knowing she had a friend nearby could help.

Suddenly, goosebumps raised up on her arms. She felt as if someone was watching her. Glancing up from her shopping list, she noticed a man wearing a purple hoodie at the far end of the aisle. He seemed to be staring straight at her. Or maybe behind her. She turned to see if there was someone behind her, but the aisle was empty. When she turned back, the man was gone.

The hairs on the back of her neck raised. Halfway down the next aisle, she turned — and there he was again. She wasn't imagining it!

An older woman came around the corner, and they bumped carts.

"Oh, I'm sorry," Denise said.

The woman gave an apologetic smile. "My fault."

Denise turned and looked behind her. The man in the purple hoodie was gone again. She made her way to the checkout counter and loaded her groceries onto the conveyor belt. Glancing from one side to the other, she finally spotted him in the back of the store, staring at her.

She whispered to the cashier. "Do you see that man back there?"

The cashier looked up, then back where Denise pointed. "No. Was someone bothering you?"

"No, I … never mind." She handed the cashier her credit card and loaded her groceries into the cart, while keeping an eye out for the man in the purple hoodie.

She jumped when a horn blasted. She looked up to see Helen's husband Ronald pulling up beside her. He waved and rolled down his window.

"Sorry. Didn't mean to startle you."

"Oh, I was just waiting for my ride." She pointed to

her grocery bags. "I just picked up the ingredients to make dessert for the barbecue tonight."

Ronald frowned. "Tonight? No, it's tomorrow night."

"No," Denise corrected him. "It's definitely tonight. Connor even said he'd be home in time to go to the barbecue."

Ronald shook his head. "Tonight is Saturday. The barbecue is on Sunday. You had your company party last night, and Sandra and Diego are at her mother's tonight."

"When did it change?" Denise asked.

Ronald gave her a puzzled look. "It didn't change. It's always been Sunday."

"But … I just talked to Helen this morning, and she confirmed it was tonight."

This time the look he gave her was more concerned than puzzled. "Helen is out of town. She's flying back this afternoon."

Just then her ride pulled up. Denise rushed away, her mind swirling. If Helen was out of town, then who was she talking to today? She vividly remembered Helen wielding that golf club through her entire house. There was no damn way she'd imagined that.

Visibly shaken, she loaded her few bags into the car and gave the driver her home address. How could she be so mistaken? Both Connor and Helen had mentioned the barbecue tonight. But if Helen was at her mother's house, it was even more confusing. She couldn't have imagined that entire scenario today.

When the driver dropped her off, she went inside and dropped the grocery bags on the counter, then marched over to Helen's house. She knocked on the door, but no one answered. She pounded harder, convinced Helen would come out and they'd have a good laugh about the misunderstanding.

Just then, Sandra and Diego came out of their house and called out, "Everything all right, Denise?"

"Yes, I'm trying to get a hold of Helen. Have you seen her today?"

Sandra shook her head. "She's out of town. At her mother's, I think." She turned to Diego for confirmation.

He nodded. "Yes, her mother's been sick lately. She said she'd be home in time for the barbecue tomorrow night."

Tomorrow night. And Helen hadn't been home all day. What the hell was happening?

She rushed to her house, leaving Sandra and Diego staring after her. She locked the door behind her, went upstairs, and collapsed on the bed, trying to find a rational answer for all the day's events.

Had she been sleeping when she heard someone downstairs? Could it have all been a dream? But no, she remembered she'd been working in her craft room when she'd heard the noise downstairs and talked to Helen. Helen, who was supposedly visiting her mother hours away. And what about the man in purple? She'd been out in public when she saw him this time. It felt as if he was following her. But why?

Rather than sit around and worry, she decided to go for a run. She changed into her jogging clothes and pulled on a pair of sneakers, then set out at a comfortable pace until the endorphins kicked in. Soon, she was running with the breeze in her hair and the sun on her face. Her heartbeat matched the rhythmic stomp of her shoes on the sidewalk. The fresh air and sunshine did wonders to elevate her mood.

Before long, she found herself in an unfamiliar area of the housing development. The lots had been cleared, but there were no houses or foundations built. It was just wide-open space. She stopped to get her bearings and heard a rustling sound behind her. She spun around, but no one was there.

Stop being so paranoid.

She looked around, trying to place which direction she'd gone. Perhaps the smartest thing to do was simply to turn around and retrace her steps until she found her way back home.

But instead of running, she strolled casually, focusing on the surrounding sounds. Birds chirped in the trees, and something howled in the distance. A dog maybe, or worse yet, a coyote. Hadn't Connor said there were wild coyotes on the outskirts? She'd have to remember to ask him later that night.

She turned a corner and recognized the street where a cluster of houses was under construction. There was the one where she'd seen the man in the purple hoodie. She crept up and cautiously pushed aside the flap of tarp over the open doorway.

It was empty inside. If there'd been a squatter or a stalker, there was no sign of them now.

Relieved, she turned. Now that she had her bearings, she knew exactly how to get back to her cul-de-sac. She picked up the pace and jogged all the way back to her house.

When she passed Helen's house, all her fears came back. The run had only camouflaged them temporarily. There was no sign of life in Helen's house. Helen wasn't there. Had probably never been there. Which meant she'd invented the whole thing.

She was going crazy.

Chapter Eleven

THE SUN WAS SETTING when Connor finally came home. Denise heard him calling her name downstairs, but she didn't have the energy to reply. Nothing made sense anymore, and she wasn't sure what was wrong with her. She just wanted to be alone. But that wasn't going to happen. She heard his footsteps on the stairs. Then he peeked into the room. "Hey, everything okay?"

She didn't respond.

He stepped closer to the bed and studied her face. "What's wrong? The groceries are sitting on the counter. Did you forget them?"

She couldn't explain. If she tried, he'd think she was crazy. Maybe she was.

The bed dipped as he sat beside her. "Trust me, Denise. Whatever it is, I can help."

She sniffed, then sat up. "You know how I keep asking you about the photo on the wall?"

"Yeah."

"Sometimes when I look at it, it looks different."

He took her hand and squeezed it. "Different how?"

"Like, sometimes Laura seems to be smiling, and other times she looks angry."

"Angry? Angry at you?"

When he put it that way, it seemed rational that she'd interpret her sister's smile as anger. Why wouldn't she be angry?

"Maybe it's just the way the light hits it," Connor suggested.

Denise shook her head. "No. It's more than that. Sometimes the flowers are different. Sometimes Laura's smile changes. It's just … it's like someone is changing the picture."

He snorted. "That's silly. Why would anyone do that?"

"I don't know." Denise shook her head. "Did Laura ever tell you about some of the things my mother did when she was having mental lapses? When her schizophrenia first started getting noticeable?"

Connor looked away, probably because the last thing he wanted to hear right now was to hear that his wife was going crazy. "No, she never talked about it."

"Never?" That was odd. Denise and Laura talked about it all the time. It seemed like every time they talked about it, they remembered something new that should have been a clue to her mother spiraling out of control. Like the time she had them huddle under their beds all day because she was convinced a bomb was going to fall. Or the time she had them lay on the floor and pretend they were dead when their father was coming home from work. One time, she didn't get out of bed for almost an entire week. And yet they didn't realize until it was too late how serious her mental issues had become. "It's not just the picture," she told Connor. "What about the toothbrush? Remember I was convinced they were yellow. Then they were blue. Now they're yellow again." Once she started, she couldn't stop. "And then there's Helen. I saw her today. I talked to her. But according to her husband, she's not even in town." A sob ripped her throat. "I'm afraid, Connor. I'm afraid I'm turning into my mother."

Connor brushed his fingers through her hair. "No, don't think like that. You're just tired, that's all. And all the stress of the 80th anniversary. Plus, we're coming up on the anniversary of Laura's passing. It's a lot to handle."

She nodded. "Maybe you're right."

His voice was hesitant. "Have you been able to find a new therapist?"

"Nope, not since Doctor Corning retired."

He gave her a pointed look. "Maybe it's time to find a new one."

No question about it. He was right. Today had convinced her she needed to talk to someone. "I'll start looking tomorrow."

"I'll help in any way I can," he assured her. He pulled her close and held her until her trembling stopped. "Now let's go downstairs and put those groceries away."

In the living room, Connor took the picture off the wall. "Why don't we put this away for now? It might be better for both of us."

On the one hand, Denise was grateful, but on the other, she felt like it was an admission that she was losing it, like Connor was humoring his crazy wife to avoid triggering another one of her episodes.

Connor pulled bananas out of the grocery bag. "Why did you buy bananas?" he asked. "You don't even like them."

It was true, Denise couldn't stand bananas, but Laura had loved them. She ate them as snacks, sliced them into her cereal, and put them in peanut butter sandwiches.

Had she subconsciously bought the bananas for Laura?

"Honey?" Connor prodded. "Are you in there?"

"I don't know how those got in there." Denise pulled the bag closest to her and stared in amazement — french fries, frozen peas, and pop tarts. What the hell? She didn't buy any of those things. And where were her strawberry shortcake ingredients?

"I didn't buy these," she said, the volume of her voice escalating. "I must have picked up the wrong bags."

She started digging through the remaining bags, scattering produce over the countertop. "Nothing. Nothing I bought is here." She turned pleading eyes to Connor. "I don't know how this could have happened."

"It could have been an honest mistake," he assured her. "Did you step away from the cart at any point?"

"No." She stopped and thought back. "Well, Ronald stopped by and spoke to me for a few minutes. He said Helen is out of town, but I was sure…"

He tilted his head, waiting for her to finish.

She shrugged. "It's nothing. Just a misunderstanding, that's all. Apparently, Helen is out of town. But," she continued, frowning, "I distinctly remember seeing the strawberries in the shopping bag when I got into the car."

She shook her head. Everything was all jumbled. "Didn't you say you'd be home in time for the barbecue tonight?"

"Tonight?" He laughed. "No, the barbecue is tomorrow night. That will give you plenty of time to make your dessert." He held out his hand. "Give me your shopping list. I'll run out for the ingredients."

Now she felt ashamed for being angry with him earlier when he couldn't drop everything at work to take her to the store. He was so willing to take care of her, even when she struggled to do the most basic things.

She searched through the bags until she found her shopping list. Everything was crossed off. She remembered buying each and every thing on her list. Maybe while she was upstairs, someone had switched the bags? She closed her eyes and shook her head. That was just crazy thinking. Like Connor said, it was probably an accidental mix-up.

She pulled out the receipt, hoping there was an answer there. Maybe the driver got her bags mixed up with another client. Nope. Same store, same date, same time, and all the ingredients she knew she'd bought were listed on it.

If someone had just switched the bags, how did her receipt get in this bag?

She was about to show it to Connor, but she was sure he would say something like, *it's proof that the bagger mixed things up while you checked out.* And once he'd explained it away, it would be harder to talk to him about it again without sounding crazy. She needed time to think it through and figure out what was really going on before she talked to him about it again.

She stuffed the receipt in the junk drawer before turning around to hand the list over to him. "Are you sure you don't mind?"

He leaned over and kissed her forehead. "Not at all. While I'm out, I'll pick something up for dinner, okay?"

She nodded, and a spike of pain shot through her head. She winced and dropped her hand into her palms.

"Hey," Connor said. "Are you okay? Is it another migraine?"

She nodded, each movement sending another jolt of pain through her head.

"Oh, baby." Connor reached in the drawer for a clean dishcloth and ran it under cold water. He pressed it to her forehead. "Why don't you lay down while I go back to the store and get these things on your list, okay?"

She followed him to the bedroom and sat on the side of the bed, then spotted the bottle of ginkgo biloba on his nightstand. "Have you started taking these yet?"

He grinned and shook his head. "Nah. But don't tell Frieda."

She shook out two capsules and swallowed them dry.

"Do you think they'll help your migraine?" he asked.

"Can't hurt," she replied.

She placed the bottle back on his nightstand and noticed the book splayed open on his nightstand. It was the latest domestic thriller by one of her favorite authors. She didn't even know they had that book. "Have you finished the other one?" she asked.

"What other one?"

She tried to remember the title. "Something about archetypes."

"Oh. *Making Workspace Archetypes Work for You*. That's next up on my list once I finish this one."

Denise stared at the cover. It didn't look familiar, and it certainly wasn't the same book he was reading in bed last night. "But I thought you were almost done with that one?"

"Nope. Haven't started it yet. First, I need to find out whether the maid or the wife killed the husband in this one."

She made a mental note to look up the side effects of the anti-anxiety pills she'd stopped taking. Could withdrawal symptoms include migraines? She hoped so, because if this was a sign that there had been more wrong with her than a concussion and the doctors *had* missed something...

She tried to remember if her mother had suffered from

migraines in the days before they'd realized her mind was deteriorating. She didn't think so.

Connor urged her to lie down on top of the covers, then placed the cool dishcloth over her forehead. "Try to get some rest. I'll be back in a few hours. I'll grab some takeout after picking up the groceries.

She shook her head. "I'm not hungry. Just get something for yourself." As she heard Connor's footsteps recede, she closed her eyes and tried to sleep.

When she woke, it was dark. Connor snored softly beside her. She'd slept straight through dinner and now she was wide awake at — she reached for the phone on the bedside table and checked the time — four in the morning.

She tossed and turned until she realized there was no going back to sleep. She slipped quietly out of bed and left the bedroom without waking Connor.

Downstairs, she opened a notebook and made a list of the things she needed to talk to her new therapist about: the toothbrush, the photograph, the imaginary man in the purple hoodie. Her old prescription, and the migraine. Helen.

Maybe with the right prescription and enough therapy, she'd be able to get behind the wheel of a car again. But first, she had to find someone she felt comfortable talking to.

She put the list away. With nothing better to do and hours to fill, she decided to make the strawberry shortcake for the barbecue. Checking the refrigerator, she saw that Connor had gotten everything on her shopping list. She'd thank him in the morning.

That other receipt still bothered her. She opened the junk drawer — but the receipt that proved she had bought the ingredients for strawberry shortcake was gone. In its place was the receipt for the bags with the bananas and peas in them.

She tore the kitchen apart, doing her best to keep quiet so that she wouldn't wake Connor up. She even went through the trash, in case she'd thrown away the wrong receipt. But she found nothing.

Is this what it had been like for her mother?

Chapter Twelve

DENISE WAS FRYING bacon when Connor came downstairs in the morning, determined to keep him from suspecting that his wife might be going crazy.

"Well, this is a surprise," he said. "Smells delicious." He poured himself a cup of coffee and sat at the table. "What did I do to deserve this?"

Denise flipped the bacon over, cooking it crisp just the way Connor liked it. "Well, for one thing, you picked up the groceries I needed to make dessert for the barbecue tonight." She stopped and frowned, spatula frozen midair. "It *is* tonight, right?"

"The barbecue? Of course."

"Of course," she repeated, relieved that at least she wasn't confused about the dates this time.

"But instead of Glen's house, the barbecue will be in Helen and Ronald's backyard. They want to welcome the new people to the neighborhood."

She had too many questions.

Helen was back?

Why did they switch it from Glen's house?

And what new people? She didn't remember hearing about any new people.

Instead of asking any of these questions and looking foolish or crazy, she simply nodded and pretended she'd known all along. "How many eggs would you like?"

"Two is fine," Connor said. "Over easy."

Was he looking at her differently? Did he realize she was only playing along and had no memory of anything he'd just talked about? Or was she imagining that too, like she'd imagined the different expressions on Laura's face in the wedding photo?

She opened the refrigerator to get the eggs, relieved to see that her strawberry shortcake was wrapped and ready to take to the barbecue. At least she hadn't imagined making it during the night.

She cracked three eggs into the frying pan, then plated two for Connor and one for herself, along with some bacon strips on each plate. Then she joined Connor at the table.

He eyed her dish, then shook his head. "Well, that didn't take long."

"What?"

"The whole vegan thing. I figured you'd give in eventually." He chuckled. "Don't feel bad, though. Bacon has a way of seducing even the most die-hard vegetarian."

Vegan? She remembered reading a blog post about veganism earlier in the week, debating pros and cons (and ending up on the pro side). But she didn't remember telling Connor that she was considering trying it. And she definitely wouldn't have made strawberry shortcake for the picnic, because the cake had eggs in it. Eggs weren't any more vegan than bacon.

Denise pushed the bacon around her plate. Should she pretend she'd just forgotten, or go along and not eat the bacon? She pushed her dish aside, her appetite forgotten. One more thing to add to the growing list.

Maybe she should journal everything that happened during the day to cover these memory lapses.

"I guess I'm not hungry after all," she said. "I think I'll take a shower."

Upstairs, she shook two more ginkgo capsules out of the bottle. She went to the sink and cupped water in her hand, then swallowed the pills. Maybe they'd help her memory issues. In the meantime, she'd take Connor's advice and find a new therapist.

Glancing up, she was taken aback. For a moment, it seemed as if Laura was in the mirror. She blinked, then her own reflection stared back at her. People had always said they looked similar, but Laura was willowier and more self-assured.

Denise realized that their similarities were more striking since she'd lost weight while hospitalized. Her hair had grown longer as well, more like Laura's rather than her old pixie cut. No wonder the sight of her own reflection had jarred her for a moment, making her think she'd seen a ghost.

Ghosts. That was ridiculous.

She stepped out of her clothes and into the shower. It felt refreshing and her mind cleared, whether the result of the shower or the ginkgo she wasn't sure, but it felt good to be clear-headed again. After showering and choosing an appropriate outfit to wear to a backyard barbecue, Denise went into her office and grabbed a fresh notebook. She'd promised herself she was going to start journaling, mainly to keep track of events, so she could refer back when her brain felt muddled or confused.

Whatever was happening to her — dementia, withdrawal, brain damage or worse, the same schizophrenia her mother had suffered from — the evidence would be there in black and white.

Once she knew for sure, then she would talk to Connor about it.

JOURNAL: *Sunday*

Woke up early and made my famous strawberry shortcake. It's in the refrigerator to bring to the barbecue this afternoon, which is at Helen and Ronald's house. Connor said we're going to meet some new neighbors. I don't remember hearing about new neighbors moving in, but the more people here, the better I'll feel. It's weird living in a place where most of the houses are unoccupied. Weird and scary.

THERE. She felt better having written things down. Now all she had to do was refer back to her journal when things didn't make sense. She placed the journal on the shelf, then went through her orders for the day. There was an order for one of her favorite projects, a Tree of Life wall hanging. It was time-consuming to make, but she found the intricate pattern relaxing and the result was always stunning. She wrote back to the customer that the order would be ready in a week, then set to work choosing cords and setting up her workspace.

Before long, she was in the flow, knotting and twisting with ease. Time slipped away while she worked. She was surprised when Connor peeked in the doorway and announced it was time to go to the barbecue. Had she been working that long?

She stood up and stretched, surprised at how much she'd accomplished in a few short hours.

"Looks great," Connor said.

She smiled and nodded. "Yes, it does."

"How much do you charge for that piece?"

"Oh, this one is about a hundred dollars." Not that it mattered. She still had a regular paycheck coming from Grady Oil, despite the fact that she'd stopped coming in. Connor's decision, probably. But the online shop had started because she loved to macrame but didn't have room for all the pieces she made. This way she could share them with people who appreciated them. The money she made was simply pocket change. The truth was, she'd do it for free.

She joined Connor and went downstairs to get the covered pan containing the strawberry shortcake. Connor poured chips into a bag. "Here," he said. "You take the chips and I'll carry the cake. It looks heavy."

They walked to Helen and Ronald's backyard, where they were joined by Glen, along with Sandra and Diego Parker. Connor brought the cake into the kitchen so Helen could put it in the refrigerator until dinner was over. Denise put the bowl of chips on the picnic table, next to the sliced watermelon and potato salad. The enticing aroma of barbecued chicken filled the air.

She walked over to the barbecue where Diego was grilling. "Smells wonderful," she said.

"Thanks. I bought a new grill for the occasion."

Helen joined them. "More like he used the occasion to buy the new grill he's been eyeing." They both had a chuckle over that.

Denise reached out for Helen's hand. "How is your mother doing?"

"Better," Helen replied. "I may have to head back soon for another visit."

"Let me know if there's anything I can do."

"I will. Thanks." Helen turned and waved to a couple entering the yard through the open gate in the fence.

"There's the new neighbors," she told Denise, leading her by the hand and introducing her to them. "Denise, this is Cora and Bruce. They've just moved to Dallas from Los Angeles."

"Nice to meet you," Cora said with a shy smile. She was petite, with fair skin and blonde waves that framed her face. She looked like a porcelain doll.

"She'll be teaching at the local elementary school this fall," her husband explained.

Helen smiled. "That's lovely." She turned to Bruce. "And what will you be doing here in Dallas?"

"I'm a psychologist," he said. "I belonged to a large practice in LA, but I'm looking for a smaller workload here. I'll be turning the den into a home office, so if you know of anyone looking for a psychologist, I'd appreciate a referral."

How convenient, Denise thought. Here she was planning on finding a new therapist, and one simply drops in her lap.

Before she could give it more thought, Diego called out that the chicken was done. He carried the platter to the table. Denise put a drumstick on her dish, ignoring Connor's questioning glare. Even if she had told him that she was thinking about seeing if a vegan diet agreed with her, it's not like she'd signed a contract agreeing do it. So she was going to enjoy this juicy barbecued chicken. And why did he care anyway? He wasn't a vegan.

She added a dollop of potato salad, a handful of chips, and a slice of watermelon to her dish and sat between Connor and Helen. Then she turned to Helen and smiled.

"I had the strangest dream." It was the only way she could think of to ask about the other day without sounding crazy. "I thought someone was in the house, and you came over with a golf club to investigate."

Helen laughed. "We don't even own golf clubs."

"Yeah. Besides, you were away at your mother's. But the dream was so vivid."

Connor reached over and patted Denise's hand. "You've been having a lot of little slips these days. I wish you'd see someone about it."

Denise struggled not to show her annoyance. It was one thing for Connor to say it to her, but another to embarrass her in front of the neighbors. Was he really still annoyed about the vegan thing?

Helen leaned close. "Didn't Bruce say he was looking to expand his practice locally?"

Denise nodded. It would be convenient. She wouldn't have to drive to a therapist's office in town. But it might be a little weird opening up to someone she'd see socially. What if he told the rest of them that she was crazy? Or worse, what if she decided that he wasn't the right therapist for her, and then she had to see him every day after rejecting him?

"That sounds like a great idea," Connor said with enthusiasm. "Why don't you talk to him after dinner about making an appointment?"

"Maybe," she said, then dug into her chicken to avoid having to talk about it.

When dinner was over, Helen excused herself to bring out the dessert. Denise followed her into the kitchen. Helen took a lemon cake out of the refrigerator. "That looks delicious," Denise said. "I'll grab the strawberry shortcake."

"Oh, you made strawberry shortcake too?"

Too? What did Helen mean?

She opened the refrigerator and searched for her strawberry shortcake, but it was nowhere to be found. "I thought Connor said he was going to put it in the refrigerator?"

"He did," Helen gestured to the lemon cake. "It's right here."

Denise felt a tiny flare of pain in her head. *Not another migraine.* Was it possible that the migraines and the memory slips were connected?

She would have to track that in her journal too.

But Helen was watching her, as if waiting for a reply. "No, I brought strawberry shortcake, not lemon."

Helen glanced from Denise to the lemon cake and back again, as if that was explanation enough that Denise was mistaken. They stood there awkwardly, then Helen excused herself and went outside, carrying the lemon cake.

Denise began to pace the length of the kitchen, wringing her hands.

She remembered the picture on the vanilla cake box. She remembered washing and chopping the strawberries. She remembered putting that very same lid on that very same pan, and there had been a strawberry shortcake in it.

Even if Connor had accidentally bought a lemon cake and she hadn't noticed, she knew for a fact that they didn't have fresh lemons in the house, and there had been fresh lemon zest dotting the glazed lemon cake.

There had been no lemons in the grocery bags they'd gone through together. The only fruit had been bananas.

She was about to walk back home to double check the receipt, which she'd left in the junk drawer, when Bruce entered the kitchen to grab a cup of coffee. "Coffee and dessert," he said with a grin. "Two of my favorite things."

He glanced at Denise and frowned. "Hey, are you all right?"

Denise blinked back tears of frustration and shook her head. "No. I can't seem to keep things straight lately. Ever since the accident."

"Do you want to talk about it?"

His voice was kind and gentle, all the encouragement she needed to open up. She needed to talk to someone, and Bruce might just be the right choice. But then she caught herself. If she started explaining everything now, someone would probably come back to see where they were, and everyone would know she was going crazy.

"I'm sorry," he said, backing up. "My professional habit just kicked in there. I didn't mean to intrude."

"No," she replied. "I think maybe you're right. I would like to talk about it." She cleared her throat, not wanting him to think she was asking for a favor. "In your professional capacity, of course. Could I make an appointment?"

"Of course. We just moved in, so my calendar is wide open."

"How about tomorrow? First thing?"

"Let's say 11:00. How does that sound?"

"Perfect," Denise said. "I'll see you then. Let's go back to the barbecue for now."

They made their way back to the picnic table, where Helen was cutting the lemon cake into slices and passing them out. Everyone, including Connor, commented on how light and tasty it was. He had bought the strawberries — how could he believe that she'd made lemon cake? Was it possible he had switched them for some reason?

She couldn't see him doing that, mostly because he almost never cooked, even when it was something as simple as cake from a mix. Ever since he'd checked her out from the hospital and brought her home with him, he'd either ordered takeout or eaten whatever she'd cooked.

She couldn't even remember him making himself a sandwich. Only microwaving takeout or brewing a cup of coffee before work.

Also, he would've had to do it while she was working on the Tree of Life design. And he would've had to buy an identical cake pan, or thrown out her strawberry shortcake so he could make the lemon cake in the same pan.

But if he'd done that, the cake would've still been cooling on the counter unglazed when she'd come downstairs, and the pan had completely cold when she'd removed it from the fridge.

Which was more evidence that she was losing her mind.

Denise took the plate that Helen offered. It would have looked suspicious if she didn't eat her own dessert. She took one hesitant bite. Then another. It was very good. Much better than anything Connor could've made on his own.

Soon they said their goodbyes, and Helen sent the remaining lemon cake home with Denise. When they walked in the door, the first thing Denise noticed was the picture hanging back on the wall. Seeing it up again was like a sucker punch to the gut, stealing her breath as she froze, staring at it. Another flare of pain in her head, bigger this time.

She turned to Connor. "I thought you got rid of it?"

He tilted his head and gave her a pointed look. "Why? You agreed to keep it up."

"Yes, but we talked about it. You said if it bothered me, we could take it down."

"When?"

When? Denise stared at him. But he already thought her memory was slipping, so there was nothing she could say to prove that he was the one who'd forgotten this time. "Never mind."

She turned and carried the remaining lemon cake to the refrigerator. Her recipe book was on the counter, opened to the lemon cake recipe. She had no memory of performing any of those steps last night.

Then she flipped to the strawberry shortcake recipe and stared at it. She clearly remembered making it, each and every step of the way.

She slammed the book closed and put it away. Thank goodness she'd made an appointment with Bruce for tomorrow. She'd add the lemon cake switcheroo to her list of things to talk to him about.

And Connor putting the picture back up. She went back into the living room and stared at the picture again, which was back to the way she remembered it. Her sister's face filled with joy, starting a new life with the husband she adored. Laura had been wearing their mother's pearls that day, even though it was Denise's turn. She'd placed them around her sister's neck on the morning of her wedding day. It seemed appropriate, standing in for their mother since she couldn't be there with them on that special day. The pearls were the one thing that connected the three of them.

"Where did they go?" she murmured, staring at her sister's image. "I know I saw you wearing them when we got in the car." Her heart lurched and her shoulders slumped. "I miss you so much, Laura. I wish you were here."

Connor stepped into the room behind her. "Everything okay here?"

She turned and gave him a half-hearted smile. "Yep. Just talking to myself."

He rubbed her shoulder. They stared at the picture together for a long, silent moment. "I miss her too," he finally said, his voice breaking.

And that right there was the one thing they would always have in common. She leaned against his chest, no longer angry with him. Because even if he was being a little annoying about her slips, he was also clearly worried about her, even in his grief. And he understood how much losing Laura had wounded her. Every couple had little disagreements, but theirs were smaller than most. And given how much stress he was under, with work and the hostile takeover, he still went out of his way to take care of her.

"I still can't believe she's gone," Denise said. "I expect to pick up the phone and hear her voice, or turn a corner and see her coming into the room."

"Yeah." And then, almost as an afterthought, he pulled her close. "But I have you, and that eases the pain."

She wanted to believe that, but something about his comment felt insincere, almost as if he'd rehearsed and was just waiting for the right moment to toss it out casually. Suddenly, she didn't want to be around Connor. She just wanted to be alone and try to collect her thoughts.

She'd been all over the place emotionally today, happy one minute, angry the next, and it was hard not to feel like she was overreacting to something that was clearly intended to make her feel better, even if it had been rehearsed. It showed he was trying, didn't it?

But she couldn't shake her desire to get away from him. All she could do was try to hide it.

"Want to watch a movie?" he asked.

"No, I think I'm going to go catch up on some orders."

He glanced at his watch. "This late?"

"It relaxes me," she said.

He gave a dismissive shrug, as if she'd personally rejected him, which was funny considering how much time he spent at work leaving her alone. But in his mind, work was work, while what she did was just a hobby that took time away from him.

She refused to feel guilty about needing time alone after a hectic day and went upstairs to her craft room.

Instead of working on her macrame, however, she pulled out her journal.

SUNDAY NIGHT

Today was surreal. Everything I thought I knew was turned on its head. I'm seriously concerned about my mental health at this point. My mother had mental issues. Is it hereditary? Could I be deteriorating the same way that my mother did? She was paranoid, she struggled to tell what was real, and she didn't care how badly she scared Laura and I. Am I scaring Connor?

The good thing is one of my new neighbors is a therapist. I've been putting off making an appointment with a new one, but the timing couldn't be better. I spent a little time talking to Bruce, and he made me feel at ease. I think we can work well together. Maybe he can put some of my fears to rest.

Like the fear that I'm hallucinating during the day. The whole episode with Helen. Was she here, or was she with her mother? Had she gone all Terminator in my house with a golf club that she claims they don't even have? But it felt so real. Lately, I don't know what's real and what's not. Dreams? Hallucinations? Memory issues? I'm not sure which one is worse.

The thing is, my feelings toward Connor are changing. He's acting suspicious. One minute, I think he loves me. The next, he looks at me as if he's gauging my reaction to something he said that directly contradicts the way I remember it. It's as if he's playing a prank but he's the only one laughing. Sometimes I just go along so I don't sound crazy contradicting everything he tells me.

It'll be good to talk to Bruce tomorrow and get a professional opinion.

DENISE HEARD Connor coming up the stairs. She closed the journal and tucked it at the bottom of a basket of yarn.

She wasn't sure why, but she didn't want Connor reading it.

She heard him go in the bathroom, then he stepped into the room holding her pills and a glass of water.

"Didn't want you to forget your pills," he said. "I know it's been a long, hectic day."

She had never told him that she'd stopped taking them, fearing that perhaps they were the cause of her slips. But she'd gotten worse since she stopped, and she still wasn't sure if maybe that was the reason she was losing her grip on reality.

Maybe it wouldn't hurt to try them again and see if everything went back to normal?

She pasted on a smile and took the pills from his hand. "Thank you."

He stood there waiting while she took a sip of water and swallowed the pills, then took the glass from her hand, saying, "I'll slip this in the dishwasher and start it."

After he was gone, she questioned his behavior for the first time. Was he taking care of her — or manipulating her?

Chapter Thirteen

THE NEXT MORNING, Connor was dressed and ready for work before she got out of bed. Even though she'd had a good night's sleep, she felt groggy, thanks to the pills he'd given her.

Connor leaned over and kissed her on the forehead. "I'm going to work, sleepyhead. What are your plans for today?"

"I made an appointment to talk to Bruce. I think it's time to see a new therapist."

"That's a great idea. You can tell me all about it tonight. I'll be home for dinner."

She smiled. "I'll make lasagna."

"Perfect," he called over his shoulder. "See you tonight."

Unable to go back to sleep, Denise staggered out of bed. Her head felt twenty pounds heavier, and she had to blink several times in order to keep things in focus. She felt drugged, which was odd, but she'd had a glass of wine at the barbecue last night in addition to the pills, which might have strengthened their effect.

She made her way to the bathroom, where she swallowed her vitamin but skipped the anti-anxiety pill, since last night's dose still seemed to be in her system. Then she brushed her teeth. Yellow toothbrush. Maybe things were finally getting back to normal. She stripped out of her night clothes and stepped into the shower, setting the stream as hot as she could stand it. She let the water soothe her body and soul until she started to feel human again.

She was just stepping out of the shower when she heard her name called.

"Denise?"

She looked around. Was that Laura's voice? She pulled a towel around her and went to the doorway. "Laura?"

No answer.

Goosebumps rippled her skin. She was sure she'd heard Laura's voice. She backed against the wall, her body shaking, every nerve alert. Her voice came out in a whimper. "Laura?"

She didn't know whether she wanted to hear a reply or not. She'd give anything to hear Laura's voice again, but not back from the dead. Laura must surely blame her, not only for the accident, for killing her and her unborn baby, but for taking her place in Connor's life.

With her back against the wall, she slid down until she was sitting on the cool tile, sobbing. "I'm sorry, Laura. I'm so sorry."

She waited for Laura's ghost to come and take revenge. Time slipped by, and she grew so cold that she started shivering, but nothing happened. Laura did not appear to exact her revenge.

Finally, feeling foolish, Denise stood and wrapped the towel tighter around her to warm her body. With hesitant steps, she walked out of the bathroom, searching for any sign of Laura's ghost.

Nothing.

It had to be her guilty imagination. Laura wasn't here, she couldn't be, and Denise was embarrassed that she'd let her imagination run away with her. Guilt and shame, those were what was haunting her, not her sister.

She looked around the bedroom. Nothing was disturbed. There was no sign of anyone or anything having been in there. She grabbed some clothes from her closet and quickly changed.

Downstairs, she went right to the picture on the wall. There was no mistaking the malevolence in her sister's face today. She reached up and stroked her sister's cheek. "I'm sorry, Laura. If I could take it back, I would. Please forgive me."

She couldn't bear to see her sister's face so filled with anger and hate. She took the picture off the wall and placed it face down on the kitchen counter. She brewed a cup of coffee, then went to the refrigerator for creamer. And there, staring her in the face, were the remains of a *strawberry shortcake*.

What the hell?

She rubbed her eyes. When she opened them, the cake was still there.

"No." She shook her head. "No, no, no."

She grabbed the dish and dumped the cake in the garbage with a satisfying thump. She rinsed off the plate and put it in the dishwasher. She'd hoped it would be out of sight, out of mind, but she kept replaying the conversation in Helen's kitchen over the lemon cake, where Helen had looked at her with pity when she'd insisted that she'd made the strawberry shortcake. She remembered the big fuss Connor had made over the lemon cake. And she definitely remembered eating a piece herself, then later, finding her recipe book open to the lemon cake recipe.

Bruce had been there. He had eaten the lemon cake. Surely, he would confirm that she was remembering it correctly.

She went back to the refrigerator for the cream, stirred it into her coffee, then sat and sipped while drumming her fingers on the table. She glanced at the clock. There were still two hours left before her appointment with Bruce. She decided to add these new developments to her journal. On her way to the craft room, she stopped by the bathroom to take one of her anti-anxiety pills, to counteract the shock of finding the strawberry shortcake.

Then she pulled the journal from its hiding place in the basket of yarn and began to write.

MONDAY MORNING

I'm hearing voices. I swear I heard my sister calling me. It's not possible, but I know my sister's voice. My imagination is playing tricks on me. Did my mother hear voices too?

Yesterday, I vividly recalled making a strawberry shortcake, but Helen brought lemon cake out of the kitchen and assured me that's what Connor had given her. So we all ate the lemon cake, and I brought the leftovers home. Today, the remains of the strawberry cake were in the refrigerator. I can't explain it.

And the picture has changed again. It was horrid and hateful. I think Laura blames me for everything. Why shouldn't she?

SETTING THE JOURNAL ASIDE, she tried to finish the Tree of Life project, but had a hard time focusing. Finally, she stood up and stepped away from the craft table before she messed everything up. Pacing back and forth, she went over everything in her mind. There was only one explanation. She was losing her mind.

She picked up the journal and clutched it to her chest. Bruce would either confirm it or help her find a plausible explanation that she hadn't thought of.

Downstairs again, she marched toward the wall where the picture normally hung. She stared at the empty space. It wasn't on the wall, or on the counter where she'd left it. She searched the room, but it was nowhere to be found. A few days ago, she would have been terrified that someone else was in the house with her.

Today, it was just one more thing to add to the journal.

A few minutes before eleven, she headed over to Bruce and Sandra's house and rang the bell.

Bruce opened the door and glanced at his watch. "Punctual. I like that!"

He stepped aside and gestured for her to enter.

The layout was exactly like her house. Even the walls were the same shade of beige. "Wow, it's like déjà vu," she said.

Bruce laughed. "Cookie cutter. That's how these developments are. They use a few different models over and over, and some are simply mirror images of others. I guess they expect once you buy the house, you'll put your own personal stamp on it. Choose your own wall colors and decorations, and no one will notice that your house is identical to theirs."

Denise laughed too, but it gave her a strange feeling in the pit of her stomach. There was no reason for it. A house was a house. But seeing how much Bruce and Sandra's house looked like her own was a strange feeling.

"Even the furniture," she said.

"Well, what there is of it. We left most of our things in storage in California. Just in case this didn't work out here."

Denise pointed to an oak armoire. "We have the same piece in our house."

Bruce nodded. "Most of this stuff came with the house. I guess these were the model homes for the neighborhood and were all staged pretty much the same."

"We bought our house fully furnished as well," Denise said. "We both wanted a fresh start." Truth was, it would have felt weird living with Laura's furniture, her hand-chosen china, and her Laura Ashley bedding. But irrationally, Denise still had the urge to get them out of storage, just to have something familiar around her.

She'd told Connor that she wanted to paint their front door turquoise, but she hadn't done it. And aside from the things she'd bought for her workroom, she hadn't replaced any of the generic furniture in their house, even though they could easily afford it.

Why not?

Maybe it was all connected, her conflicted feelings about moving on from her sister, the migraines, the hallucination. And her guilt at the center of it.

She would almost rather hear that there was a medical reason for all of this.

Because if all of this was caused by guilt, didn't that mean this was her punishment for killing her sister?

For a fraction of a second, she was tempted to tell Bruce she'd changed her mind.

But then he said, "Why don't we go upstairs to my office?"

And Denise found herself following him upstairs.

His office was located in the same area as her craft room. Like the rest of the house, the office was sparsely furnished — a couch, two chairs and a wooden desk with a small potted succulent on one corner.

He pointed to the plant. "Housewarming gift. I've been

told they're impossible to kill. But I'm up for the challenge."

She laughed. "We have that in common. My sister always said I was like a plant hospice. They came to me to die."

"And your sister?"

"Oh, she had the greenest thumb in the world. She could pick up a broken toothpick from the sidewalk, stick it in dirt, and grow an oak tree."

"Your sister is…?"

"Gone." But she wasn't ready to talk about Laura yet. Or at least, not about the accident. She turned to the wall and studied the framed diplomas on the wall. "You seem so young to have a doctorate degree," she said, changing the subject.

He shrugged and grinned. "Not as young as I look." He gestured across the room. "Have a seat wherever you're comfortable."

There were two chairs against the opposite wall on either side of a bookcase filled with medical texts. She chose the closest chair and Bruce sat across from her. She expected him to pull out a notebook or recording device, but he simply chatted as if they were having an informal conversation rather than a session.

"So, tell me about your family."

Denise shifted in her seat. "There's not much to tell. My mom died of breast cancer when we were kids. She had, umm, some mental problems."

Even though he was a therapist and she'd come to him for help, it was hard for her to admit that. She'd spent so many years trying to hide her mother's decline from others. It had been the family's shameful secret, before the diagnosis had finally come.

Bruce nodded. "We'll come back to that later."

"My dad was barely there. He was a workaholic and spent most of his time at the company."

"That's Grady Oil, right?"

"Yes, how did you know?"

"You told us you were at the 80th anniversary party the other night. How long has the business been in your family?"

"Oh right. Yes." This was something she could talk about. "My grandfather started the business and passed it down to my dad. It's always been in the family. When my father died of a heart attack five years ago, my sister and I inherited Grady Oil. We each owned equal shares, and then…"

He waited, giving her space to compose her thoughts. She forced herself to say it.

"Then my sister died in a car accident. Her shares were equally divided between me and Connor, who she was married to at the time."

"Your sister was once married to your husband?"

Denise felt her stomach curdle. "I know how it looks, but all we had was each other and the business. Connor took the reins and kept everything going while I was recovering. I don't know what I would have done without him after Laura's death."

Bruce nodded. "No children?"

"No." And there wouldn't be, either. The accident had taken more than her sister. It had also taken away her ability to bear children.

"So, there's no other family left?"

Denise shook her head. "Not that I know of. Each of my parents was an only child. When they died, it was just Laura and me."

"Do you want to talk about Laura?"

Did she? Isn't that why she was here? "Laura was older

than me by a few years. She was everything I wanted to be — smart, pretty, and confident. Everyone loved her." She swallowed. "But no one loved her or looked up to her as much as I did."

And that was something no one could understand. It wasn't just guilt that gnawed at her heart, it was losing the one person she loved most in the world, the one person she emulated and wanted to please.

She remembered Laura leaning over, her hair falling in effortless curls around her face as she studied Denise's report card. Ignoring the row of C's, she pointed out the one B+ grade. "Wow," she'd said. "You must be really good at art."

She'd shrugged. "I guess."

"Can I see some of your drawings?"

Denise hadn't shown anyone the pictures she drew. They were her little secret. She opened her sketch book and turned the pages as Laura exclaimed over each and every one. "You're very talented."

Laura's compliments had set a fire under her. From that point on, Denise would leave little drawings on Laura's desk. She'd raised her grade in Art Class from a B+ to an A, hoping to make Laura proud.

She hadn't picked up her sketch book since Laura died.

Thankfully, Bruce moved on, probably sensing how hard it was for Denise to talk about her sister. That was the opposite of what her last therapist would've done. Dr. Garcia always wanted her to confront the hard emotions. All Bruce seemed to care about was her family history.

Maybe he liked to get to know his patients before he got into the therapy?

"What about friends?" he asked.

"I don't really have any friends," she said.

"Why not?"

She shrugged. "I never really had a lot of friends. I guess I've been a loner most of my life. My sister was my best friend." She picked at a piece of lint on her pants. "I was in the hospital for months after the accident. I had a broken leg, a fractured collarbone, a fractured pelvis, and uterine bleeding which resulted in a hysterectomy."

"Head injury?"

"Yes. I had a concussion. I guess that could be the cause of a lot of my memory problems, right?"

He nodded noncommittally. She waited for a moment, to see if he would elaborate on the possible connection, but he just stared at her.

"Anyway, at first people came by, sent cards and flowers. But eventually they stopped. Connor was the only one who kept visiting."

"I see."

"And when I was well enough to go home, he was there to take care of me. I found it hard to leave the house and couldn't get in a car. I was still grieving the death of my sister and blaming myself for being behind the wheel."

"That's a lot," Bruce said.

She searched his face for any sign of sympathy or understanding, but he showed no emotion. She wasn't sure this was going to work. Her last therapist had been empathetic and understanding. She felt as if Bruce wasn't even listening to her, just making the appropriate sounds when necessary.

"So," he said, "what are your concerns now?

"There are weird things happening now," She pulled her notebook out of her purse and went down the list. "For one thing, my yellow toothbrush changed to blue, which is Laura's favorite color, not mine."

Bruce laughed. "I don't even know what color mine is."

"I do," she insisted. "And it should be yellow, not blue."

She chewed her lower lip. "Is it possible I subconsciously switched it myself because it reminds me of Laura?"

"Maybe. What else?"

What else? He didn't see that as a problem worth talking about — that she might be losing her grip on reality, when she'd already told him that her mother had suffered from schizophrenia?

She tried to give him the benefit of the doubt. Maybe he was trying to get an overview of all her problems, looking for a pattern?

Maybe every therapist had their own style and she just had to adapt to Bruce's. But she missed Dr. Garcia's thoughtful observations and quiet empathy. He'd never rushed her when she was talking about something that upset her, and he definitely never put the most difficult topics off until later.

But if she wanted to go back to her old therapist, she'd have to spend more time in a stranger's car, because she couldn't ask Connor to take time from work to shuttle her around. And since they'd moved, Dr. Garcia's office was all the way on the other side of the city, so it would be nearly an hour's drive each way with traffic. Possibly more.

She should see if Bruce could help her before she committed to that journey. Maybe he could at least give her something more effective for the panic attacks, to make the drive easier.

She sighed and glanced at her list. "There's a picture of my sister. It's my favorite picture because she looks so happy. Most of the time."

"Most of the time?"

"It changes," she said, knowing how silly it sounded. "Sometimes she looks happy and sometimes she looks angry. Sometimes the flowers are roses, and sometimes they're carnations. It looks different every time I see it."

"Could that just be caused by the way the light hits it?"

"Maybe," Denise said. "That's what Connor says." She knew that wasn't true but appreciated his support. It was enough to keep her talking. "Then there was the episode with dessert yesterday at the barbecue."

"The strawberry shortcake," he said.

A tiny part of her was relieved that he remembered it being strawberry shortcake. So, she wasn't going crazy. "Helen said I made a lemon cake."

Bruce shook his head. "I don't remember lemon cake."

"But you remember the strawberry shortcake?" Her voice was hopeful.

"I do."

"Thank you!" she cried out. "I still don't understand what happened. I specifically remember making strawberry shortcake, but Helen brought out a lemon cake and sent the leftovers home. The next morning, the lemon cake leftovers were strawberry shortcake. Connor swore I'd made lemon cake, and my recipe book was open to that recipe. I was so confused."

Bruce nodded. "A concussion, coupled with grief, can do odd things to a person's memory."

"Yes. My previous therapist talked about survivor's guilt. Could that be the cause?"

"It's a possibility."

But instead of elaborating, Bruce glanced at his watch and Denise realized her time was up. Disappointed, she closed her journal and got up to leave. At least he'd confirmed that she wasn't wrong about the strawberry shortcake. But that raised a new disquieting question: why had Connor lied about it?

And where had the lemon cake come from?

He undoubtedly had survivor's guilt too, although he'd refused to go to therapy after the accident, insisting that he would mourn Laura in his own way. Was it possible that both of them were having memory problems or hallucinations?

She didn't think so, but she didn't ask Bruce, for fear that he'd mention it to Connor. He wasn't supposed to, but he could slip. Or he could see these informal sessions as falling outside the usual patient-therapist confidentiality.

"Keep making notes of all the things you notice," Bruce said. "We'll chat again in a few days. How does Thursday sound? Same time."

"That will be fine. Thank you." That would give her a few days to decide whether it was worth continuing. It might be, if Bruce continued to confirm whether she was misremembering things.

She clearly couldn't trust Connor to do that.

Bruce walked her downstairs and held the front door open. She glanced out and saw Sandra pulling into the driveway. She walked up to the house, greeted Denise, then kissed Bruce.

Denise glanced from one to the other. *What the hell?* She peered over at Sandra and Diego's house, then back to Sandra and Bruce. "I, um, didn't realize you two were so close," she muttered.

Sandra laughed. "Of course we're close." She looked at Bruce with adoring eyes. "He's my husband."

Denise was about to argue that Bruce was *Cora's* husband. But just then Cora and Diego come out of the house arguing over garbage. Denise stared from one couple to the other. How could she be wrong about who was married to whom?

This was the kind of mistake her mother would've made on her worst days. Not even a mistake, really, but spinning a new narrative of reality that she became trapped in and couldn't be rescued from, no matter what evidence Laura or Denise offered her.

Cora and Diego walked over. "Have you heard about the garbage?"

Bruce and Sandra look confused. "Garbage?"

"Yeah." Diego was fuming. "I just heard the garbage pickup is stopping because it's not worth sending a truck into the development for only a few houses. That's downright ridiculous!"

Denise blinked. She couldn't believe they were talking about garbage when everything she knew about them had been turned upside down.

Diego stopped talking and looked at Denise. "Hey, are you all right?"

Denise tried to act normal, but everything came crashing down on her. She turned and ran back to her house, shaking her head. *No.* She wasn't all right. She might never be all right again.

She paced back and forth in her living room, stopping to glance out the window whenever she walked by. At one point she saw Cora and Diego getting in their car and driving away. She was sure Cora and Bruce were introduced as the new neighbors at the barbecue. There was no way she could have gotten that mixed up.

Could she?

She pulled out her journal and wrote down the original couples: Helen and Ronald, Sandra and Diego, and the new couple, Bruce and Cora. That's the way it had been at the picnic. But now Sandra claimed to be married to Bruce, and Diego with Cora.

Maybe they were all swingers and were pulling her leg about being married. Maybe "married" was code for swinging. Who knew? But that seemed like the most plausible explanation. For now, anyway.

With that settled, Denise decided to go for a run. It always seemed to help clear the fog from her brain. She changed into her jogging clothes and sneakers and walked out the front door.

But before she could go far, Sandra called out. "Hey Denise, could you wait a second?"

Denise stopped. "What's up?"

"I've been promising myself to get more exercise, but I keep putting it off. Would you mind if I joined you for a run?"

"Oh. Sure."

"Give me a minute to change my shoes." With that, Sandra turned and went inside.

Denise had been tempted to say no. Running was her private time to get her thoughts together. But Sandra and the others all just witnessed Denise's slip, followed by her fleeing into her house mid-conversation, and she worried that they'd tell Connor she'd had another incident. Not to mention, her abrupt departure had been rude, and turning down Sandra's request might be interpreted as doubly rude. A nice neutral conversation while they went on a short run together might make Sandra forget about her earlier departure. Or at least reassure the woman that there was no need to mention it to Connor.

So she'd tolerate company on her run today, but in the future, she'd set boundaries.

They set off at a comfortable pace. Denise purposely kept her speed down, assuming Sandra hadn't exercised in a while. She was wrong about that. Not only did Sandra keep up, but she soon took the lead, taking them in a direction Denise hadn't been before. Here, the lots were cleared, but no housing had been built. The sidewalks hadn't been built yet, so they ran on an uneven dirt path.

Denise's still-healing leg began to ache, then cramp.

She slowed down, favoring it. Sandra soon outdistanced Denise, who finally stopped to rub out the cramp. When she looked up, Sandra was gone.

Denise called out. When Sandra didn't respond, she limped to where she'd last seen her. There was no sign of her. Denise was disoriented, not sure where she was or which direction to turn, but Sandra didn't answer. Where the heck had she gone?

Her leg ached, but she was determined to make her way back without having to call for help. It took a while, but eventually she found her way to her house, her leg throbbing with each step. She couldn't wait to get inside and put an ice pack on it.

Sandra waved from her doorway. "Where'd you get off to?"

"Me? I stopped for a minute, and you were gone."

Sandra shrugged. "I thought you'd turned around and gone home."

"I wouldn't have just left without telling you." She didn't bother saying that's exactly what Sandra had done.

"Well, it was a good run," Sandra said. "We'll have to do it again some time." She waved and went inside.

Don't count on it.

But at least she hadn't had to spend the whole run making small talk with Sandra. And next time, she'd leave out the back door.

Denise went inside and grabbed a bag of frozen peas from the freezer, then sat on the recliner with her leg raised and balanced the frozen peas on it. She knew she'd overdone it running on the uneven surface, but the run had given her a taste of something she hadn't even realized she'd been craving: freedom. When she'd first come home from the hospital, Connor's house had felt like a cocoon, protecting her from the harsh outside world while she was vulnerable. But now, staying home all day, with only Connor to talk to when he could pull himself away from work, she was starting to feel claustrophobic. No, trapped. Like she'd let Connor build the cocoon walls so thick that she might never break free again.

Chapter Fourteen

DENISE LEANED BACK, relaxing into the gentle rocking of the back porch glider. This was her favorite time of the evening, just before dusk. The air was still, and the sky glowed with a lavender light. Someone had mowed their lawn, and the scent of freshly cut grass filled the air. If the color green had a scent, it would be new-mown grass.

The solitude soothed her, and for a moment she wished she could stay in the glider forever, never speaking to her neighbors again. She'd spent the day writing in her journal and escaping into fantasy fiction. Her leg felt better, but she was still favoring it. Fear simmered below the surface instead of raging out of control as it had earlier today. She was still confused, but determined to find a logical answer for everything that was happening.

Connor came home from work and joined her on the glider. He put one arm around her shoulder. "How did your session with Bruce go?"

"Fine."

"Did you tell him about the memory lapses?"

"Yeah, some of them." She didn't mention the final

mind trick — seeing Sandra and Cora trading places as if they'd been with the wrong husband all along. She'd debated telling him, and decided it was better to keep tracking things in her journal. Eventually, she would either figure out the truth for herself, or she would have evidence that Connor couldn't explain away.

But she also needed more help than Bruce could give her.

She turned to face Connor. "I think something is really wrong with me. I need to see a specialist."

Connor pulled her close. "No. There's nothing wrong with you. This is temporary. I'm sure of it." He rubbed her shoulders to ease the trembling. "When was the last time you ate?"

She shook her head. "I don't remember."

"Come on," he said, standing and helping her to her feet. "Let's go out for dinner."

"Let me go change," she said. "I'll only be ten minutes."

"Take your time."

She went upstairs and changed into a butter yellow slip dress and strappy sandals. She threw a paisley silk scarf across her shoulders and added a touch of makeup. Feeling more presentable, she made her way downstairs. Getting out of the house was exactly what she needed right now — another taste of freedom, without putting any more strain on her leg until she recovered from today's run.

She took a deep breath as she passed through the living room, noticing a framed print of sunflowers hung above the mantel where Laura's picture had been. Beautiful bright yellow petals against a blue sky. Her favorite color and Laura's. Was she hallucinating again? Replacing the guilt-inducing wedding photo with something more symbolic?

Connor followed her gaze. "Do you like it?"

She blinked. So she wasn't imagining it. Connor could see it too. "Did you do this?"

"Yes, you asked me to get a new picture for that space, remember? I saw it in the store window and thought it would look great there. I probably should have checked with you first," he said. "If you don't like it, I can return it."

"No. I love it." She turned and wrapped her arms around his waist, resting her head on his shoulder. Thoughtful Connor was back, trying to protect her from the tricks her mind was playing on her. "It's perfect."

Outside the restaurant, they ran into Alan and his wife Pamela. Denise stiffened, remembering Pamela's cruel words in the restroom the night of the anniversary party. Before she could think of an excuse not to, Alan requested a table for four.

Alan ordered a bottle of champagne, and they toasted to the success of Grady Oil. "I've admired the way you've handled those sharks nosing around." He turned to Denise. "I'm sure Connor has told you about the attempted buyout."

Denise nodded. "I don't see how that's even possible, since Connor and I hold the majority of the shares and we have no intention of selling the company." Grady Oil had been her family business for as long as she could remember. She couldn't imagine not being a part of it.

"You don't really take an active part in the business anymore, do you?" Pamela asked.

Denise heard the challenge in her voice. "Not right now."

It wasn't any of Pamela's business, and she wasn't about to explain her feelings to her or anyone else. Especially not to someone who would accuse her of killing her own sister.

"So, what do you do with your day?" Pamela asked. "Since you're not working."

Denise just stared at her, but Connor jumped in to break the silence. "Denise has an online shop where she sells her work. She makes, umm…" He turned to Denise. "What do you call it?"

"Macrame," she said, not meeting Pamela's gaze. "I find it therapeutic."

"And she gets paid for them, too," Connor said, almost sounding surprised that she'd get paid for her "little hobby."

Denise didn't expand on it one way or the other. She didn't care what Pamela thought of her. She already knew.

But she wished she didn't know what Connor thought of her business.

Denise barely lifted her eyes from her plate during dinner. Connor and Alan didn't seem to notice the silence around them as they discussed business.

"Are you prepared for the presentation tomorrow?"

Connor leaned forward, his eyes bright with anticipation. "Yeah, I have the numbers for last quarter. We had growth in revenue and profit."

"That's good, then, right?"

"Yeah, but we can't get complacent. We're still facing challenges."

"Those rumors of a planned hostile takeover."

Denise perked up. This was her chance to learn more about the possible takeover. Maybe it was time she paid more attention to what was going on at Grady Oil, instead of sulking around feeling sorry for herself.

But Connor turned to her. "We must be boring you. Why don't you ladies go ahead and order dessert while we step outside and enjoy a cigar."

If she couldn't learn more about the business, then she'd take the opportunity to set a boundary or two.

As soon as the men were gone, Denise turned to Pamela. She straightened her shoulders and steeled herself for the confrontation. "I overheard you and Kelly in the restroom the other night."

The color drained from Pamela's face.

"I heard you suggest that I purposely killed my sister." It was an effort to keep her voice from trembling.

"We were drinking. It was just, I don't know, just a joke."

"It wasn't funny."

Pamela had the decency to look embarrassed.

"I suggest you refrain from telling those kinds of jokes from now on."

"Of course," Pamela stammered. "I'm sorry." She held her breath for a moment, then blew it out with resignation. "Did you tell Connor?"

"No, but I have a good mind to give him a detailed account of what the two of you said."

"Please," she begged. "Alan would be upset if he found out. He thinks so highly of Connor, and he adored your sister."

Denise clenched her fists, her voice tight. "I adored my sister too. For you to imply that I had anything to do with her death is…"

Pamela reached out for Denise's hand, but she pulled it away and stood. "Thank you for picking up the check." She turned and walked away without another word.

Outside on the patio, she caught up with Connor and touched his arm. "I'd like to go."

"Let me just get the bill," he said.

"No need. Pamela is picking up the check." She turned to Alan. "Thank you both."

"Sure, no problem." Alan looked confused, but he clapped Connor on the back. "See you in the office."

Back in the car, Connor asked Denise what was wrong.

She stared out the window. "Nothing."

Neither one spoke the rest of the way home.

Stepping into the living room, Denise glanced at the wall. It was automatic now. She had to check in to see if the picture was changed, still there or gone. The sunflowers that Connor had brought home were still there. But she also felt a guilty twinge that Laura's picture was gone. Maybe someday she would be strong enough to put it up again.

As she started up the stairs, she caught a whiff of something sweet. The closer she got to the top of the stairs, the more prominent the scent became, until she reached the bedroom, where it was strongest. She knew exactly what it was. Daisy by Marc Jacobs. Laura's signature scent. She'd recognize that sweet, fruity scent anywhere.

"Laura?" Her voice was barely a whisper.

She walked slowly around the room surrounded by her sister's scent. When Connor entered, she gestured around the room. "Do you smell it?"

He took a deep sniff, then shook his head. "Smell what?"

"Laura's perfume. How can you miss it?"

"I don't smell anything. Are you sure?"

Denise stomped her foot. "Of course I'm sure. She's been wearing that scent since we were teenagers. The only time I can remember her being furious with me was when I took it out of her room to borrow it and accidentally dropped the entire bottle on the floor."

Sorrow gripped her chest so tightly that she thought her heart would explode. Silly to regret something as insignificant as spilling her sister's perfume, but it was only one of many regrets she felt. How many things did she wish she'd done differently? Borrowing Laura's things without asking. Copying everything Laura did ad nauseam. Constantly angling for Laura's approval, when she could've been supportive instead. Why hadn't she been a better sister?

"These hallucinations are becoming a concern," Connor said. He struck a note of pity rather than concern. Had it always been there, and she'd just been too desperate and vulnerable to notice? Or was this new?

For the first time, Denise looked at him with anger. She'd been taking his reactions to her slips as attempts to reassure, but now they felt dismissive. As if he thought she was silly — or worse, crazy — and it was his job to humor her until she came back to her senses.

"Hallucinations? If I didn't know any better, I'd think you were the one trying to make me think I was crazy."

"Hon, how can you even think that of me?"

She looked away. "I don't know what to think anymore."

"When is your next appointment with Bruce?"

The question brought even more anger rising to the surface. What was he implying? Did he think she was going crazy, or did he just want *her* to think that? She turned and stomped out the door, not wanting to be in the same room with him anymore.

Downstairs, the picture of sunflowers had been replaced with Laura's wedding picture again. Her face seemed to stare into Denise's soul. It was too much. A howl of rage escaped her lips as she tore the painting off the wall.

Outside, she tossed it onto the barbecue, squirted lighter fluid over the picture, frame and all, and set it ablaze. The fire caught with a *womp*, and flames shot straight up. The heat of the fire warmed her skin as she watched the picture burn. Charred paper floated on the breeze and sizzled when they landed on her hair. Still, she didn't move until the entire picture was burned to a crisp and the frame broken and black.

When she was sure the picture was utterly destroyed, she closed the lid of the barbecue and turned. She glanced up and saw Connor watching her from the bedroom window. Probably thinking she had lost her mind. She didn't care. Let him think whatever he wanted.

With that, she turned and stormed back into the house, locking the door behind her. She grabbed a pillow and blanket from the hallway closet, then made a bed for herself on the living room couch. If the picture came back, she'd be there to see it. And to catch whoever was putting it there.

She sat up, staring at the wall until well after midnight. When she couldn't keep her eyes open any longer, she snuggled under the blanket and drifted off to an uneasy sleep.

Chapter Fifteen

DENISE SAT up and stretched her aching back. The couch wasn't made for sleeping. She'd remember that next time. Her hair smelled like smoke. She glanced up at the bare wall. At least she'd accomplished something by sleeping on the couch, although her back didn't agree.

She heard Connor banging around in the kitchen. Stretching the kinks out of her back, she got up and joined him, grateful to see he'd already brewed a pot of coffee. She poured herself a cup as he looked over his shoulder.

"I'm sorry," he said.

She shook her head. "No, it was my fault."

"I see you had a barbecue last night."

Now that it was over, she could laugh about it. "I may have overdone it."

"Well, overcooked wedding pictures are my favorite thing on the menu."

"God, I'm so sorry. It's just that it seemed to change every time I looked at it."

Connor came over and wrapped his arm around her.

"I told you I'd take it down and put up a new painting if it bothered you."

"I know. I'm sorry." She didn't mention the picture of flowers he'd hung there yesterday. Why add more fuel to the fire? He already suspected she was losing her marbles.

"Is that the only reason you were upset last night?"

Denise debated whether to tell him or not. It wasn't as if she had any loyalty to Pamela and Kelly. Besides, Connor had a right to know what people were saying about them behind their backs.

She brought her coffee to the table and sat. "I'm not comfortable around Pamela."

Connor joined her at the table. "Oh?"

Denise decided to tell him everything. "Remember when I went to the restroom at the anniversary party?

He gave her a questioning look. "Yeah?"

She took a deep breath. "Well, I overheard Pamela and Kelly saying some nasty things."

Connor's voice bristled. "Saying what?"

Denise took a long sip of her coffee, working up the nerve to confess all. "They said I was responsible for killing my sister. That I might have even done it on purpose. And then married you when you were on the rebound. That I planned it all." There, she got it all out in one breath.

Connor pounded a fist on the table, making her cup rattle and spilling coffee. She reached for a napkin to wipe it up while Connor stood and paced around the room.

"How dare they talk about you like that!"

Watching Connor pace, Denise wondered if telling him was the right thing to do. But it felt good to know he felt protective of her reputation. He looked genuinely angry. It made her regret her accusation of last night. Her conversation with Pamela had upset her so much, it might have triggered her hallucination of Laura's perfume. And she'd taken it out on him. But he still leapt to her defense.

Instead of blaming him, maybe she should have told him about Pamela and Kelly last night.

"I'm firing Kelly," he growled. "We don't want people like that working at the company. And I don't want to work with anyone who would talk about my wife like that."

"No. I didn't want to get her fired. I just wanted you to know what kind of gossip was going around the office. Besides, this is personal, not work-related. Kelly is good at her job."

He agreed, but he was still obviously angry. "And Pamela too? Jesus, and you had to sit next to her all during dinner. No wonder you were so quiet."

"Oh, I gave her a piece of my mind when you and Alan went outside."

"Good for you. I'm glad we left when we did. If I'd known, I don't know what I would have done. I certainly wouldn't have accepted their invitation to sit with them during dinner."

Although it felt good that Connor was being protective, she didn't want him to go to war over it. "There's no need to tell Alan. I've cleared the air with Pamela. And I left her to pay the bill."

Connor laughed. "Well, that'll teach her."

Denise couldn't resist his smile. "I'm pretty sure they can afford it. But I'm glad you ordered that second bottle of champagne for the table."

She felt better having gotten it all off her chest. And Connor's reaction was endearing. She felt like she was starting to get back in control. She finished her coffee and put the cup in the dishwasher.

"You should eat something," he said.

"I'm not hungry. I'll grab something later."

She turned to Connor. "I think I'm going to call Bruce to see if I can move my appointment up."

She still hadn't talked to him about the anti-anxiety pills, or whether she should switch to something else. Something that would calm her down enough to get in the car without making her too dopey to drive.

So that she could taste freedom again.

Freedom to see a therapist who wasn't her next-door neighbor.

Freedom to see a specialist who might be able to figure out what was going on with her brain.

Freedom to take her life back, so she wasn't so dependent on Connor.

Connor came over and kissed her forehead. "I think that's a good idea. I have meetings all day, so I'll probably be back late."

When Connor left, Denise packed the bedding up from the couch and put it away. So far, so good. The wall was empty, her toothbrush was yellow, and there was no sign of Laura's perfume in the air. She thought about taking her anti-anxiety pill, then decided not to. No point in making herself dopey when she was in a better mood.

She made note of last night's events in her journal, then called Bruce to see if she could come over for another session.

"Of course," he said. "How about 11:00?"

"Perfect." That would give her time to take another run.

She changed into her running shoes and headed out. She stretched — her knee was a little stiff, but she knew the best thing to do was work it out with a short run. She avoided the area where she'd seen the man in the purple hoodie and the uncleared area where Sandra had taken her. Luckily, Sandra hadn't asked to join her this time. The fresh air and sunshine helped to clear her thoughts as she covered ground, the sound of her sneakers hitting the pavement creating its own hypnotic rhythm.

When she was ready to head back, she realized she had no idea which direction to turn. She was totally lost, and every house looked exactly the same. Since they were all unoccupied, there was no one she could ask for directions. She stopped and turned around, trying to get her bearings.

A sound in the distance caught her attention. Part bark, part scream. The sound sent chills down her spine. *Coyote?* She'd heard they roamed the area. It wasn't surprising. Since there were so few people around, they were simply reclaiming their territory. But she didn't want to run into one.

She took a deep breath and turned around, determined to retrace her steps. After a false number of twists and turns, she found herself in familiar territory and ended up back home in time to shower and get ready for her meeting with Bruce.

He met her at the front door and led her to the same office they'd been in the day before. She took the same chair, comfortable in its familiarity.

"So," Bruce said, "I'm guessing there's a reason you wanted to move our appointment up." He pointed to the journal on her lap. "Have you been keeping track of everything?"

"Yes, and things seem to be getting worse." She fingered the pages but didn't need to open the journal. She remembered everything distinctly. "Yesterday, when I left here, your wife, umm … Sandra." She glanced at him for confirmation. When he nodded, she continued. "I was under the impression that Cora was your wife, and Sandra and Diego were a couple. I'm not sure how I misunderstood. But you can see why I freaked out when Sandra came over here and said she was your wife."

She winced. "I can't trust my memories anymore."

He waited for her to continue.

She barreled on. "Then when I came out of the shower, I heard my sister's voice. Not just in my head. I clearly heard her voice. I looked it up online, and I guess it's called auditory hallucinations."

"Could be," he said.

She waited to see if he was going to elaborate, but when he didn't, she didn't take it personally. Dr. Garcia had taught her that therapy was more about talking and discovering answers for yourself rather than having judgment passed down from someone else. Maybe Bruce wanted her to keep an open mind about what she was experiencing, rather than assuming they were hallucinations.

The possibility that he might actually believe she wasn't hallucinating made her feel better.

"Then I smelled her perfume. It's a distinctive scent. I might write that off as coming from her clothes or something, but Connor put everything in storage, and even though I searched the entire bedroom, I didn't see her perfume anywhere."

Bruce sat back and let out a deep breath. It was hard to tell what he was thinking, but he didn't seem too concerned. Maybe what she was going through was a natural outcome of grief and loss.

"So," she said. "In addition to those things, there's something I need to talk about."

"Go on."

"It's about my mother. I told you she died of cancer, right?"

He nodded yes.

"Well," she continued, "before that, she was institutionalized for schizophrenia."

"Yes, you mentioned that. Are you ready to talk about that now?" Bruce leaned forward, listening intently. For the first time, he seemed to be paying close attention. She wasn't sure why it unnerved her as much as it did.

"She hated being on medication. She said she didn't feel like herself when she was taking it, that it leached the color from the world, leaving it gray and muddy. My father hired a caretaker for her, but there was this one day where she didn't show up…" Denise shivered, remembering that day so long ago. "I guess I was, I don't know, maybe six, and Laura was eight. Something like that."

She took a deep breath, needing strength to continue. "My mother was paranoid, convinced people were coming to steal us away. With the caretaker gone, she told us we were playing a game and had us climb into my grandfather's old steamer trunk. It smelled like dust and mold and something … old." To this day, the smell of vintage clothing sent Denise into a panic attack.

"My mother locked the trunk and swallowed the key. She wouldn't let us out no matter how much we screamed and cried. We held onto each other, sure we were going to suffocate and die. But at least we'd die together."

As soon as she said that, she realized that the worst part of the accident was that Laura had died without her. She fought back tears and forced herself to continue.

"It was hours later before our father came home," she continued, "but it felt like an eternity. He had to cut the trunk apart, but he finally set us free. He held us close as we cried, telling us everything would be all right. And it was. After that, he made our mother take her medication, and she seemed better, at least for a while. But Laura and I never really felt safe again after that, and neither of us could bear to be trapped in small spaces."

"And your mother?"

"Her paranoia got worse. She would do strange things that didn't make sense to me as a child, but now I know were symptoms of her schizophrenia. She was institutionalized when I was a teenager and eventually died of cancer."

"That's a lot to deal with," Bruce said.

Denise hadn't shared that story about being locked in the trunk with anyone else, not even her last therapist. "My question is … can schizophrenia be genetic? Can it be handed down from mother to daughter?"

Bruce crossed his arms over his chest. "It's possible. There's a genetic component to the illness. Individuals with a family history of the disorder have a higher risk of developing it themselves."

He seemed to be choosing his words carefully, as if trying not to upset her. Denise clenched her eyes shut. It wasn't the answer she wanted to hear, even though it was the one she had expected.

"But," Bruce continued, "it's not a given, not at all. Having a family member with schizophrenia does not guarantee that an individual will develop the condition."

Denise opened her eyes. "So, I might not have it? Something else could be going on."

She tried to think of what other options could be responsible. Early onset dementia? God, that didn't sound any better. "It could still be related to my concussion, right?" she continued. She knew she was grasping at straws, but a physical injury somehow sounded better than a genetic condition. Maybe instead of a therapist, she should just get an MRI to see if there was a physical reason for her mental agitation.

But she would have to get herself there.

"Could be," Bruce agreed. "It won't hurt to rule it out."

She made a mental note to ask her doctor for a referral. "Thank you, Bruce. I feel better now that I have a plan."

Then she hesitated. Should she ask him about the pills? "My last therapist prescribed anti-anxiety medication. Could those cause hallucinations?"

Bruce frowned, biting his lower lip before he answered. "I don't think so. Did your last therapist say that was one of the side effects?"

She shook her head.

"Then they're probably fine."

That was a relief too.

"You've been pretty isolated, and it's easy for your imagination to play tricks on you when you're all alone," Bruce said. "Why don't you spend more time with the girls? It's lonely for them in this neighborhood too. You might find that company keeps you more firmly anchored to reality."

Bruce stood and ushered her out of the office. "Glad I could help. You can call me any time."

As she was leaving, she spotted a photo of Cora and Bruce on the hallway armoire. It looked like a wedding photo. Cora, not Sandra. Should she confront Bruce about the discrepancy, or should she keep quiet? She had written down in her journal that he was married to Sandra after her last visit — she had it in black and white as proof. That wasn't a memory slip or a hallucination. Unless she was hallucinating right now.

She reached out and touched the photo. It was solid. It seemed real.

If she assumed that she wasn't crazy and or suffering

from a physical injury, then it meant that someone was messing with her. But why?

How could anyone benefit from confusing her about whether Bruce was married to Sandra or Cora?

Bruce had said that she needed to stop isolating herself. Maybe she would take his advice and get to know both Cora and Sandra better. See if she could figure out what was really going on between the three of them.

Back at her house, she went into the neighborhood group chat and invited Cora, Sandra, and Helen for dinner that night. Since Connor had said he'd be home late, it was a good time for a girl's night.

All three got back immediately and said they'd be there.

Chapter Sixteen

DENISE SPENT the afternoon making her special pasta sauce. The kitchen was fragrant with the scent of garlic, sausage, and tomato sauce. She hummed as she cooked. The kitchen was always her favorite place. She'd fallen in love with cooking when she was a teenager. There was something intensely satisfying about taking the freshest ingredients and making a mouth-watering meal. It had been awhile since she'd allowed herself the luxury of cooking. She'd gotten out of the habit of spending time in the kitchen when she lived by herself, as it was seldom worth cooking for one. And it hadn't seemed important since she'd moved in with Connor, who seemed to prefer takeout. She'd been assuming that he liked bringing food home because he was trying to take care of her, but now she wondered if it was more about being in control of what he ate.

Or maybe it was just habit. When Laura had been alive, they'd both worked late, so maybe he was just used to neither of them having time to spend in the kitchen.

Denise promised herself that she was going to get back

in touch with her inner chef now that she was back on her feet.

She added spices to her sauce and set it to simmer on the back burner while she prepared the meatballs. Helen had offered to bring dessert, Cora was bringing garlic bread, and Sandra was bringing wine. All that was left was to chop vegetables for a green salad.

A string of fairy lights adorned the outdoor patio, and lanterns cast a romantic glow over the table. Denise put four place settings on the table. The other women showed up at the same time, almost as if they planned it. Cora carried a covered basket of garlic bread, while Sandra held up a bottle of wine.

"I hope you like red," she said.

"Perfect," Denise replied, carrying wine glasses to the table. "It'll go well with pasta."

Helen carried a covered cake dish.

"I'll put dessert on the counter," she said, making her way inside. "I made strawberry shortcake."

Denise stopped what she was doing. A chill raced up her spine. Suddenly she wasn't so sure it was all in her imagination. It was too much of a coincidence that Helen brought strawberry shortcake after the mix-up the other day. Was she trying to taunt Denise? Could she have been the one in the purple hoodie? Had she lied about coming into the house with a golf club?

And what about the wives' musical chairs? Were they doing it on purpose? But why would the neighbors mess with her like this? Was it some kind of fucked-up prank?

Did they all hate her for some reason and want to harass her into leaving the neighborhood?

That was the kind of paranoid thought that would have driven her mother to pull another terrifying stunt that got the dosage of her medication increased. And had eventually led to her being institutionalized.

Denise pasted on a smile when they were all gathered around the table. "Thank you all for coming. I was hoping we could all get to know each other a little better now that we're neighbors."

They raised their glasses and toasted. "To new friends."

"This is lovely," Helen said, looking around. "Remind me to tell Diego I want to spruce up our patio."

Diego.

She looked over at Cora, who appeared totally innocent. So yesterday when Cora was supposedly with her *husband* Diego, either it was an elaborate charade, or she was having a psychological break of some kind. Sandra didn't react either, more evidence that she was in on whatever was going on.

Denise was determined to get to the bottom of it.

She asked Helen how her mother was doing.

"Better," Helen replied. "It's hard because she lives in Houston and had a stroke recently. That's why I've been running back and forth."

"I'm sorry," Denise said. "If there's anything I can do…"

Helen smiled. "Thank you." She broke off a piece of garlic bread and swirled it in the sauce on her dish.

Denise turned to Cora. "And you're a teacher, right?"

Cora looked confused. "No, I'm a dentist."

"Oh, I thought Diego said you were a teacher."

Cora shrugged. "I don't remember telling Diego my job."

But wouldn't he know that if he was her real husband? Denise was sure that if she consulted her journal, it would tell her that Cora was lying. Who really belonged to whom? It was like those hurricane projections — spaghetti models, all twisted and braided and curling back on themselves.

Sandra piped up. "I'm a teacher. Maybe that's why you were confused."

Denise took another sip of wine, watching the three of them over the rim of her glass. She wasn't convinced at all that she was the one who was confused.

Helen reached over and patted her hand. "I get things mixed up too. Mostly names. The older I get, the less I can remember."

Yeah, that made her feel better. Denise pushed the salad greens around her dish, stabbing a forkful with more force than necessary before eating it.

"Besides," Helen said, "didn't Connor say you'd had a concussion recently?"

Had he? Or was that something Bruce had shared with them? Either one felt like a betrayal. As her husband, Connor was supposed to have her back. And as her therapist, Bruce was supposed to keep what she told him confidential.

"That's true," she said, but didn't elaborate.

Denise paid special attention to everything that was said over dinner. She'd make notes later on. The only way to find the truth was to keep track of everything that was said and done.

An hour later, Denise opened a second bottle of wine. By now the women were giddy, but Denise had taken care to nurse her first glass throughout the evening, to be sure that she wouldn't become distracted or forget anything. Every time the conversation slowed, she asked one of them another question. Who was Sandra's favorite student? What had inspired Cora to become a dentist? How did Helen meet Diego?

Sandra talked at length about precocious little Miri,

who apparently read like a high school student even though she was in third grade and who had taught herself the flute.

Cora claimed to have an aunt who'd left her enough money to pay for college, and it had been enough for dental school but not med school.

Helen told a story about meeting Diego at a college party and skipping out because neither of them wanted to be there.

There were no discrepancies in any of their stories, but Denise was more interested whether those stories would change the next time she asked.

As day turned to dusk, the women began clearing the table. There were now three empty wine bottles on the counter, and only a handful of crumbs were left on the strawberry shortcake plate. Denise continued to pretend that she was as tipsy as the others, eager for them to leave so she could write everything she'd learned in her journal.

Soon, Connor came to the door carrying a large package, and the women gathered around him.

"What do you have there?" Helen asked.

"A new painting," he said. "For Denise." He tore the paper off and unveiled a painting of sunflowers identical to the print that was on the wall yesterday before her impromptu bonfire. "What do you think, Denise?"

She blinked. "It's, umm … it's fine."

"Fine?" Connor shook his head. "You wanted a new painting for the wall over the mantel. Don't you remember asking me to get one?"

Denise's stomach churned, but she didn't want to call him out in front of the other women and give them reason to think she was having another slip. Or to let on to Connor that she'd realized what he was doing, presenting the same painting as if it was new.

So she kept up the pretense that she'd drunk too much. She waved a hand and stumbled forward. "Do what you want with it."

"Fine," Connor said. "I'll go hang it up."

She wobbled her head and smirked, "*I'll go hang it up*," she repeated with a drunken slur.

Connor scowled at her, then turned on his heel and left the room.

The rest of the women made excuses and scattered like roaches when the lights came on. Denise watched them go, then took a deep breath and followed Connor into the living room. He'd hung the painting on the wall and was tilting each corner trying to make it level.

He turned and scowled. "Look, I had a shit day at work. I just wanted to do something nice for you, and all I get is attitude."

"I'm sorry," she said, not mentioning that this was the second incarnation of the sunflower painting he'd hung on the wall and risking another conversation where he accused her of forgetting or worse.

"Yeah, well I'm sorry you don't like it. Tomorrow you can drive to the store and buy something you like more."

Low blow. He knew she couldn't get behind the wheel of a car, whether to buy a new painting or anything else. But she chose not to react. All she wanted was to go upstairs and write everything down before she forgot. But she didn't want him to discover what she was doing, so she would wait until he'd gone to bed.

"I'm just going to straighten this painting and go to bed."

Perfect.

"Fine," she said. "I'm going to clean up the kitchen. I'll be up later."

Denise took her time, hoping Connor would be asleep

when she went upstairs. After the kitchen was spotless, she tiptoed upstairs and checked that their bedroom light was off. It was, so she hurried to her craft room and locked the door, then retrieved her journal to record everything she could remember the other women telling her. She mentioned the sunflower painting, too. Then she headed into the bathroom. There in her cup on the counter was a blue toothbrush. Her shoulders sagged as she stared at it in disbelief. It had been yellow this morning. She decided that she would double check in her journal tomorrow, then brushed her teeth, took her pills, and went to bed, sliding between the sheets silently so as not to wake Connor.

Chapter Seventeen

THE NEXT MORNING, Denise woke up feeling groggy again, even though she'd only had one glass of wine to drink last night. Maybe the pills had a cumulative effect, making her dopier the longer she took them. They did dull her anxiety, but she still didn't know if they might have caused the hallucinations — Laura's voice, her perfume, the changes to the wedding picture. Or maybe it was quitting them that caused those.

She rolled over and snuggled under the blankets. She wanted to stay in bed all day. Surely, nothing strange would happen if she didn't get up. But if she stayed in bed, one day might turn into two, then two days into a week. Just like her mother.

Connor called from downstairs. "Denise, I'm leaving in a few minutes. I've made breakfast."

She yawned and stretched. Her back ached. She stood up and tried to stretch the kinks out. The mattress felt different. Softer. She pressed her palm on it and pressed down. Softer. No wonder her back hurt. She'd have to tell Connor it was time to get a new mattress.

"Be down in a minute," she called back.

She took care of her bathroom needs, washed her face, and brushed her teeth before heading downstairs.

Connor gave her a bright smile. "There you are, sleepyhead." He handed her a cup of hot coffee. "Look, I'm sorry for losing my temper yesterday." He rubbed the frown lines on his forehead. "It's the takeover threat at work. It's stressing me out."

"I'm sorry, too." Then, to test his reaction, she added, "I think these pills are making me worse. Maybe I should stop taking them."

"No!" Connor's shout was unexpected. "I mean, the doctor said they were necessary. I wouldn't go fooling around with them if I were you. Don't you remember what a mess you were before Dr. Garcia prescribed them?"

"But they don't seem to be helping at all. I'm hearing things and seeing things that aren't there. I'm confused most of the time and can't seem to get my bearings." She paused, maybe a bit dramatically, to get her point across. She wanted Connor to think she was still as confused as ever. "And I heard Laura's voice. I smelled her perfume. I think … I think her spirit is haunting me."

Connor put an arm around her. "Don't blame the pills. Blame the concussion you suffered after the accident. It takes time for your brain to heal completely. Plus, you're still grieving. I'm not surprised that you see evidence of Laura everywhere. Remember what your therapist said about survivor's guilt?"

Denise gave a nod of agreement and walked Connor out. He opened the door. Denise's mouth dropped open as she stared outside, dazed and confused. The coffee cup fell out of her hand, smashing on the steps and splattering hot coffee all over her legs. *What the hell?*

She pushed Connor aside and rushed out the door.

This wasn't her house. They were standing in the doorway of Sandra and Diego's house!

She turned to Connor. "Why are we here?"

"What? Where?"

"In Sandra and Diego's house."

"We're not. This is our house."

She pointed to the house two doors down at the end of the cul-de-sac. "*That's* our house!"

His voice was dangerously quiet. "Denise. This is our house. We moved here four months ago."

Now she really did wish that she'd painted the front door turquoise, because then he wouldn't have argued with her. She shook her head back and forth. "No, no, no. I know where my own house is." She took off down the street.

Connor tried to stop her, but she shook him off. The door was unlocked, and she barged inside. Instead of Sandra and Diego, she'd interrupted *Helen* and Diego eating breakfast. Unbelievable. Spouse-swapping or lying about their jobs to prank her was one thing. Stealing her house was an order of magnitude crazier.

"Denise?" Helen's face held both suspicion and surprise. "What are you doing here?"

She glanced at Connor behind Denise and gave a slight nod.

Denise stormed toward the table. "The question is, what are *you* doing in my house?"

"Your house? This is our house. Diego and I bought it shortly after you and Connor moved in."

Diego? "Don't you mean Ronald?"

Helen laughed. "Why in the world would I mean Ronald?"

That's when Denise spotted the wedding picture over

159

the mantel. It was Helen and Diego. She shook her head. No, this wasn't possible.

She took the stairs two at a time, Connor trailing after her. The office was different. All her macrame projects were gone. Including the yarn basket with her journal. Instead, there was a sewing machine in the corner, bolts of fabric and a half-finished quilt.

Her head spun. How was this possible? She could believe that she was forgetting what color her toothbrush was, or what Cora did for a living. But believing that someone else had stolen her house? Or that the house she'd woken up in belonged to somebody else?

That was the kind of paranoid delusion that her mother would have.

A dizzy wave of fear whooshed through her. What if she had inherited her mother's mental illness and all the little discrepancies she'd been recording were the warning signs of her impending break from reality?

No! I'm not crazy. I am not my mother. There has to be a rational explanation for this.

"I was making that for you," Helen said, joining Connor. "It was going to be a surprise."

"Fuck the quilt! What the hell is going on here?" She looked from Connor to Helen and back. "Why are you all messing with me?"

Connor reached out. "Denise, calm down. Let's just talk about this for a minute."

Helen took a step back. "Maybe we should call an ambulance."

"No." Connor shook his head. "She'll be fine. I'll take care of this."

Oh no, you won't. Denise pushed her way past Connor and Helen and ran down the stairs. She passed Diego watching her from the kitchen, a look of amusement on his face. What was so damn funny?

She didn't stop to ask, but kept running faster and faster. She knew she could outrun both Connor and Helen if they were following. She ran until her breath caught in her chest and her legs grew numb. Finally, after what seemed like hours, she took refuge in one of the partially developed houses on an unnamed dead end. She curled up in a corner while her body shook with exhaustion.

As she was catching her breath, she caught sight of a shadow passing in front of the open doorway. Her body on full alert, she waited to see if it was Connor coming to have her committed. Not that she'd blame him. The world had gone topsy-turvy and her emotions were out of control.

But it wasn't Connor. The wind blew the plastic covering the doorway, and she saw a coyote standing there. Its eyes were wild, its mane shaggy. She could count the ribs on each side. The poor thing must be starving. No wonder it was roaming the development in search of food.

They locked eyes. The feral animal howled, making the same sound she'd heard the other day. It was almost as if the coyote was trying to tell her something. *If it was even real.* She blinked and the plastic covering flapped shut, then blew open again.

There was no sign of the coyote either inside or out.

Chapter Eighteen

DENISE BLINKED HER EYES, she was crouched in the corner like a hunted animal. What the hell? She'd fallen asleep in an empty house with wild coyotes roaming the grounds? That, if anything, was proof the pills she was taking were too strong. That had to be the explanation. Because the alternative was that this was the beginning of her descent into the insanity that had destroyed her mother's lives, and nearly destroyed hers and Laura's.

What about last night? Was it possible she'd slept through the night while Helen and Connor switched houses? That was too ridiculous to even consider. Why go to that trouble just to freak her out?

It had to be the meds.

She heard Connor and Helen calling in the distance. She didn't want to see either of them right now, but she didn't think it was safe to stay here much longer. Who knew when the coyote would be back, and this time he might decide she looked good enough to eat.

She pulled her phone out of her pocket and checked her messages. Seventeen missed calls from Connor. Several from Helen. She deleted them all. Then, at the bottom, a call from Raquel. She stared at the message for a long moment. Raquel left a voicemail.

She scrolled through her voicemails, ignoring the ones from Connor begging her to come home. She played Raquel's voicemail, relieved and somehow hopeful to hear her familiar voice.

"Hi Denise. I've been thinking, and you were right. I did abandon you during the worst time of your life. It was selfish, and I'm so sorry." There was a moment of silence, then the voicemail continued. "I'd like to make it up to you. I mean, if you want. Maybe we could go to lunch sometime or something. Anyway, let me know."

Remembering Bruce's suggestion that she not keep isolating herself, she decided to call Raquel back. She had no friends right now — not even Connor — and Raquel had nothing to do with any of this. Maybe someone from the outside looking in could help her figure out what was going on.

Unless Raquel was in on this, and Connor had somehow convinced her to call Denise because she'd been ignoring his attempts to find her. But that seemed paranoid too. How would Connor know Raquel? She was *mostly* sure that she hadn't told him about seeing her in the post office again. And she definitely hadn't mentioned her during the long recovery from the accident.

She wasn't sure if she was falling deeper into paranoia — or seeing reality for the first time since Laura had died.

She hit the redial button and chewed her lip waiting.

"Hi," she said when Raquel answered. "I got your message."

"Oh good. I hope you know I'm really sorry. I couldn't believe Laura was gone, and I didn't know what to say or how to behave."

"I understand." She wasn't just saying it, she really did. It was Denise's own sense of loss and guilt that had made her blow Raquel's absence up into some kind of betrayal rather than just the discomfort of dealing with a grieving person.

"I was about to head out and take the baby to the park. Would you like to meet us there?"

Denise was forced to admit that she didn't drive. "Not since the accident."

"Oh. Then I'll pick you up." There wasn't any judgment in Raquel's voice. She simply accepted and offered to drive. Denise gave her the address of her house, or at least the house she went to bed in last night. If the rest was a hallucination, she'd deal with that later.

"I'll be there in thirty minutes," Raquel said.

"I'll be ready," she replied. Denise had no idea which direction would take her home. Then, with the phone in her hand, she had an idea. She put her address into Google maps, which gave her specific directions to her house. Why hadn't she thought of that before?

Following the map, she was able to find her cul-de-sac with no trouble. The neighborhood seemed exceptionally quiet. She glanced from one house to another, unsure of which one to enter. Should she go to the house she thought of as her own? The one she went to sleep in last night? Or should she go to the house where she'd gotten out of bed this morning? A bed that certainly *wasn't* her own — it was far too soft. The house that she was convinced belonged to the Parkers.

She stood, undecided. Then she saw Helen peeking out the window from what should have been her and Connor's house. She turned instead and continued on toward the house Connor claimed was theirs. She could hear him on the telephone. She stepped inside to find Connor pacing the living room. He glanced at her, then spoke into the phone, "Never mind. She just came home."

He turned and scowled at Denise. "Jesus Christ, you scared me. I was just calling the police."

"I went for a run," she deadpanned.

"A run? You've been gone for four hours."

She turned to go upstairs. "I'm going to take a shower and change."

"Denise…"

But she kept going. She wouldn't give him the chance to chastise her. She undressed and stood under the hot shower until she felt like herself again, letting the hot water wash away her remaining tears.

Changing into a clean outfit, she went back downstairs and walked past Connor, who stood with his hands on his hips.

"I'm going out," she said.

"Out? Where? You don't even drive."

Denise kept going, giving the minimal answer to his questions. "A friend is picking me up."

"What friend?" He looked surprised. "Are you sure that's a good idea?"

Was he truly surprised, or did he know that Raquel was coming because he'd asked her too?

No, she wasn't going down that rabbit hole. Not until she saw evidence that Raquel knew Connor.

She kept going. Outside, she saw Raquel parked in Helen's driveway and made her way over. "Sorry. I gave you the wrong address."

She'd explain the mix-up later.

"No problem." Raquel opened the passenger door and Denise looked inside, finding a tiny, wide-eyed child tucked into a car seat.

"This is Lily," Raquel said. "She's eleven months old."

Denise smiled. "Hi Lily."

Her heart swelled when she realized Lily was about the same age Laura's child would have been if not for the accident.

The baby gurgled and cooed. Grief nearly brought Denise to her knees. Instead, she slid into the passenger seat and managed to comment. "She looks just like you."

Raquel laughed. "Yes, my mini-me." She backed out of the driveway. Denise couldn't hold it together any longer. It was as if she'd crawled through the desert and now found herself on a fresh oasis, a place where she could finally let down her guard. She tried to hold the tears back, but they bubbled up, first tightening her throat, then scalding her eyes until she couldn't hold back any longer. She sniffled back a sob.

Raquel pulled over to the side of the road and parked the car. She turned and wrapped her arms around Denise, letting her cry until there were no tears left.

Chapter Nineteen

ONCE DENISE HAD her emotions under control, Raquel drove them to the park. She put Lily in a stroller, then they walked together silently. But it was a comfortable silence. Denise knew Raquel would let her talk when the time was right.

"I was a shitty friend, huh?" Raquel started.

Denise looked at the baby in the stroller, then back to Raquel. "I didn't even know you were pregnant. I guess you had a lot to deal with too." It wasn't like her to be so judgmental without seeing the other person's point of view. "And I could have reached out, but I was too caught up in my own issues to realize that other people were hurting as well."

The truth was, she'd been leaning on Connor for so long that she'd forgotten how good it was to spend time with a girlfriend. This was the best she'd felt in months.

They made their way to an empty bench and sat. Raquel gently rocked the stroller until Lily was sound asleep. It seemed as good a time as any for Denise to unload everything that had been on her chest.

"I've been having a hard time lately. I can't remember things, and what I do remember gets mixed up and muddled. Sometimes reality changes so fast, I feel like I'm going crazy," she began. Then she told Raquel the rest, starting with how Connor had bought the house without consulting her and ending with this morning's debacle.

Raquel nodded. "Something similar happened to me when I was going through postpartum depression. I went to my sister's and commented on a beautiful hand-embroidered tablecloth she had. She gave me a strange look and told me I had made it for her. I had no memory of doing it. Zero." She shook her head. "The brain can do funny things."

"Yeah, I guess." Denise's phone vibrated, and she pulled it out of her pocket. It was Connor. The second she answered, he demanded to know where she was. She snapped, "I'm out. With a friend."

"Out with this mysterious friend I've never met. Do you think that's wise?"

Why wouldn't it be? Was he angry because she'd stepped out from under his control?

"I'm fine," she said. "I'll see you when I get home."

When she hung up, Raquel gave her a questioning look. "He's not taking advantage of you, is he?"

"In what way?"

"I don't know. It's just weird how he's almost afraid to let you out of his sight."

Denise didn't admit she was thinking along those same lines. "He's always been a bit overprotective. We went through a lot after the accident. But he was always there to take care of me while I recovered. I'm grateful."

"Grateful enough to marry him?"

Maybe if someone else had asked that question, she would have defended Connor. But Raquel had been so accepting and nonjudgmental, Denise was able to consider the question seriously. Would she have rushed into marriage if Connor hadn't proposed to her the way he did? She remembered the intense pressure she'd felt to say yes, feeling manipulated into becoming his fiancée while simultaneously recognizing how he'd done everything right — her favorite restaurant, a ring most women would've killed for, surrounded by friends and colleagues. It should have been magical, but instead, it had made her feel trapped, in the same way that she felt trapped now.

"Have you seen a therapist?" Raquel asked. "If not, I have someone I could recommend."

"I'm seeing someone already."

Raquel gave her a long, hard stare. "Someone Connor recommended?"

"No. It's a neighbor who just moved in."

"One of the neighbors playing musical chairs with the other wives?"

Denise shrugged. "Well, when you put it that way."

"Okay," Raquel said. "Enough with the interrogation. I guess I'm just a little skeptical because everything you're telling me sounds pretty suspicious. I'm not so sure it's all in your imagination." She patted Denise's hand. "What does this therapist say about all this?"

Denise took a deep breath and let it out with a sigh. "He says it's probably a combination of grief and the concussion I suffered during the accident. But it could be genetic too. He suggested it wouldn't hurt to get checked and to rule out brain damage. Maybe an MRI?"

"Might be a good idea. Once you rule out other possibilities, you can focus on the most logical one."

"That I'm going crazy?"

"Or maybe that someone wants you to think you're going crazy."

Denise was afraid to agree with her, because that was the kind of thing her mother would've said during an episode. She wanted to believe that it was true, but she was also terrified that wanting to believe it meant she had inherited her mother's illness. And that Raquel might be enabling her paranoia.

So instead of agreeing, she said, "It feels good to talk to someone about it. Keeping it all inside makes my brain go in circles."

"I'm here for you now. I promise." It was hard to mistake the sincerity in her voice. "And I think it's good that you do some things for yourself. Sounds like Connor is keeping you on a short leash."

Denise stopped herself from arguing that Connor was just worried about her. When had that become her instinctive response to any criticism of his behavior? Raquel was right. Connor *had* been keeping her on a short leash, and she'd only noticed that recently.

Before Denise could argue, Lily began to whimper.

"Look who's up from her nap," Raquel lifted the baby from the stroller and held her close. Lily immediately started cooing and nuzzling Raquel's neck.

"Aw, she's such a good baby."

"She sure is." Raquel gave Denise a questioning look. "Would you like to hold her?"

"I don't…" Lily turned and gave her a bubbly smile. "Yes, I'd like that."

She took Lily from Raquel's arms and snuggled her close. Lily lay her head on Denise's shoulder and cooed. Denise felt something soften inside her. Yes, there was still a sense of loss, but there was also hope.

"You're a natural," Raquel said. "Do you think you'll have kids one day?"

"I can't." It was hard to say the words out loud. "I had

a hysterectomy after the accident." She inhaled the baby's sweet scent and brushed her lips over Lily's downy hair. "But maybe I could adopt one day." She knew she could easily fall in love with a baby that wasn't her own. She was already half in love with Lily, and she'd only known her for an hour.

Raquel took the baby from Denise and put her back in the stroller. "We'd better get going. She'll be hungry soon."

They made their way back to the car, tucked Lily in her car seat, and started back. When Raquel pulled into the driveway of the house where Helen lived now, Denise didn't correct her. She hadn't explained the revolving houses, knowing it would sound completely insane and not wanting Raquel to decide that she was crazy, so she had no idea which house she should go to.

After getting out of the car, she leaned in the window. "Thanks so much, I really enjoyed it."

"Let's do it again tomorrow, okay?"

Denise smiled her first genuine smile in months. "I'd love that." She blew Lily a kiss, then waved goodbye to Raquel. She glanced at her house, then at Helen's house. She had a 50/50 chance of getting it right. Since she'd left what should have been Helen's house before Raquel picked her up, she figured that was the right choice. She walked over, opened the door, and stepped inside.

Helen was coming down the stairs. "Can I help you?"

Damn. "No. Wrong house."

Helen nodded, as if that happened all the time. Denise couldn't help but notice her eyes were red and swollen. Had she been crying? "Is everything alright?"

"I'm fine," Helen said. "I just had an argument with Connor."

"Connor? Why were you arguing with Connor?"

Helen looked away, guilt written all over her face.

"Jesus, what's wrong with me? Not Connor. I meant Ronald. I had an argument with Ronald." She rubbed her eyes. "I guess I need some sleep."

Ronald, not Diego.

Denise was glad she wasn't the only one who seemed confused for a change. Maybe that was supposed to be the next part of the prank, pretending that Helen was married to Connor and Denise was married to someone else, and Helen had botched it by saying it too soon.

She turned and walked back to the house at the end of the cul-de-sac. Her house. Just as it always had been. Except for that gaudy picture of sunflowers Connor had hung on the wall.

Connor looked up from the couch, clicked the remote, and turned the television off. "I wish you'd told me where you were going."

"Why? I'm an adult."

"I just worry about you. What if you have another episode while you're out?"

"I was with a friend. If I'd had an *episode*, as you call it, I'm sure she would have taken me to the hospital." Her voice was steely. "Or to a psychiatrist, if that's what you're worried about."

"Look, I just want you to be safe."

"Don't worry about me. I can take care of myself." The words sounded right, but was she 100% sure it was the truth?

She turned and stomped up the stairs. He'd already dampened the good mood she had from spending the afternoon with Raquel and Lily. Maybe working on her macrame would help her get some of that good mood back.

First, she needed to update her journal, adding the details she could remember: Sandra's suspicious misdirection on their run, waking up in the wrong house, Helen's latest husband switch, and most of all, reconnecting with an old friend.

SPENDING *time with Raquel today was nice. Very nice. It was as if no time at all has passed, and we picked up where we left off. I realize I've cut myself off from most of the people I knew before the accident. When I wasn't with Laura, most of my time was spent with people from the office. Not really friends, as evidenced by the fact that I hadn't sought any of them out, especially now that I don't go into the office anymore.*

But talking to Raquel was comfortable. I opened up in more ways than I thought possible. She encourages me to look at things in a different way. I need a different perspective. And Lily. What a darling. She's already stolen my heart.

I'm really looking forward to spending time with them tomorrow.

SHE CLOSED the journal with a smile, feeling optimistic for the first time in months.

Chapter Twenty

DENISE WORKED LATE into the evening, stopping only to make a quick sandwich for dinner. She passed Connor in the hallway, and they simply nodded to each other without speaking. She waited until he was asleep before crawling into bed, her eyes tired from knotting macrame, but at least her mind was calm once again.

When she woke the next morning, Connor was already in the shower. As she dressed, she thought about skipping her pills, but Connor's warning still rang in her ears. If the pills were helping at all, what would her world be like if she stopped taking them?

She decided that it was time to get an expert opinion on that. And that expert was neither Connor nor Bruce.

She went downstairs before the alarm went off, put the coffee on, and waited for Connor.

He was showered and freshly shaved when he came downstairs. Denise offered him a cup of coffee as a peace offering. "Sorry for being a bitch yesterday."

He took the cup and grinned. "Me too."

"You're sorry I was a bitch?"

He laughed. "No, sorry I was a dick."

"Fair enough." She reached out her hand. "Friends?"

He pulled her into his arms and gave her a warm hug. "More than friends."

Denise wondered if all marriages were like this, filled with ups and downs, arguments then make ups. Connor had accepted her apology without demanding an explanation. Maybe he just didn't want to know how crazy she was. Or maybe he was afraid of starting another fight?

She wished Laura was there to ask: *Did you and Connor fight like this too?*

"What are you up to today?" he asked.

She lifted one shoulder. "I don't know. Probably working on some macrame projects."

"Is that why you were up so late last night?"

"I had lots of orders to fill." It was only a little white lie.

He held her gaze for a moment, then turned to leave. "I'll probably be late again tonight. I have a meeting with Jose and Sarah. Don't hesitate to call if you need me."

After Connor left, she went upstairs and reached for her journal. It wasn't on the shelf where she'd left it last night. She checked her worktable, then the floor. Odd. She distinctly remembered putting it on the shelf beside the cord that had arrived from the craft store yesterday. She turned and spotted it across the room. Had she put it there and forgotten? Or had someone been reading it?

Not that it mattered if Connor had read it. It wasn't like a diary or journal where she vented a lot of her feelings about him. Just a place to make notes on her forgetfulness and other strange things happening around her. Even though he wasn't aware of everything she'd recorded, it would be obvious to him that she was trying to track her memory slips and other problems. She picked up the journal and flipped through the pages. Nothing seemed to have changed. But she still felt a sense of violation.

She was glad now that she hadn't written her suspicions about him down. She would be more careful to hide her journal in the future.

Thinking back to something her first therapist had suggested — that she try writing a letter to Laura to help assuage her guilt — it had seemed like a terrible idea at the time, but now maybe she was ready to express her feelings on paper. Maybe doing that would help her get over some of the guilt she still felt. She picked up a pen and began writing.

DEAR LAURA,

I miss your face. I miss the sound of your voice. I miss knowing that the person who knew me as a child and young adult is gone, and now those memories you held of our lives growing up are gone as well. I wish I could bring you back. I wish that it was me instead of you that lost your life. No. I wish neither of us had died and we'd still be together. Sisters forever.

Next week is my birthday. It won't be the same without you making that stupid pineapple cake you thought was so wonderful. It kinda was, but only because you made it for me. I doubt whether Connor will even remember. And to be honest, I just want the day to go by without anyone even noticing, because another birthday only reminds me that you'll never see another one. Next year I'll be the same age you were when…

SHE STOPPED. She couldn't go on. Tears streamed down her face, and her breath came in shallow bursts. She reached for a tissue and wiped her nose. Would the tears ever end? Was she doomed to living a life of grief and guilt for all eternity?

She put the notebook away, this time tucking it in her lingerie drawer. Not that she was hiding it or anything. She just didn't want to misplace it again.

The morning flew by while she worked on some less intricate orders for plant holders. She made one in sunny yellow with a smiley face bead woven into the design. This one would be for Lily's room.

It was nearly noon when Raquel called asking if it was too soon to swing by.

"Not at all," Denise replied. "I'll be ready in ten minutes."

She hung up and combed out her hair, then brushed macrame lint from her black pants. She was ready when Raquel pulled up in Helen's driveway. Denise stepped outside and waved.

Raquel got out of the car and met her halfway. She pointed to Helen's house. "I thought you lived there?"

"Nope, this is my house."

"That's odd. I could have sworn I picked you up over there yesterday."

Denise shrugged. She wasn't ready to tell Raquel about waking up in the wrong house yet. Not until she'd confirmed another suspicion. Because once Raquel knew, she could decide Denise was crazy and there would be no going back to being friends after that.

"I'm so happy to see you." She peeked in the backseat. "Where's Lily?"

"Oh, I left her with my mom. I thought we'd have a girl's pamper day. My treat."

"Aww, I was looking forward to seeing her." She reached in her tote bag and pulled out the smiley face plant holder. "I made this for her room."

Raquel took the plant holder and admired it. "You made this? I love it!" She leaned forward and gave Denise a warm hug. "Thank you."

It wasn't often Denise had the pleasure of seeing someone receive one of her projects. That was the one drawback of having an online marketplace. There was no real one-on-one interaction.

Their first stop was Raquel's hair stylist. "She's an absolute artist," Raquel said.

The stylist ran her fingers through Denise's hair. "I know just the perfect cut for you," she said. "And this color washes out your complexion. What would you think about some highlights around your face?"

Denise shrugged. "Sure." It didn't matter one way or the other, but when the hairdresser was done and Denise looked in the mirror, she barely recognized herself. The cut framed her face, and the highlights complemented her skin tone.

"Wow, she really is an artist," Denise said.

"Told you!" Raquel preened in the mirror, admiring her new cut as well. She caught Denise's eye in the mirror. "You know, with that haircut and highlights, your resemblance to your sister is uncanny."

Denise studied her reflection. It was true. Her face was leaner, and with the new hairstyle, she looked even more like Laura than before. She smiled at her reflection, and it was almost as if her sister was smiling back at her. Did she like it?

She decided that it made her feel closer to Laura.

When Denise tried to pay, Raquel insisted it was her treat. She put her wallet back in her cross body. "Next stop, Belleza."

"Oh, that's one of my favorite stores. I haven't been there since…"

"Mine too," Raquel said, ignoring the rest of the unfinished sentence. She put the car in gear and drove off. "Do you have to be home at any special time?"

"Nope. Connor is working late again."

Raquel nodded, a hint of disapproval on her face. "My mom has Lily for the whole day, so I don't have to be home any time soon either. How about we go to lunch after we shop?"

"Sounds wonderful." She'd meant to ask Raquel to take her to a pharmacy, but Denise couldn't remember the last time she'd been out to lunch with anyone. Connor was usually at work, and she didn't know any of her neighbors well enough to suggest a lunch date. It would be so nice to enjoy a normal day out, doing normal things. They could always stop on the way home.

"Do you have a special place in mind?" Denise asked.

"No, you choose," Raquel said. "You probably have more experience eating out than I do."

"You don't eat out much?"

"Not usually, no. Connor will bring home takeout occasionally. But for the most part, we're homebodies."

"Hmm."

"What?"

"Nothing. It just seems to me that Connor and Laura were out all the time. Drinking, dancing, partying, or just hanging with other couples. They were anything but homebodies."

Now that Raquel mentioned it, Denise realized she was right. She even use to tease them about never being home. And now Connor hardly ever left the house. Other than Grady Oil's anniversary celebration, they barely went anywhere. Of course, during the first few months of her recovery, she'd been on crutches and in a lot of pain. Hobbling from the couch to the bathroom had been all she was up to then, and Connor left the house every day to go to work or do the errands she was unable to do because of her inability to drive a car.

But there was nothing stopping them from going out now — except Denise's need for *support* to tolerate being in a car.

Even today, she'd needed one of her pills in order to be okay while Raquel drove them around.

"That might be partly my fault," she admitted.

While Raquel parked the car, Denise answered a call from Connor. "Where are you?" he asked.

"Out with a friend."

"I thought you were working in your studio today?" His voice was tight, almost accusatory.

"I changed my mind."

"Well, I would have liked a heads up."

"Why? You're at work, so what does it matter if I'm home or not?"

His voice softened. "I just worry, that's all. You haven't been yourself lately." He cleared his throat. "That's why I asked Sandra to keep an eye out."

"Keep an eye out? You mean spy on me? Did she call and tell you I'd left the house?"

He was silent for a moment, which seemed like answer enough.

"It's not spying," he finally said. "I just asked her to make sure you were okay."

"I'm just fine," Denise said with more force than she had planned. She hung up the phone. When Connor tried calling back, she turned it off.

"Everything okay?" Raquel asked.

Denise shook her head, "I think you're right. I think he wants to keep me at home where he can control me. He says it's because he's worried about me, but this possessiveness feels more like he has me on a leash."

Raquel gave her a knowing glance. "That's the impression I was getting."

Denise tucked the phone back in her pocket as they entered the store. Before long, she had half a dozen outfits to try on. She and Raquel entered the fitting rooms together and posed with different outfits to get the other's opinion. So far Denise hadn't found anything that screamed "Buy Me!"

Then she tried on *the* dress. The one that Raquel had insisted was made for her. Royal blue, with a twist front and plunging neckline. It fit her body perfectly, hugging her curves and falling just above the knee. She turned and the dress swirled around her like magic. It was love at first sight.

She stepped out of the fitting room and Raquel gasped. "Oh my God. That dress was made for you!"

Denise couldn't agree more. There was only one problem. "Do you think they have it in a different color?"

"Why? That color brings out the blue in your eyes. It's perfect for you."

Denise took a deep breath. "Blue was Laura's favorite color." She'd told Raquel about the disappearing toothbrushes, but it probably didn't seem like a big deal to her for each sister to have *their* color. "I always avoided wearing blue because, I don't know … it just felt wrong."

Raquel took hold of Denise's shoulders and turned her to the three-way mirror. "What do you think Laura would say if she saw you in that dress?"

And just like that, Denise knew exactly what Laura would say: *My favorite color on my favorite sister.*

Your only sister, Denise would reply. And they'd laugh and hug, and Denise would buy the damn dress because it was never a competition between them. They had each other's backs. Always.

"She'd tell me to buy it if it made me feel pretty."

"Does it?"

"Absolutely." So she bought the dress, and Raquel convinced her to wear it to lunch because it made her eyes sparkle and brought a smile to her face.

Lunch was at a quiet cafe that Raquel recommended. It was cozy and inviting, with soft lighting and intimate seating arrangements perfect for private conversations. They talked about Lily, and Raquel made motherhood sound like the most enjoyable job on earth.

Then they talked about Laura, and for the first time, Denise was able to talk about her sister and remember the good times instead of focusing on the accident. What they *didn't* talk about was Connor. Raquel didn't push, leaving Denise to ponder all the things Raquel had said in earlier conversations. Even though she could make a good excuse for Connor's behavior, Raquel encouraged the seed of doubt that had been growing in Denise's mind ever since she'd detected that false note in his voice when they were looking at the wedding picture and he'd said insincerely that having Denise helped ease the pain of losing Laura.

But Denise was still afraid to give herself permission to indulge in the kind of paranoid thinking that the seed of doubt could lead to.

So they stuck to safe subjects, bouncing around all over, from gossip about old schoolmates, to the rising price of eggs, to movies they'd seen recently. It felt comfortable and natural. Time flew by. It was the best day Denise had had in a long time, despite the fact that they'd been driving all over the place. Somehow Raquel's presence made it easier to control the anxiety that her pills didn't suppress, and as soon as they were out of the car, she was fine.

She checked her watch, surprised at the time. She'd wanted to ask about stopping at a pharmacy, but it was later than she'd meant to stay out. Connor would be home from work soon. "I suppose I should get back."

"Yeah, I miss my little peanut," Raquel said with a grin. "But that doesn't mean I don't appreciate a day off with a friend."

A friend. Denise liked the sound of that.

Raquel dropped Denise off at the right house this time. Or so Denise hoped. She leaned into the driver's window. "Thanks for lunch. I had a great time. It's the most fun I've had in a while."

"Let's do it again. How about a weekly walk in the park with Lily?"

"I'd love that." She watched Raquel back out of the driveway and waved, then heard a gasp behind her.

She turned and saw Connor, his face pale, eyes wide as he stared at her. "Laura?"

"Huh?"

Then recognition came over him. "Denise? What are you doing?"

"What?"

"It's not funny." He turned to leave.

She grabbed the back of his shirt until he turned to face her. "I don't know what you're talking about."

"The hair. The dress. You look exactly like Laura. What the fuck is wrong with you?"

He turned and marched into the house, leaving Denise frozen in place. A few minutes later, he came back out with his keys, got in the car without saying a word, and drove away.

Not sure what else to do, Denise went inside. She checked the hallway mirror. Connor was right. She looked like an imitation of Laura. And not a good imitation, either. Yes, her hair was similar, and since she lost weight, her body was more willowy like Laura's was. Had she subconsciously tried to mimic her sister's look? Was she trying to *be* her?

Maybe some part of her had thought that would fix the problems that she and Connor had been having.

Or maybe bringing Laura back to life by pretending to be her for a few hours was a way of assuaging her guilt.

Either option was seriously fucked up.

She rushed upstairs, pulled the dress over her head, and tossed it in the laundry basket. She changed into her usual leggings and t-shirt, then spritzed her hair to comb out the blow dry. When she checked the mirror, she looked and felt more like herself. Sitting on the edge of the bed, she realized it was time she faced some of her past. Otherwise, she'd never get better.

There was a vintage hat box on the top shelf of her dresser in a delicate primrose print. She and Laura had found it at a yard sale a few years ago and fallen in love with it. That's where they put their treasures: special pictures of days they wanted to remember, receipts they saved "just in case," and little mementos too sweet to throw away. It was one of the few items she'd brought back from the cottage.

She pulled it down from the closet and placed it on the bed. After staring at it for a few minutes, she took a deep breath and lifted the cover. The first things she saw were clippings from the accident with glaring headlines: *Local CEO and Unborn Child Dead, Highway Miracle: One Survivor, Mechanical Failure Blamed for Horrendous Highway Collision.*

She didn't remember seeing these articles. Had Connor tossed them in there? She pushed them aside, barely glancing at the black-and-white photo of her mangled car. She dug deeper into the box. There were photos of her and Laura. In one, she was pointing to Laura's belly, both of them smiling.

Connor was right. Her hair did look like Laura's. But she hadn't planned it. The hair stylist had chosen the cut to go with her face — she had the same facial structure as Laura. And she'd questioned the blue dress when Raquel had first spotted it. It wasn't as if she was trying to mimic Laura. It was just so pretty. But Denise knew she'd never wear it again.

She pulled out a birthday card. It was the card that had started the whole pineapple birthday cake thing, a tradition that Laura refused to let go of. On the front of the card was a picture of a pineapple with the saying, "Be a pineapple. Stand tall, wear a crown, and be sweet on the inside."

Denise smiled. It was the summer she'd turned eighteen. Laura had made a pineapple upside-down cake for her birthday, but she didn't quite manage the upside-down part. It was a mess, but the most delicious cake Denise had ever tasted. Because her sister made it. After they'd gorged on pineapple cake, there was the ceremonial exchanging of the pearls as Laura's six months ended and Denise's began.

She opened the card, shocked at the sight of Laura's loopy writing. She traced her finger over the signature. "I miss you so much, Laura."

There'd be no pineapple cake this year for her birthday. No card. No pearls. She put the lid back on the box and replaced it in her closet. Enough feeling sorry for herself, she decided. She straightened her spine, determined to make things right with Connor. She hadn't meant to upset him, but she did owe him an apology. It had to have been a terrible shock to come home from work and see her looking like a pale imitation of his dead wife. And given how short she'd been with him on the phone when he'd said Sandra was keeping an eye on her, he'd probably assumed she was doing it to punish him.

That was also the kind of thing her mother would have done on a bad day.

At first, she wasn't sure he would answer her call. When he did, his voice sounded angry. "What do you want?"

"I want to apologize. I honestly wasn't trying to upset you. I guess I just wasn't thinking how it would look."

"I may have overreacted," he admitted. "It was such a shock seeing you like that."

"I let the stylist choose my haircut and color. And my friend picked out the dress. It was an accident." She paused, but he didn't say anything more. "Will you come home? Please?"

Silence. Then, "I'll be there in half an hour."

"Have you eaten?"

"Not yet."

"I'll take something out for dinner. Steaks on the grill?"

"Sure." This time, Denise heard the smile in his voice. "That sounds great."

Denise changed into a swingy sundress in shades of pink and plum. Definitely not blue. She made baked potatoes, tossed a salad, chilled a bottle of wine, and seasoned the steaks. When Connor arrived home, everything was ready.

Connor grilled the steaks to perfection. Everything was perfect. And yet they walked around each other like polite strangers. Denise still had doubts, and obviously Connor had other things on his mind.

They both started to speak at the same time.

"You first," Connor said.

Denise took a deep breath. "I always looked up to Laura. I wanted to be just like her. And yes, there were times I copied her hair or makeup. But not today. At least not purposely." She was willing to admit that it may have happened on a subconscious level to herself, but she wasn't ready to admit it to him. Not until she was sure he wouldn't use it against her later.

"I believe you," Connor said. "But you can imagine what a shock it was to see her ... *you*." His voice cracked. "My heart broke all over again."

"I'm sorry." She was. She hadn't meant to cause him pain.

"On top of that, things are going downhill at work. The vultures are circling, and I'm not sure how long I can hold them off."

"What can I do?"

He chewed on his lower lip, staring into the distance. "I was just thinking. What if you were to sign your shares over to me?"

Denise frowned. "I'm not sure what difference that would make."

"Well, it would give me more leverage to fight them off."

"Why does it matter if the shares are yours or mine?"

He sighed, like he was trying to be patient. "Everyone knows that you haven't been involved in the business since the accident. Maybe you can be persuaded to sell. But they know there's no point in trying if I'm the one they'll have to convince. They'll go sniffing around somewhere else and leave us alone."

Denise sipped her wine to avoid answering. She didn't want to start another argument, but his argument didn't make sense. Let them think what they wanted. She wasn't selling. "I'll think about it."

Connor looked away, then back again. "That's all I ask."

While Denise was clearing up the dinner plates, she heard Connor talking on the phone.

He joined her in the kitchen. "That was Helen and Ronald. They invited us over for a drink."

It was still Helen and Ronald? Okay. "Sure, sounds good."

They walked to the house where Helen and Ronald now lived five minutes later. Denise looked around. The furniture was the same. Helen and Ronald's wedding picture was on the wall. Everything was as it should be. Or was it? Denise's head spun from trying to keep everyone straight, along with their spouses, and the houses they lived in. She wished she dared carry her journal around with her, but that would invite too many questions. And possibly provide proof of her insanity, if Denise's worst fear turned out to be true.

Helen brought out a cheese platter and poured wine all around. "How are you doing?" she asked Denise.

"Okay, I guess." Her shoulders clenched and her fists tightened. She was wiped out from the argument she'd had with Connor, but she couldn't afford to let her defenses down around any of them.

"Sandra said you were out running and got lost?"

"I didn't get lost. The leg I broke was slowing me down, and Sandra left me behind," she blurted out.

Connor quickly interrupted. "Now, that's not what happened," he said. "Sandra said you went off without her and she couldn't catch up to you, so she came home and waited."

Denise stared in amazement. When had he talked to Sandra, and if he had, why hadn't he asked her for her side of the story? "Are you going to believe her over me?"

Connor hesitated. "Well, you have been having memory issues." He turned to Ronald and laughed. "She thought Cora was married to Diego and Sandra to Bruce. She just can't keep anything straight these days."

Ronald laughed along with Connor. Denise felt tears stinging her eyes. It was one thing for Connor not to believe her, but to make her the butt of his joke was too much to take. All the good feelings from their make-up dinner fled, leaving her thinking of the things Raquel had said about him being too controlling and keeping her on a short leash.

Did he think that humiliating her was going to make her more dependent on him?

Well, it wasn't working. It was making her mad again.

"Come help me in the kitchen," Helen said, leading Denise away. Once they were out of earshot, she whispered, "Tell me what's going on."

Denise wondered if she should tell Helen the truth, or if that would be a terrible mistake. Out of all the neighbors, Helen seemed the most sympathetic. Or the most patronizing. Denise couldn't decide which.

She decided that it was safer to play the confused innocent than to confide her suspicions.

"It's everything. Like Connor said, I can't remember who is married to who, and it seems like I wake up in a different house every morning. My sister's picture keeps changing, and now I'm hearing her voice and smelling her perfume." She choked back a sob that wasn't entirely fake. "I think I'm going crazy. Connor wants me to keep talking to Bruce, but I don't think he knows what's going on with me either, and … I don't know."

Helen put her arm around Denise's shoulders. "I don't think you're going crazy."

"Then how do you explain all this?" She waved her arms to encompass everything that had happened. "Remember the desserts? I know I made a strawberry shortcake, but you brought out a lemon cake." She shook her head. "There's no other explanation."

Helen's cheeks were flushed and her brow furrowed. "Maybe there is," she said. She handed Denise a wet paper towel to wipe her eyes. "I want you to go back in there and act like nothing's happened. I'll see if I can get to the bottom of this."

Denise could imagine what Helen could do to "get to the bottom" of anything, unless it was to confess that there had been two cakes. But her sympathy had seemed genuine. Denise took Helen's advice and went back to the living room, acting as if nothing had happened.

Every now and then she'd catch a strange look pass between Helen and Connor. There was something there she couldn't decipher, but her instincts told her that if push came to shove, she'd have Helen on her side.

When they were back home, Denise confronted Connor. "I can't believe you made it look like I was a mental case in front of our neighbors."

Connor shook his head. "There you go, making a mountain out of a molehill. It was just a joke. We all have memory lapses at one time or another."

Except that they all knew she hadn't been experiencing the kind of everyday forgetfulness that most people did.

Denise simply glared at Connor until he looked away. Then she brushed past him without another word and marched up the stairs.

"Where are you going?" he called.

"I'm going to bed."

"I thought we were having a discussion."

She turned, eyes narrowed. "Go talk to your buddy Ronald if you want to have a discussion. I'm done."

She went upstairs and climbed into bed without changing out of her clothes.

Chapter Twenty-One

DENISE WOKE UP GROGGY, as if she was swimming up from beneath the ocean's depths, even though she'd skipped her pills. She couldn't remember when she'd woken up clear eyed and ready to start the day. Lately, all she wanted to do was stay in bed and let the world go by without her. And she had no idea if that was depression or the result of the medication. Maybe it took more than a day to get the drug out of her system.

She heard arguing. At first, she thought it was the television downstairs, but then she realized it was coming from outside. She rolled out of bed and peeked out the window. The bedroom was dark. Who was out there arguing in the middle of the night? She squinted but couldn't make out the figures on the lawn. One of them might have been Connor, and she couldn't tell who the other person was.

Fractured phrases drifted up. She could barely make out the words. "...has gone too far ... practical joke ... not what I signed up for..."

She went downstairs and opened the door, but there was no one on the front lawn. She was sure she'd heard

Connor arguing with someone out here. Where had he gone?

"Connor?"

No answer. She shook her head and went back inside. As long as she was up, she might as well make coffee. She went into the kitchen and turned on the light, but the coffee machine wasn't where it should have been. A fancy espresso machine stood in its place. She went to the cabinet, but her favorite mug wasn't there. As she looked around, she realized this wasn't her kitchen.

Not again.

She peeked into the living room. The furniture looked the same, but most of the models came furnished, so that wasn't unusual. She swiped her eyes and stared into the dim room. Over the mantel was the gaudy print of sunflowers that Connor had hung on the wall. She rubbed her forehead and checked the garage. Their car was in there. What the hell was going on?

She went outside and looked over at the house she'd fallen asleep in. How did she get here?

Sandra came outside and gave her a worried glance. "Laura, is that you?"

Denise froze. "What?"

"Laura, what are you doing outside like that?"

Denise realized how she must look. She'd just rolled out of her bed and was standing there barefoot in the clothes she'd worn yesterday. But that didn't explain why Sandra had called her Laura. And Sandra hadn't even known Laura, so it couldn't be a case of her looking like her sister.

"I'm not Laura," she said.

Sandra stepped closer, talking slowly as if she were a toddler. Or a crazy person. "Okay, what would you like me to call you?"

Denise stepped back. There was something threatening in Sandra's stance.

"Denise. My name is Denise." Her voice rose stridently. "You know me. I'm Denise, your neighbor."

Just then Diego came outside and asked what was going on. "What are you two doing out here in the dark?"

Sandra's voice lowered theatrically, but Denise could still make out her words. "I think Laura is having a breakdown."

Denise screamed, "I'm NOT Laura! And I'm not having a breakdown!"

But deep down inside, she wondered: *Am I?*

Both Sandra and Diego looked at her with equal measures of scorn and pity. Denise turned and raced inside the house. She slammed and locked the door behind her. Retracing her steps, she went back to the bedroom.

There was someone in the bed. She was sure she'd been alone in bed when she woke up. Then who…?

She turned on the bedside lamp to get a better look.

Connor jerked a hand over his eyes. "What the hell, Laura?"

Denise stared at him, dumbfounded. "What?"

"You're shining the light in my eyes, for God's sake."

"No," she said. "What did you call me?"

"Your name." Connor sighed and sat up. "What's this all about?"

"What name did you call me?"

"Laura, of course."

"No," she cried, then ran to the bathroom. She stared at her reflection. Laura's face stared back. No, she wasn't Laura, despite the similar haircut. It was her own reflection. At least she thought so, but now everyone had her confused.

Connor appeared in the doorway.

She looked at him with pleading eyes. "I'm not Laura. I'm Denise."

Connor shook his head. "Oh hon, Denise was killed in the accident. This is all a psychotic break. You want her to be alive so much, you've convinced yourself you're Denise. But trust me. You're Laura, my wife."

How could he believe any of this?

Denise wondered if this was how her mother had felt when her father had tried to talk her out of her paranoid delusions. Like she'd woken up in a reality so distorted that it felt like it had been designed to torture her?

"No. No, no, no!" Denise shook her head fervently from side to side. "That's not what happened. I was driving and the brakes failed. Laura was killed along with her unborn baby." She realized there was a big hole in his theory. "If I'm Laura, then where's my baby?"

Connor blinked, as if holding back tears. "You miscarried after the accident. We were devastated."

Denise gulped back a sob. He had an answer for everything. But there was no way he could convince her that she was Laura, no matter how hard he tried. She knew who she was. She just didn't know why he was doing this to her.

As far as she could tell, *he* was the one having the psychotic break. Induced by the shock of seeing her dressed and done up like his dead wife.

Except that would mean Sandra and Diego had to be having psychotic breaks too. Because they'd been calling her Denise since they moved in.

But what was more likely — that Denise was having a psychotic break and hallucinating all this, or that the entire neighborhood was having one at the same time?

Why was this happening to her?

She ran across the hall to her studio. All signs of her macrame were gone, even the shelving they had installed to hold her cords and yarn. It was just a regular office with a small desk in the corner and a laptop sitting on top.

"Where are my things?"

"What things?"

"My macrame."

"I didn't know you'd taken up macrame," he said, scratching his head. He reached out to take her arm. "Let's get you into bed."

She pulled away. "I don't need to go to bed. I need you to admit I'm Denise, *not* Laura."

"Okay," he said to mollify her. "But I think you need professional help. I'm calling Bruce first thing. If not…"

Her heart hammered in her chest. "If not, what?"

"If not," he said, "I'll have no choice but to have you sectioned."

"Sectioned? You mean involuntary commitment?"

He nodded. "I don't want to, but you leave me with no other choice."

Committed, just like her mother. Her worst nightmare.

Denise stepped back. This wasn't the Connor she knew. Her husband. Laura's husband. This man was a stranger. "How dare you threaten me!"

"It's not a threat, Laura. It's for your own good. Do you know how crazy you sound saying you're Denise, your dead sister?" His voice rose in volume. "You need to deal with your grief. It wasn't your fault Denise was killed when you were driving."

Denise put her hands over her ears. She wouldn't listen. None of what he was saying made any sense. When Connor moved closer, she scooted around him and ran into the bathroom. She locked the door with a satisfying click and leaned against the wall, her head spinning. She slid down until she was sitting on the cool tiles, her body shaking with rage.

She could hear Connor on the phone but couldn't make out his words. Was he following through on his threat to have her committed? She wrapped her arms around her knees and rocked back and forth, repeating over and over, "I'm Denise, I'm Denise, I'm Denise."

Who would believe her? Who could she turn to?

Five minutes went by. Then ten. Just when she thought it might be safe to leave the bathroom, there was a knock on the door. "Laura? It's Bruce. Can you open the door?"

Bruce? He, of all people, should know who she really was. She covered her ears, refusing to open the door. Let them break it down.

And that's exactly what they did. It crashed inward with a splintering sound, then Bruce was crouched beside her. "Hey, Laura."

"I'm Denise."

Bruce looked up at Connor, who simply shrugged. His eyes were red and swollen. "I don't know what to do."

Bruce turned back to Denise, his voice gentle. "I'm just going to give you something to help you sleep," he said.

Denise nodded. Maybe that's all she needed. She just wanted this nightmare to be over with.

Bruce pulled out a needle and pricked her arm. The next thing she remembered was being carried to bed and hearing Connor and Bruce's voices as they left her alone in the room. Then she slipped into blissful unconsciousness.

AS SOON AS Raquel saw Denise's name come up on her phone, she smiled and answered. "Hey girl, I was just thinking of you!"

But it wasn't Denise on the other end. "This is Connor. Denise is, umm … unavailable."

"Oh?"

"I didn't have your number, so I'm using her phone."

"I see."

"The thing is," Connor continued, "when Denise came home after the two of you went shopping, she had a bit of a breakdown. She thought she was Laura. The hair, the dress. I couldn't convince her otherwise."

That wasn't the way Raquel remembered it — Denise had been completely aware of who she was when Raquel had dropped her off — but she let Connor continue. Maybe something had happened after she left. And Denise had said that his controlling behavior was coming from a place of caring.

"Denise is very vulnerable right now," he said. "She needs some time to adjust and to heal."

"What are you saying?"

"I'm simply asking you to give her some space. She seems more agitated after spending time with you. It's hard for her."

Raquel remained silent.

"I'm asking as a concerned husband."

Connor sounded sincere. Did she believe him? Maybe. Maybe not. She'd honor his request for now, but if there was any indication that he was lying, or if Denise reached out to her for help, nothing Connor could say would stop her from being there for her friend.

Chapter Twenty-Two

DENISE WOKE to find Bruce asleep in a chair next to the bed. She cleared her throat, and he opened his eyes. "You're awake."

"Yes."

"How are you feeling?" The concern in his voice was genuine.

"Scared," she says. "Last night was surreal, at least what I remember of it." Already the memory was fading, as if it was a dream. Connor had seemed so different. She hadn't felt safe with him. "Where's Connor?"

"Who?"

"Connor."

Bruce shook his head. "I don't know anyone named Connor."

She sat up and pulled the blankets tight around her. "Connor, my husband."

Bruce looked confused. "*I'm* your husband."

Denise screamed.

She jolted awake and jerked up in bed, the sound of her screams echoing in her ears. Just a dream, just a dream, she told herself. This whole episode was one long, crazy dream.

Bruce was asleep in the chair next to her bed. A sickly sense of déjà vu washed over her. She stared at him, then cleared her throat. He opened his eyes. "You're awake."

It was happening again. Just like in her dream.

"How are you feeling?" he asked.

Her voice quivered. "Who are you?"

"I'm Bruce. Your therapist."

"Not my husband?"

He laughed. "No. Connor is your husband. He left for work already. Said something about a big meeting he had to attend. I told him I'd stay here with you."

"And I'm Denise, right?"

"That's right. Did you think you were someone else?"

She shook her head. "No. Bad dreams."

"You've had a rough night," he said. "I'm going to give you a new medication for anxiety and confusion. I think the ones you've been taking have been doing more harm than good."

"If you think that will help." She was running out of options.

"I'll get the prescription filled this afternoon." He stood up to leave. "We don't think you should be alone, however, so Helen is going to stay with you."

Why didn't they think she should be alone? Did they think she was going to hurt herself? Or did they just want Helen to spy on her, like Sandra had spied on her?

"Why don't you get dressed," he said. "Helen will be over in a bit."

After Bruce left, Denise got out of bed. She looked out the window, remembering the argument she'd heard last night. She noticed she was still in Bruce and Cora's house. She went into the bathroom, where a blue toothbrush sat on the counter. She didn't even care anymore. She stepped into the shower, feeling absolutely spent. The needle-spray pounded her skin, energizing every cell in her body. She took her time washing and conditioning her hair, somehow feeling the need to get back in touch with her body. *Her* body. Not Laura's or anyone else's.

Feeling clean and refreshed after her shower, she dressed and went downstairs. Out of habit, she peeked into the living room. On the wall was the picture of Laura on her wedding day. The one she'd burned in the barbecue. She shook her head, not trusting her own memory. Maybe that had been a dream as well.

She followed the sweet scent of cinnamon and found Helen in the kitchen making breakfast.

"I hope you're hungry," Helen said. "I have pancakes and sausage, plus cinnamon rolls in the oven."

"Sounds good," Denise said, sitting at the kitchen table. To be honest, she didn't have much of an appetite, but didn't want to hurt Helen's feelings after she'd gone to all the trouble to make a nice breakfast. "Did Connor eat before he left for work?"

"I don't know. He was gone before I got here."

"Oh."

Helen brought over a cup of coffee. "I'm worried about you."

Denise lifted one shoulder in a shrug. "It's this medication I'm taking. Bruce thinks it's giving me hallucinations or something. He's changing my prescription today, so I should be better soon." At least, she hoped so.

Helen filled her dish and brought it to the table. Denise took a bite, but it was tasteless. She had no desire to eat, and even her coffee grew cold on the table.

Her phone buzzed and she checked her messages. Nothing from Connor. Nothing from Raquel, either.

She pushed her phone aside, wondering if she'd done something to upset Raquel. She didn't think she had, but there were a lot of things she either couldn't remember or remembered incorrectly. And her head was already starting to pound again. She felt like she was trapped in a nightmare. And while she hadn't taken her pills, Bruce had given her a shot of who-knew-what last night.

Maybe the new pills would be better.

Helen took a seat across from her, glancing at Denise's uneaten food. "You know, I was thinking. Maybe we could go away for a few days. Have a bit of a girl's getaway. Wouldn't that be fun?"

"Just you and me?"

"Yeah, what do you think?"

Denise thought about it. She'd grown to trust Helen despite their misunderstandings. "Yes," she said. "It does sound nice."

"Why don't you go pack a bag? We can leave now."

"Now?"

Helen smiled. "Sure, why not? We can text Connor, tell him we're driving down to Houston for a few days. I need to drop by and check on my mother, then we'll hit the spa. Or whatever you want to do."

But Denise was having second thoughts. "What's the hurry?"

Helen glanced right and left, then lowered her voice as if they were co-conspirators. "I just think with all that's happening, it will be good for you to get out of the house. Get some fresh air. A new perspective."

That sounded good. Could she trust Helen, who'd moved into her house and acted like she'd been there all along? Who'd made her think that her strawberry short-cake had somehow become lemon cake?

More than she could trust Connor, who'd tried to convince her that she was her dead sister.

And once they were out of town, she could decide what to do next.

"Okay. Maybe you're right."

"Great. Why don't you pack an overnight bag, and I'll meet you back here in twenty minutes."

After Helen left, Denise dumped her breakfast in the trash and her coffee down the sink. The thought of eating made her stomach roll. She was stacking the dishwasher when she heard someone at the front door.

She opened the door to Sandra, who held out a bouquet of sunflowers.

"Hi," she said. "I brought you these. Bruce said you had a rough night, and I thought these might cheer you up."

"Thank you." Denise felt a familiar sense of foreboding. The bouquet was exactly like the painting Connor had hung up on the wall, right down to the arrangement of the sunflowers.

Had Sandra seen the painting before Connor had brought it home? She didn't remember Sandra being in their house during the time that it had been up on the wall.

"Hey," Sandra said. "Did I see Helen leaving just now?"

"Yes, we're going on a trip together. I just need to pack a few things."

"Really?" Surprise was evident on Sandra's face. She glanced over at Helen's house, frowning. "I didn't know you two were going anywhere. Does Connor know?"

"I'm going to call him." Although it wasn't clear why Sandra cared whether or not she'd told Connor she was going, unless she was still spying on Denise for him. "Helen thought it might be a good idea to get away for a few days. Get a new perspective on things."

"Oh, I see." Again she shot a questioning look over toward Helen's house. "Do you want me to wait with you until Helen gets back?"

"No, that's not necessary. I'm just going to throw a few things in an overnight bag. But thanks for the offer."

"Diego and I will be at home if you need anything," Sandra as she headed out. "Let us know if you change your mind."

What the hell? Did Connor have a whole neighborhood watch committee keeping an eye on her?

She closed the door, maybe a little too hard, then went into the kitchen and put the flowers in water. She placed the vase on the center of the dining room table, refusing to look over the mantel in the living room. If there was an identical picture of sunflowers on the wall, she might just lose it completely.

She went upstairs to pack a small overnight bag. Should she pack her medication, or wait until Bruce got back with the new prescription? She glanced in the mirror at her reflection. Her face was pale, her hair hung limp, and there were dark bags under her eyes. She wobbled, nearly losing her balance, and decided to lay down for just a minute or two to get her equilibrium.

Just for a minute, she told herself, then closed her eyes. When she opened them again, she sat up in bed and checked her phone. Two hours had passed.

She rubbed the grit from her eyes. Why had Helen let her sleep? Where was Helen? Denise raced downstairs, but there was no sign of her. She ran outside, momentarily disoriented. Which house was Helen's? She couldn't remember. She stared at each house on the cul-de-sac.

That one used to be her house, which meant Helen's house would have been right next door.

She walked to the front door, hoping she had the right place. There was no answer when she rang the doorbell. She tried knocking instead, and when her fist banged on the door, it swung open. "Helen? Are you here?"

She stepped inside. The house was deathly quiet. She glanced around and saw Helen's wedding picture on the wall in the living room. At least she had the right house.

She went to the foot of the stairs and called. "Helen, are you up there?"

No response.

Denise had a bad feeling about this. Maybe Helen had just stepped out? But something told her it was worse, much worse.

Her fears were confirmed when she went upstairs and peeked into Helen's bedroom.

Helen lay dead, sprawled across the bed, her face frozen in terror. Angry red bruises circled her neck. Denise rushed to the bed, hoping beyond hope that Helen was still alive. Her skin was cold, so cold. She felt for a pulse, checked for breath, and stared into Helen's wide open, lifeless eyes. She'd probably been dead for hours. Murdered.

Denise let out a strangled scream.

Chapter Twenty-Three

DENISE RAN SCREAMING from the house. She cried out for help, but the streets were silent and empty. Where was everyone? She raced down the street to her house and ran upstairs to get her phone from the nightstand, but it wasn't there. She searched the whole house, from top to bottom. She turned in circles. Had she dropped it when she'd run out to find Helen?

Desperate, she left the house and ran down the street to Bruce and Cora's house. She pounded on the door. Bruce opened, his eyes wide when he saw the state she was in. "Denise, what's wrong?" he asked.

"I can't find my phone. You have to call the police."

"The police?"

"It's Helen!" she cried. "Someone killed her!"

It seemed surreal. She hoped it was another nightmare and she'd wake up and find Helen waiting for her to get up so they could leave.

"Are you sure?" Bruce led Denise inside and made her sit.

"Yes. It looks like she was strangled. There were marks

around her neck. Her face was twisted and her tongue was sticking out."

Cora came out and listened while Denise tried to convince Bruce to call the police.

"I thought Helen was going to her mother's this morning," she said.

Helen had mentioned checking in with her mother. Maybe that's what she had told Cora?

"She invited me on a trip today." The shock was beginning to set in. Her body trembled. "We were going to go on a girl's getaway. Then I fell asleep, and when I woke up, I went over there and found her."

"Listen," Bruce said, "Helen has epilepsy. Maybe she just had an episode."

"No," Denise sobbed. "She was dead. Definitely dead."

Cora grabbed Bruce's arm. "Call the police."

"But what if she's just having an epileptic seizure?" Bruce asked.

"Then the police will take care of her."

"No. It'll take them too long to get here. I'm right here." His face was set with determination. "I'm going over."

"Wait." Cora reached into the cupboard and pulled out a gun. She handed it to Bruce. "Take this."

He nodded and took the gun. Denise and Cora watched him go. Cora wrapped her arms around Denise, who was still shaking.

"Who could have done such a thing?" Denise cried. After finding Helen dead, she'd lost all hope. And without hope, there was only despair.

Only moments later, Bruce came back.

Denise and Cora looked at him expectantly.

He shook his head. "She's not there."

"Did you look in the bedroom?"

"I looked in the bedroom, the bathroom and the back-yard." He shook his head. "There's no sign of her, dead or alive."

Denise shot up in her chair. "That can't be. I saw her!"

She marched over to Helen's house, determined to prove what she'd seen was true. Cora and Bruce followed behind. Denise pushed the door open, half afraid to enter the house. Inside, she rushed up the stairs. The bed was empty, just like Bruce said. The cover was neatly pulled up, not rumpled the way it had been when Denise found Helen there.

Denise reeled back. She turned in circles, searching for any sign of Helen. She couldn't have just gotten up and walked away.

"See?" Bruce said. "She's not here."

Cora piped up. "Maybe you imagined it."

Denise turned to her. "I didn't imagine anything. She was here. She was real." Her voice was emphatic, a hollow wail.

"I'm sorry," Cora said, wringing her hands together. "It's just that I saw Helen leave for her mother's house last night."

"No, she was here this morning." Then she remembered. "Sandra saw her too."

She rushed down the stairs and into the street, then stopped. Which house was Sandra's? She saw Bruce and Cora watching her, concern on their faces. Pretending a confidence she didn't feel, she walked toward the closest house.

"That's not Sandra's house," Cora called out. She pointed to the next one.

Denise changed course and knocked on the door. She waited, tapping her foot, then knocked again, louder this time. Finally, Sandra opened the door wearing nothing but a bath towel. "Geez, patience. I just got out of the shower."

Denise pointed to Cora and Bruce standing behind her. "I need you to tell them you saw Helen this morning."

Sandra gave her a blank stare. "I don't know what you're talking about."

"This morning," Denise said, her voice rising. "You came over and brought flowers. You said you saw Helen leaving. Remember?"

"Nope."

"Oh, come on! You were there. Helen was there. And now she's dead. I'm not crazy!"

Sandra locked gazes with Cora and Bruce. She shrugged her shoulders. "I've been home all morning. Besides, where would I even get flowers that early in the morning?"

Anger burned through every inch of Denise's body. "I'll prove it," she said, marching back to her house.

"That's not your house," Cora said, as if speaking to a toddler.

Bruce touched her arm and pointed. "That one."

Denise went inside, her gaze touching on everything familiar. Everything except the vase of sunflowers from Sandra. And there on the table was her phone. The phone she'd searched for and couldn't find anywhere.

She let out a frustrated scream.

Bruce sprinted across the room and held her arms. "Calm down. I'll call Connor."

"No. Don't call him. Just leave me alone."

When they didn't move, she shooed them out the door. "Go on. Leave! Just leave me alone!"

They backed out the door, eyeing her with suspicion. Denise didn't care what they thought, what anyone thought. She knew she wasn't imagining things. There had to be an explanation. She just had to find it.

She picked up her phone and called Raquel, but the phone went right to voicemail. "Raquel? It's Denise. I need to talk. I could really use a friend right now."

She dropped the phone, then sat on the floor and sobbed.

Chapter Twenty-Four

BRUCE MUST HAVE CALLED CONNOR, because he came home shortly after. He sat down on the floor beside Denise and put an arm around her shoulder. She leaned into him, unable to talk, unable to stop the tears from flowing.

He held her, talking soothingly until she finally stopped crying. "I've made an appointment for you to see a doctor," he said. "Tomorrow afternoon."

She nodded, too drained to speak.

"I can't get out of my meeting with the lawyers in the morning, but I was able to reschedule the afternoon so I can take you to your appointment."

"You don't have to. I can take an Uber"

"Of course I do. We'll go to the doctor. Everything will be fine. We'll get through this together, okay?" He brushed the hair back from her face and stared intently into her eyes. "I can have Sandra stay with you in the morning while I'm gone."

Not Sandra. Denise never wanted to see her again.

She shook her head. "No, I want to be alone." She lifted her eyes, imploring. "Helen is dead."

He didn't say anything one way or the other. Denise figured Bruce had told him all about her meltdown and the fact that there was no evidence that Helen was even home, let alone dead. But she had to say it aloud, if only to prove to herself that she hadn't imagined the whole thing.

After sitting with her for a few more minutes, Connor stood up. He reached in his pocket and pulled out a bottle of pills. "I forgot. Bruce was on his way over when I got home. He gave me these pills. Said you were expecting a new prescription."

Denise remembered Bruce telling her he'd give her a new prescription. It seemed like ages ago, but it was just this morning. "Yeah, he thinks maybe the other pills were causing the memory issues and confusion."

Connor checked the label, then brought her two pills with a glass of water. She swallowed them one at a time, then handed the glass back to him.

"Why don't you go lay down for a bit?" he suggested.

"I took a nap earlier."

"Yeah, but you've had a stressful afternoon. The bottle says these pills may make you drowsy."

She gave a weak smile. "I don't plan on operating any heavy machinery any time soon."

He smiled back. "Well, at least you haven't lost your sense of humor."

Connor helped her stand and reached out to steady her when she wobbled.

"Woah, maybe those pills are stronger than we thought," Denise said.

"I gotcha." Connor put an arm around her waist and walked her up the stairs. He nuzzled the side of her neck and whispered softly in her ear. "Everything will be alright, Laura."

Denise didn't have the energy to argue. She felt as

fragile as a dandelion, her thoughts and memories scattering in the wind and disappearing before she could catch hold of them. "I think I'm very tired," she said. "I think…"

But she never finished the thought.

The next thing she knew, she was waking up in total darkness. Not a pinpoint of light anywhere. She tried to sit up, but her head hit something solid. She reached up and rubbed her forehead until the pain faded, then dug in her pocket for her cell phone.

The light switched on for only a moment, then the cell phone died. She realized she hadn't charged it in days. But that brief flash had shown her she was surrounded by wooden slats. She reached up and her fingers hit something hard. Wood. She was trapped in a wooden box.

She screamed. "Hey, let me out!"

God, what was happening? Had she been buried alive? How could this be happening?

She banged harder on the wood, feeling more claustrophobic as time passed. "Connor! Connor, get me out of here!"

Surely someone would hear her with all the noise she was making pounding and screaming. Her breath came in short, shallow gasps. Was she running out of air? Her head felt as if it weighed a hundred pounds. She wondered if she'd given herself another concussion when she banged it against the wood.

"Connor, please?" Her voice came out weak and pleading. She was losing energy and could feel her body going soft. She stopped banging uselessly on the wood and slid her hand down the side. A splinter pricked her skin with a sharp burst of pain. Despite her efforts to fight her way out of the box, her body was giving up on her. Fog shrouded her brain and she felt herself swirling down, down, down into oblivion.

Chapter Twenty-Five

DENISE WOKE STILL TRAPPED in the nightmare, surrounded by impenetrable walls, her knuckles raw from scraping and her voice hoarse from screaming for help.

Light penetrated her still-clenched eyelids and she sat up, gasping for air. She was in bed.

Connor jerked awake beside her. "What's wrong?"

"I was trapped. Locked in a box." She stuttered, trying to shake the vestiges of what must have been a drug-induced nightmare. "I couldn't get out. I cried out for help, but no one came."

Connor pulled her close and held her as she trembled.

"It's okay," he said. "I'm here. I've been here all night.

"But it was so *real*."

"Just a dream," he said. "You've been right here by my side all night long."

Dream? Or hallucination? She couldn't tell what was real anymore, and that terrified her. Was this how it had been for her mother?

"I want to go to the doctor," she said.

"Okay. I'll make an appointment."

She blinked. "I thought you did already?"

"Nope, this is the first we've talked about it. Up until now, you didn't want to see a doctor. Honestly, I'm a little surprised you've changed your mind."

She sat up and shook her head.

Connor got out of bed and went into the bathroom. She heard him brushing his teeth. When he was done, he came out and suggested they go out to dinner that evening. "How about that seafood restaurant you like so much?"

Still sitting on the side of the bed, Denise shook her head. It felt stuffed with cotton. "No, I don't like seafood."

"Since when?"

"My whole life."

Connor laughed. "Don't be silly. You love salmon."

Salmon. That was Laura's favorite. She felt panic whirling through her. It was happening again.

She was *Denise*. Why did he keep confusing her with Laura? Was he punishing her for the haircut and the blue dress? She'd explained that it was an accident, and he'd said he believed her.

But maybe she'd dreamed that too.

Connor stared at her, waiting for a response. "Right," she said. "Salmon is my favorite."

He smiled at her. "That's my girl. Now get up and get dressed. I'll see about making that doctor's appointment."

He came over to the bed and rested a hand on her belly. "How's the baby doing today?"

Baby? Denise caught her breath. "Are you saying I'm pregnant?"

His smile faltered. "You're starting to scare me, Laura." He rubbed her stomach. "Three months along."

Three months. That's how far along Laura was when the accident had happened. And he'd called her Laura.

She closed her eyes and took a deep breath, pushing Connor aside.

"I have to use the bathroom," she said. "I'll be down in a minute."

Once Connor was out of the room, she stood on wobbly legs and made slow progress to the bathroom. By now she barely noticed or cared whether the toothbrush was yellow or blue. There were more important things to worry about … like dead neighbors and people confusing her with Laura. She leaned forward and stared in the mirror. Her hair was a mess, her face gaunt, but damn it, it was still *her*! Not Laura.

"I *am* Denise," she said at her reflection, repeating it over and over like an affirmation. "I *am* Denise. I *am* Denise."

It didn't matter what Connor or anyone else thought. She knew who she was, so whatever game they were playing wasn't going to work on her. She'd play along with them for now, but she'd get to the bottom of this one way or another. Maybe Connor was the one having a psychotic break, not her. She reached up to touch the bags under her eyes. That's when she noticed it.

The splinter.

She reached for a pair of tweezers and pulled the sliver of wood from her finger. If being trapped in a locked box was just a dream, then where did the sliver come from? She pondered the question as she put antiseptic cream on her finger, then went back and checked all around the bed for any signs of wood. Nothing. Someone would have had to move her from her bed to the wooden box somewhere, then bring her back. Why would anyone go to the trouble?

To make her think she was losing her mind?

She couldn't think of another explanation.

After dressing, she joined Connor downstairs. They

were back in the house at the end of the cul-de-sac. She walked down the hallway barefoot and stubbed her toe on the hallway cabinet.

"Damn," she cried out, hopping on one foot to the sofa, where she sat and rubbed her throbbing toe.

Connor popped his head out of the kitchen doorway. "You okay?"

"Yeah, just stubbed my toe."

She stood and limped to the window. Ronald was pulling out of his — *her* — driveway. She waved and he waved back. Helen wasn't with him.

Connor joined her. "Everything okay?"

"Yeah. I was just thinking of inviting Helen and Ronald to join us for dinner." She turned to watch Connor's reaction. "Would that be okay?"

He blinked, then his expression changed. But for a moment she'd seen a different side of Connor, there and then gone. In its place, he'd plastered on the good ol' homeboy smile. "I'm pretty sure Helen is still visiting her mother. Maybe when she comes back."

"Yes," Denise repeated. "When she comes back."

But Helen wouldn't be coming back, would she? And Denise suspected that Connor knew that.

He kissed her on the forehead, promising to call the doctor from work. "Don't forget we're going out for dinner."

She nodded and watched him leave, then closed and locked the door behind him.

Back in the hallway, she checked her reflection in the mirror. She still looked a little gaunt, but definitely more herself. The image behind her was different, however. That's when she realized why she'd stubbed her toe on the cabinet. It wasn't in its usual place. She pushed and tugged each corner until she had it far enough away from the wall to look behind it.

There on the wall was a nail hole, which had been hidden behind the mirror of the cabinet. Denise ran her finger over it. There was no reason for a nail hole to be there. The only reason was that was where Helen's wedding picture had hung.

A chill ran over her body. She hadn't imagined it. Here was proof that this was originally Helen and Ronald's house. Just like the splinter of wood in her finger was proof she hadn't imagined being trapped inside a box. She wasn't going crazy.

Then a morbid thought hit her. If these things were real, then it was possible that every hallucination she'd had was real as well. Like finding Helen strangled and lying dead on her bed. The same bed she was on only moments ago. Denise shivered.

There had to be more clues. She checked outside. Ronald's car was still gone. Maybe she'd find something there. She slipped out of the house and across the cul-de-sac to what should have been her own house. The door was locked.

She scurried around to the back door, but that was locked as well. She looked around, her eyes lighting on a metal lawn ornament. She was just about to grab it and break a window when she got an idea. Since this was originally her house, wouldn't her house keys still work? And wouldn't that be more proof that she was right all along?

She ran back to the other house, grabbed her keys, and slipped her phone in her pocket. Before going outside, she scanned the street to make sure she was alone, then walked right up to the front door, unlocked it, and went inside.

The entryway was exactly like her house, right down to the cabinet she'd stubbed her toe on, which was now where she remembered it being. And there on the wall hung Helen and Ronald's wedding picture, in the exact same place she'd found the nail hole in the other house.

That made three confirmations that it wasn't all in her imagination. What she needed was proof, something she should have been looking for all along. She pulled out her camera and snapped a photo of the wedding picture. She'd get the placement of the other nail later. For now, she needed to explore more before Ronald came back.

She went from room to room, searching for more evidence. At first, there was nothing of interest. Helen and Ronald didn't have a lot of possessions either. Their home looked eerily identical to her own. No wonder it was so easy to be confused.

Then she hit the jackpot in Ronald's office. He'd left his computer on. There on the screen was the image of Laura on her wedding day, but in this version, she had flowers in her hair and blood running from her eyes, a macabre rendition of the original. Denise reached out for the mouse and started clicking through pictures.

There was Laura in her wedding picture, the original shot. Then the same image but cropped, so she was closer with the pink carnations Denise had seen the first time the picture changed. Then closer still, Laura's face manipulated to a mask of anger. Every single picture Denise had seen changed was there in the photo editing software. All except this last one with the bloody eyes, which she assumed would have been used to scare her next.

Denise brought a composite of all the images on the screen, then took a picture. More evidence that she was being gaslighted.

She turned to leave, but her eye caught a flash of purple in the half-opened closet. She opened the door fully. There was the purple hoodie she'd seen following her everywhere. So it had been Ronald all along. One more piece of evidence slipping into place. She took a picture of the hoodie as proof that she hadn't been imagining it, then turned to leave.

She started downstairs and heard a car pull onto the driveway. She rushed down the rest of the stairs to the back door. She heard Ronald talking to someone on the phone and stood perfectly still, straining to listen.

"I don't give a fuck," he swore. "Can you imagine what I thought when she said that?"

She'd never heard him so angry.

"You better!" he shouted.

Denise hurried out the back door before he caught her snooping. She patted her pocket to make sure she still had her phone with her. It was all the evidence she needed.

"Laura?"

Denise froze. She turned to find Sandra watching her with suspicious eyes. She was about to correct her when she realized she had no idea how many people were involved in this charade. Better to go along with them before they suspected she was on to them.

"Yes?"

Sandra frowned. "Is everything alright?"

Denise nodded. "I just got confused. These houses all look the same." She did her best to look confused and dazed. "These medications don't help."

Sandra looked relieved. "Want me to walk you home?"

"Yes, thank you."

When they got to the house at the end of the cul-de-sac, Denise turned and smiled. "Thanks, I've got it from here."

Sandra stood outside watching for a moment, then disappeared. Once Denise was convinced Sandra was gone, she began searching the house for any other clues.

Living room, kitchen, studio, bedroom. Nothing. There had to be more. She just had to find it.

Connor's housecoat was hanging in the bathroom. She shut the door and heard something bounce against the wall. She reached over and checked the pockets. Inside she found a small device. It looked like a remote control, but when she hit the button, nothing happened. And then it did. "Denise?" It was unmistakably Laura's voice.

Goosebumps broke out along her skin. She played it over and over again just to hear her sister's voice. Her heart hardened when she realized this was what Connor had played to make her think her sister's ghost was calling her.

She put the recording device back in the pocket of Connor's housecoat. Laura's ghost wasn't haunting her. Laura's picture wasn't mysteriously changing. And she wasn't losing her freaking mind.

Back in the bedroom, she stared at the bottle of ginkgo biloba. She put it in her pocket, along with the pills Bruce had prescribed. She should have had them checked by someone she could trust right from the beginning. But how could she have known that Connor would try to make her believe she was crazy?

She called the one person she thought she could trust. There was no answer, so she left a voicemail. "Raquel? I need you. Could you come get me? Please."

She put the phone back in her pocket and went into the kitchen. There was nothing to do but wait. She made herself a cup of tea and waited for Raquel to call back. If she didn't hear from her in ten minutes, she'd call for a driver, but she really wanted to lay it all out for Raquel and get her opinion. She wondered whether or not Connor had made a doctor's appointment for her. If so, he could be home before she had a chance to do everything she needed to.

When Raquel called back, her voice was strained. "Denise, I just got your message. Are you okay?"

"I need a ride. It'll only take a little while. Can you help me?"

Raquel hesitated.

"Please. I'll explain on the way."

"Okay," Raquel said. "I'll be right over."

Chapter Twenty-Six

DENISE WANTED to rush to the car when Raquel arrived, but she played it cool in case the neighbors were watching, walking to the car as if she had all the time in the world. She got in the passenger side and kept her eyes forward. She spotted Sandra watching from her front door. As Raquel backed out of the driveway, Denise let out a sigh of relief.

"You want to tell me what's up?" Raquel asked.

"It's a long story. But I think with your help, I can finally get some answers."

Raquel turned and gave her a long look before turning back to watch the road. "Connor called and threatened me."

"Oh?"

"He told me to stay away from you. Said I was getting in the way of your recovery." The edge of Raquel's lip turned down. "I was scared."

"I'm sorry you had to go through that. I've been scared too. But not for much longer. I promise he won't threaten you again. I'm going to be leaving him, but not until I get some answers."

"Why don't you leave him today? I'll take you anywhere you want to go. I think he's dangerous."

"He is. But there are things I have to do first."

"I'm sorry for staying away," Raquel said. "But I'm here now. Just tell me what you need."

Denise smiled gratefully. "Thank you. Right now, I just need a ride to the pharmacy." She quickly explained her suspicions about the pills Connor had been giving her, and Bruce's new prescription, along with all of the unusual things that had been happening.

"And you think Connor is behind it all?"

"Yes, and if all goes well today, I'll have proof."

"I think you're right," Raquel said with a nod. "I suspected him all along." Raquel pulled up to the pharmacy. "I'll wait."

"No. I'll get a lift back. Thanks for the ride, but it's going to get crazy from here on in."

Raquel refused to take no for an answer. "You're not doing this alone. I wasn't there for you when you needed me, but that changes today."

Denise leaned over and gave her friend a hug. "Thank you."

With those parting words, she got out of the car and didn't look back. She needed a clear head for everything coming up. She marched to the pharmacist and placed the pills on the counter. "I think my life is in danger," she said. "My husband says these are ginkgo biloba pills, but I think they're something else. Can you confirm that for me?"

The pharmacist took one look at the pills and shook her head. "This is oxazepam. It's a type of benzodiazepine."

"Aren't those addictive?"

"They can be. Are you suffering from anxiety?"

"I was," Denise admitted, but if that's what they were for, why would Connor lie? Why not just tell her the truth? She'd probably have taken them anyway.

Then it occurred to her, maybe it wasn't about just these, maybe it was the combination of these with the pills Bruce had prescribed. She dug into her purse and retrieved that bottle, then put it on the counter.

"What about these?"

The pharmacist checked the bottle. There was no label or directions on the bottle. She poured a few pills into her hand and examined them, then went to her computer and typed something.

"Scopolamine," she said. "What did you think you were taking them for?"

"Depression."

"These aren't going to do anything for your depression, unless you're depressed because you have irritable bowel syndrome. And mixing oxazepam with scopolamine can actually increase the severity of depression. In the right dose, scopolamine by itself can cause psychotic behaviors in some people."

"I should have known," Denise said. She smiled, knowing once and for all she wasn't crazy and that Connor had been lying about her having a psychotic break. They were drugging her to make her think so.

He'd threatened to have her committed, too. She wondered if he'd planned to force her to take the pills before the doctor's appointment, in order to fool the doctor into thinking she'd inherited her mother's schizophrenia.

"Are you in danger?" the pharmacist asked.

She laughed bitterly. "Not anymore."

"I should report this," the pharmacist said, giving Denise a knowing look.

"I'll take care of it," Denise said. "I promise. Thank you for confirming my suspicions."

She left the pharmacy and got into Raquel's car.

"Well?"

"The pharmacist confirmed my suspicions. Connor has been drugging me all along."

"Bastard."

Denise nodded. She opened her journal and went over the list of everything that had happened over the last few days, filling Raquel in as she went down the list. Knowing what she knew now, it all made sense, and she was able to put all the clues together. Most of them, anyway. She had enough proof to move forward.

"You think Connor killed Helen?" Raquel asked.

"I do," Denise said. "I think she was in on it, but felt he'd gone too far. She had convinced me to go away for the weekend, which was just an excuse to get me away from him." Denise felt sadness tinged with a sense of guilt. "She paid for trying to help me."

Raquel nodded thoughtfully.

"Which is why I didn't want you to get too involved," Denise added.

"I appreciate it, but I'm already involved. So, what's our next step?"

Denise reached into her purse and held up a key. "I slipped this off Connor's key ring this morning. It's the key to the storage unit where he put all of Laura's belongings."

Raquel plugged the address into her GPS and took off, but not before reaching out and giving Denise's hand a gentle squeeze. Denise was grateful for the support. It felt good to have someone on her side.

Walking into the storage unit was like slipping back in time. Everything she saw or touched brought back vivid memories. Like the dress Laura had worn at her birthday party when Denise had put their mother's pearls around her neck. She'd worn them all day long.

She held up a porcelain teacup in a delicate floral pattern. "This was her favorite teacup," she told Raquel. "Every evening, she made a cup of Earl Grey, along with the one sugar cookie she allowed herself as a treat."

"Just one? No wonder she stayed so slim."

Denise unpacked another box and found Laura's high-school sweatshirt. It still carried Laura's scent. She buried her face in the folds and breathed in, feeling Laura all around her.

"I thought it would hurt more to touch her things," she said. "But it doesn't. It's like having her close again."

"It's good to revisit happy memories," Raquel said, giving Denise a hug. "It can help the healing process."

Denise picked up the few things that meant the most to her. "I'd like to keep these for now I'll come back for the rest when this is all over."

Raquel searched around for something to put them in.

"How's this?" she asked, holding up a blue tote bag."

Denise smiled. "That's the bag she took back and forth to work. She carried it everywhere." She reached out and stroked the leather handle, then opened the bag and found a manila envelope from their lawyer's office tucked inside.

She unfolded the first set of papers. Her mouth fell open.

"What is it? Raquel asked.

"Divorce papers. Laura was going to ask Connor for a divorce."

"You didn't know?"

"I had no idea."

Raquel made a humming sound. "Do you think she'd already told him before the brakes failed on the car?"

Denise shook her head. The implication was too

horrible to think about. Had it really been an accident, or was Connor desperate to hang onto their marriage? Why?

The answer leapt to mind immediately – so he could inherit Laura's shares. Together, Connor and Denise shared a controlling interest in the company.

But when she read the next set of papers, she felt like her heart was going to explode with rage. They were a notification to Connor that Laura had changed her will so that her shares in Grady Oil stock were left to Denise, not split between Connor and Denise. And they were dated shortly after the accident.

Connor had led her to believe that Laura's stocks were left to him in her will. He'd purposely misled her. With Laura's stocks reverting to Denise, that left Connor without a single share in the company. Not only would that have been a blow to his ego, but it meant the only way he could get controlling interest in the company was to marry Denise. He'd been manipulating her since the day he showed up in the hospital, grooming her so she would trust him. All this time, their marriage was a sham so he could get his hands on her shares.

He had killed Laura to keep her from divorcing him, believing that he would inherit her shares. But then Laura's lawyers notified him that the will had been changed and that all shares had gone to Denise, he'd married her so that he could get to the shares that way.

How stupid was she? She'd fallen for all of his tricks. And now, because there was no way he could get her to change her will, it looked as if he'd come up with another way to get his hands on controlling shares of Grady Oil stock. Make her think she was crazy and have her committed. If not voluntarily, then involuntarily. He'd pretended that Laura had never told him about their mother's schizophrenia, but now Denise would bet everything in this storage locker that she had, and that's how he'd come up with his plan to gaslight her.

Bastard.

She returned the papers to the tote bag and added the mementos she'd put aside. "Let's go," she said, her voice steel.

As she turned to leave, she spotted the bottle of Laura's perfume lying on top of an unopened box, as if it had been thrown there in a hurry. Connor must have sprayed the house, then returned it here after letting Denise believe that Laura's spirit was haunting her. She grabbed the bottle of perfume and added it to the tote bag.

Just as they got in the car, Connor called from work.

"Why did you leave the house?" he asked. "I told you I'd be home early today."

"I didn't leave the house," Denise lied. "I'm sitting right here in the kitchen."

"What? Sandra said you were acting odd and that you left with a friend. I assumed it was Raquel."

So he had Sandra spying on her, just as she suspected. "I don't know what Sandra is talking about. I'm home. I'll see you when you get here."

She disconnected the call, then turned to Raquel with a cold smile. "Two can play at this game."

Raquel gave her the thumbs up sign, then pulled out of the parking lot. Denise had Raquel drop her off at the entrance to the cul-de-sac, then snuck around the back yards and entered the house through the back door. She hid the tote bag in the back of the pantry closet, then tossed a package of frozen chicken into the crockpot.

Then, as if she'd been there all along, she casually walked out front to see Sandra talking on the phone while pacing up and down in front of her house.

"No, I'm telling you, I saw her leave! Don't you dare accuse me of lying. This is your fucking plan and I'm—"

Denise called out, "Sandra? Everything alright?"

Sandra looked up from her phone, a stunned expression on her face, then mumbled. "She's here, gotta go."

She turned the phone off and shoved it in her pocket, then walked toward the front door. "Hey, Denise. I didn't realize you were home."

Denise frowned. "Denise? You must be confused. I'm Laura."

"Oh. Yeah. Right."

Denise smiled and started walking toward Bruce and Cora's house.

Sandra called after her. "They left."

"What?"

"They went back to California."

Denise put on a frown for Sandra's sake, but that just confirmed what she'd already suspected — that Bruce was in on it too, and that he'd chickened out when Helen had disappeared. She had to assume that everyone in the neighborhood had been in on it.

But she couldn't let Sandra know she knew everything.

"Why did Bruce and Cora leave?" she asked. "Bruce was my therapist. I was supposed to talk to him this afternoon."

Sandra shrugged. "Don't know. Some kind of emergency, I guess."

Before she could grill Sandra for more information, Connor pulled up. He rushed out of the car and apologized for being late. Denise glanced at her watch. It wasn't that late.

"Did you know Bruce and Cora left?" Sandra asked him.

For once, it was Connor who looked confused. "They didn't tell me they were leaving."

Sandra smirked in Connor's direction. "Guess I'm telling you now."

Denise noticed a strained tension between the two of them that she couldn't figure out. Sandra spun on her heel and walked away without even a goodbye.

Connor put his arm around Denise and walked her back to the house. "How was your day?" he asked.

"Great. I worked in the craft room completing macrame orders."

"All day?"

"Yup. It relaxes me."

Connor looked as if he didn't believe her. *How does it feel?*

"Oh," he said, "I was able to get you a doctor's appointment for tomorrow afternoon. I'm taking the day off so I can bring you. Maybe we'll go out to eat afterward."

"At my favorite seafood place?" She couldn't resist pushing his buttons. Two could play at this game. And she was going to make sure he lost.

"Sure, if that's what you want."

She linked arms with him. "That's exactly what I want. They have the best salmon there."

They walked into the house arm in arm. To anyone watching, they looked like the perfect couple, but no one would know the secrets and lies that bound them together.

"What's for dinner?" Connor asked.

"I put a chicken casserole in the crockpot this morning. It'll be ready in half an hour."

They went into the kitchen and Connor lifted the lid. The chicken was raw. He held up the outlet cord. "You forgot to plug it in."

Denise feigned confusion. "Oh no. I don't know what's wrong with me lately. I keep forgetting the simplest things." She looked in the crockpot. "I'll just put it in the oven. It'll only need an hour or so to cook."

Connor patted her on the shoulder. "It's okay. I'm not that hungry anyway."

How had she ever thought he was sincere?

Denise made a big production of pre-heating the oven and scraping the crockpot ingredients into an oven-safe dish. Little did he know, she'd simply tossed it in less than fifteen minutes ago and purposely left the crockpot unplugged.

She opened a bottle of wine and poured two glasses. "It's a beautiful evening. Why don't we sit on the porch while we wait for dinner to be ready?"

Denise walked outside without waiting for Connor. She sat on the patio loveseat and took a sip of her wine. After a few minutes, Connor joined her. She moved aside to give him room. "That's strange how Cora and Bruce left so suddenly, isn't it?"

Connor looked as if he'd had the rug pulled out from under him.

"Yes, very strange." He joined Denise on the loveseat. "Didn't you have an appointment with him later this week?"

"Today, actually. You think he would have told me, right?"

"Maybe I should give him a call."

Denise waved away his concern. "Oh, I wouldn't bother. They're probably still on the road. Maybe Sandra's wrong and they're just out for the evening. They'll probably show up in the morning with a logical excuse."

"Probably." Connor tipped his glass and drained the wine. He stood up. "I'm going to get a refill. Want more?"

Denise shook her head. "Probably not a good idea to drink too much along with my medications."

"You're probably right," Connor said.

Once he was in the kitchen, Denise followed and opened the door a crack. She pressed her ear and listened.

"That's not part of the plan," Connor hissed. "You get your ass back here and finish what we started or else."

Denise smiled and sat back on the loveseat. Good. Whatever Connor's plans were, they were falling apart. She had a feeling that tomorrow's doctor's appointment was part of the plan as well, but she wasn't going to play into his hands.

When Connor returned, she was still on the loveseat sipping wine. She could feel the anger surging off him. His fists were clenched, his face set in a frown. "Have you taken your pills today?" he asked.

She gave a slow nod, hoping she looked dazed. Of course she hadn't taken her pills and didn't intend to take another one ever again.

He patted her shoulder. "Good girl."

She fought the urge to bark like a dog. She had a feeling he wouldn't appreciate the humor in his current mood.

Tomorrow, he was going to try to have her committed. If she'd still been taking the pills and insisting that what she saw was true, his plan might have worked. But now that she knew better, she had her own plan.

And he was not going to like it.

Chapter Twenty-Seven

THE NEXT MORNING, Connor woke her with breakfast in bed. Pancakes with sprinkles and a candle burning in the middle of the stack. "Happy birthday!"

With all that was going on, Denise had totally forgotten. She was surprised that Connor remembered her birthday at all. Last year, she'd been unconscious in the hospital when her birthday rolled around. By the time she was mobile, it had come and gone with no one noticing.

She rubbed her eyes. It felt good to wake up clear-headed instead of foggy and confused. But she didn't want Connor to notice. "My birthday? Are you sure?"

"Positive," he said. "How could I forget?"

Denise sat up and smiled at him, reminding herself that his movie-star handsome face hid a vicious, manipulative man. "Thank you."

She smiled and blew out the candle.

"Did you make a wish?"

"Oh, I certainly did. But I can't tell you or it won't come true."

She ate every last bite, glad to have her appetite back.

She would have asked for more if Connor hadn't looked at her clean plate with suspicion.

"Guess I was hungrier than I thought," she said, rubbing her belly.

After a moment he grinned. "Gotta keep your strength up." He took the empty tray from her lap. "I'll bring this downstairs. Take your time getting ready. The doctor's appointment isn't for several hours."

She got up and went into the bathroom, then dug into the tissue box for the yellow toothbrush she'd picked up at the pharmacy yesterday. She brushed her teeth, smiling at her reflection in the mirror, then put the toothbrush back in its travel case and hid it in the tissue box. Let him try to find that one and exchange it for blue. It was one more way to prove to herself that she wasn't imagining things.

She went to her dresser and there, sitting on top, were her mother's pearls.

"Oh my God, oh my God!" She couldn't believe it. Last year at this time, she was in the hospital and the pearls were the last thing on her mind. She remembered at one point asking Connor about them and he said they weren't found at the scene of the accident, even though she insisted Laura was wearing them that day.

Which meant he'd been lying about them missing when her body was removed from the car. No doubt the only reason he'd brought them out now was to make her grateful to him, so she'd cooperate with his plan to have her committed. *Bastard.*

But she was glad that he did, even if his reason for doing so was malicious. She put them around her neck and felt a warm glow, as if her mother and sister were holding her close. There was something soothing about their familiarity. They gave her courage, as if both her sister and her mother were adding their strength to her own.

"I miss you both," she whispered, clutching the pearls. "And I'll make you proud. No one will take advantage of me ever again."

She put on a light summer dress and went downstairs, smiling all the way. She stroked the pearls, already warmed by her skin. She never wanted to take them off.

Downstairs, she wrapped her arms around Connor. She was grateful to have the pearls back, and she tried to channel that gratitude into the façade she was putting on to fool him.

"Thank you," she said. "This was the best birthday present you could have ever given me."

He stared at her neck, his eyes wide. "I … I didn't give you those."

"Of course you did. They were right on my dresser." Was this part of his plan to make her think she was going crazy?

He did a complete one-eighty after that. "You're welcome. I knew how much they meant to you."

"Where did you find them? I was sure Laura was wearing them the day of the accident."

"They … turned up in the storage unit."

Denise took a deep breath. "You know what? I think maybe I'm ready to go through Laura's things and see what we want to keep."

"Oh, I don't think you're ready for that yet. The grief is still fresh. It will only cause a setback."

Denise didn't argue. He didn't know she'd already gotten everything she needed from the storage unit. Now that she had the pearls that meant so much to both her and her sister, nothing else was going to spoil her mood today.

She caught Connor watching her carefully throughout the day. He must have suspected something was different. Maybe she wasn't acting as groggy as usual. Maybe she

236

wasn't sleeping as much. She made a point to act confused about simple things and "forgot" where she'd put her phone at least twice, which seemed to relax him.

By the time they were ready to leave, she was a nervous wreck, trying to decide how Connor expected her to act as opposed to how she *thought* she should act. It was a relief when they finally reached the doctor's office.

When the receptionist called her name, Connor stood. "I'll come with you."

She reached out for his arm. "No. I'll be more comfortable talking to him alone."

Connor tried to argue, but she stood firm.

Dr. Vargas made her feel at ease the moment he walked in the examining room. He held out his hand to greet her and smiled. His grip was warm and reassuring.

"Your husband updated me on some of the problems you've been having when we spoke on the phone. Before I authorize tests to rule out a medical condition, let's go over some of those issues."

Denise nodded. It would be best to hear what Connor had told him so that she could deny everything, or at least have a credible explanation for why she reacted the way she did.

"He said you thought you heard your sister calling you?"

Denise laughed. "Well, I did hear Laura's voice. I'll admit it was shocking at first and freaked me out, but then I realized Connor was watching a video of her on his computer. That's what I heard."

"He also said you thought you *were* your sister."

Denise put on a shocked expression. "No, that's not true at all. A few times he's called me by my sister's name, but that's understandable, considering he was once married to her."

Dr. Vargas checked his clipboard. "What about thinking your neighbor was dead?"

"Well, it turned out she was epileptic and had a seizure, then passed out. But she sure looked dead to me. Our neighbor, who is a doctor, went over and checked on her. She was frazzled, but fine." Denise smiled and rolled her eyes. "I guess I overreacted."

"And the pictures? He said you claimed they kept changing."

"Yeah, it seemed that way. Turns out it was just the way it looked in different lighting. I think..." She lowered her voice to a murmur. "I think it just seemed that way because it was around the anniversary of her death, and I couldn't even look at the picture without crying."

He nodded. "That must have been very hard on you."

"It was. But I feel as if I'm getting through the initial stages of grief. I'm learning to accept that my sister is gone, and I'm working on moving on with my life. I've been in therapy."

"That's a healthy attitude." He made a note on his clipboard. "One more question, if you don't mind me asking."

"Okay."

"Do you have thoughts about hurting yourself?"

She laughed in a way she hoped came off as charming. "No, not at all."

"Anyone else?"

"Never."

"Well, Denise. I think you're doing exceptionally well for someone who's been through so much."

"Thank you. I think so too."

She stood and he shook her head. He walked her to the receptionist's desk. "It was lovely to meet you. If you need anything else, please call."

Conor stopped pacing and met her in the waiting room. "What did he say? Do we need to make another appointment?"

"No need," she said. "He gave me a clean bill of health."

"What?" Connor was clearly confused. He looked as if he was going to run back and double check with the doctor. "But what about your memory slips? And the picture? And thinking you're in the wrong house."

"Oh, he said it was probably a lack of sleep. Nothing to worry about."

"Nothing." Connor shook his head. "Really?"

Denise scowled. "You know, I'd almost think you weren't happy to hear that."

"Of course I am. I've been so worried. You know that."

"Fine," she said. "Let's go."

They reached the car, and Connor held the passenger door open for her. He got in the driver's seat and drove home, looking very irritable. Denise could tell he'd been counting on a different prognosis. Too bad for him.

Connor pulled up to the garage. She reached into the back seat for his coat and found a manila envelope underneath it.

"What's this?" she asked.

He gave her a puzzled look. "It's the paperwork we talked about the other night."

She shook her head and did her best to look confused. "I don't remember."

"The contract," he said, speaking to her as if she was a toddler. "The contract we talked about, to turn over your shares of Grady Oil."

"Why would I do that again?"

"I explained this all to you the other night. Don't you remember?"

Of course she remembered, but he assumed she was still under the drug's influence, so she'd assume it was her memory at fault. Play along, she reminded herself.

"Could you remind me again?"

He took a deep breath and let it out with a sigh. "Because with your shares and mine, I can fight off the hostile takeover. It's just a formality. You're still owner of Grady Oil."

When he'd proposed it before, she'd been confused, but unsure whether there was something she just didn't understand about hostile takeovers. But now she had to hide her fury. Did he think she was stupid on top of being drugged?

But that was exactly what he thought. *Play along, play along.*

"Of course. Now I remember."

Connor's smile had an evil glint. "I'm just trying to protect the company."

"I know you are." She smiled stupidly at him. "You're so devoted to the company."

They went inside and he handed her the contract and a pen. "Just sign here."

Denise sat at the kitchen table and tapped the pen on the surface, then made a show of hesitating. "I wonder if Laura would want me to. Isn't there any other way to stop the hostile takeover?"

Connor stared at her. She could tell he was losing patience. "I've tried everything else. This is the only option." He pushed the papers closer. "The deadline is tomorrow, or the contract expires."

Denise put down the pen. "I'm hungry. Do we have any lunch meat?"

"But…"

"I'll let you know before your deadline," she said, then got up and walked toward the kitchen. Then she called over her shoulder. "Oh, I asked the doctor about that ginkgo biloba."

Connor remained silent.

She let him stew about it for a minute, then added. "He said they were safe and it wouldn't hurt to take them."

He let out an audible sigh of relief. *Gotcha, you bastard.*

But on the kitchen counter was an appliance she'd never seen before with a bow on top. "What's this?"

Connor came up beside her. "It's your birthday present. An air fryer."

She reached up and touched the pearls at her neck. "You shouldn't have. The pearls were the best gift of all. I don't need anything else."

Connor stared at the pearls around her neck, a puzzled expression on his face. "But I didn't … I mean, I know you wanted an air fryer."

Did she? "It's lovely. Thank you. I'm sure I'll air fry … something." She smiled and gave him a kiss. "I really do appreciate it."

"Well, not tonight," he said. "Tonight we're going out to dinner, remember?"

"Of course." She pretended to yawn. "Would you mind if I took a little nap first? I'm so tired all of a sudden."

This time Connor's smile was real. He gave her the doggie head pat again. "Good girl. Get some rest. Our reservations are for six o'clock. I'll get you up when it's time to go."

She leaned against his chest, grateful he couldn't see the disgust on her face. How had she let him treat her in such a condescending way for so long?

She pretended to sleep when Connor checked in on

her, but for the most part, she was doing research on her phone and doublechecking the details of her plan. By the time Connor came in and said it was time to get ready for dinner, she was as ready as she was ever going to be.

It was hard not to show her excitement over dinner. She wanted to dance and scream that her long mental imprisonment was about to be over. But she had to pretend her world was dull and colorless for Connor's sake. The last thing she wanted was for him to catch on. Not until she'd put her plan in motion.

All through dinner, Connor had been staring at the pearls around her neck. Fingering the pearls, her entire attitude had changed. It was a sign. Laura was letting her know that everything would be alright.

"How's your salmon?" Connor asked.

She flaked a piece off with her fork. "It's very good. But I filled up on salad, so I'm not sure if I can finish it." He was used to her not having much of an appetite due to the pills, so it wasn't hard to cover her dislike of salmon by feigning no appetite.

"We can always take it home."

She pushed her dish aside. "That sounds good."

"Dessert?"

She rubbed her stomach. "I couldn't fit a single bite." Truth was, she was still hungry, but had to continue to play the part. "Do you mind if we go home now? I'm drained."

Connor paid the check and helped her to the car. She leaned on his arm for support. "I think we need to find another doctor," he said. "Obviously, you're still weak and confused. I'll see if I can get another appointment with someone else."

"Whatever you think is best," she murmured.

Connor gave her a squeeze. "Let's get you home."

Once they were back, Connor suggested watching a

movie. They sat side by side on the sofa while Connor scrolled through the list, finally stopping on the latest action/adventure movie he'd been wanting to see.

"How about this?" he asked.

Denise nodded and pulled the blanket off the back of the sofa. Wrapping it around her, she snuggled by his side, pretending to enjoy the shoot-em-up movie. She'd have preferred something with a little more drama and romance, but she was only half paying attention to it anyway. The hardest part of her plan was that it required her to wait and play dumb for a little while longer.

When the movie was over, she pretended to be too tired to stay up any longer. Connor walked her upstairs, saying he'd be up in a few more hours, but he wanted to make sure she was comfortable. He stood outside the bathroom while she brushed her teeth and shook her pills loudly out of the bottle, to be sure he heard her. She flushed them down the toilet, just in case Connor was keeping count of how many were left.

Connor peeked in. "Did you take your pills?"

"Yep."

"Good girl." He held out the bottle of ginkgo biloba. "You said the doctor told you it was safe to take these, right?

She took the bottle. "Can't hurt."

She shook two capsules into her palm and tossed them in her mouth, holding them under her tongue until Connor left the room. Then they joined the other pills in the toilet, which she happily flushed again.

When she was tucked into bed, Connor left, saying he was going to watch a little TV and he'd be up to join her in about an hour.

"I'll probably be sound asleep," she said, feigning a yawn.

He winked. "I'll try not to wake you."

Ironic, since she had no intention of sleeping. She listened for the television to come on, then relaxed. Only when she heard Connor coming upstairs did she pretend to be in a sound sleep. He checked on her, then once he was apparently convinced that she was soundly asleep, he left the room.

Minutes later, the television went off. She heard the front door open, then voices downstairs. She got up and listened at the doorway.

He was arguing with someone about Bruce and Cora leaving.

"They just took off." It sounded like Ronald. "And I think Diego is getting cold feet as well. So unless you up the pay…"

Pay? Another nail in Connor's coffin as far as Denise was concerned. Not that she was surprised. He'd spent a lot of money on his plot to get her shares. Buying the houses, paying three couples to move in next door and put on their little performance, and who knew what else.

Connor offered to pay double, but Ronald was adamant. "No, man. I want triple. I don't know where Helen is, whether she's alive or dead. Either way, she's off the payroll, so you can afford to pay me more. You can afford it. And if you don't agree, I'll have a nice little sit-down with Denise."

That was all Denise needed to hear. She tiptoed back to bed and buried herself under the covers just as she heard the two men coming up the stairs.

"Triple it is," Connor said. "But I won't be blackmailed again."

"Wouldn't think of it," Ronald answered. "Besides, we're going to be partners now."

"Fine, let's get this done."

She heard them enter the bedroom and let her body go limp. Ronald picked her up as if she weighed less than a feather. He carried her downstairs, then across the street. So this was how she kept waking up in different houses. She laid there in the new bed, listening to the sound of them moving her things from the previous house to this one.

She was still awake an hour later when Connor finished up his business with Ronald and climbed into bed beside her.

Chapter Twenty-Eight

THE NEXT MORNING, she pretended to sleep when Connor got up. She waited another half hour before getting up and joining him downstairs.

"How did you sleep?" he asked.

She poured a cup of coffee and sat at the table. "Good, but I still feel so tired. I don't know why I'm so exhausted all the time."

"Probably a side effect of the new pills Bruce prescribed. I'm sure it'll wear off after a while."

Now that she knew better, it was so obvious that Connor was lying. Why had she missed all the signs before? Probably because they'd kept her drugged up for so long.

"What are your plans for the day?" he asked.

"Nothing much. I'll just take it easy, do some reading, catch up on some of my macrame orders."

"Would you like Sandra to stay with you?"

"No, that's not necessary. I'm fine. I'll probably sleep some more later anyway. No sense having her sit here twiddling her thumbs while I sleep."

She noticed there were bananas in the fruit bowl

instead of apples but didn't comment on it. She could say she hated bananas all she wanted, but Connor would insist they were her favorite. She wasn't going to play that game with him. Better to act so docile and unaware that he was sure she was completely in the grip of the drugs.

He kissed her on the forehead. "I shouldn't have to work late tonight, so I'll be home for dinner. Have a good day."

Connor wasn't gone for more than five minutes when the doorbell rang.

Denise wasn't surprised to see Sandra waiting on the doorstep.

"Hi," she said. "I'm in the middle of baking and ran out of apples. By any chance do you have some I can borrow?"

"Nope, sorry. I have bananas, though. You can have them all. I don't eat bananas."

"Oh. No, I don't need any bananas." Sandra peeked in the open doorway, as if waiting for an invitation.

"Well, sorry I can't help. I'll see you later." Denise closed the door, not quite slamming it, but giving it a good nudge. She went to the living room window and watched from behind the curtain. Sandra looked confused and annoyed. Eventually, she turned and returned home.

Now to make her escape.

She changed into her jogging clothes and sneakers, put her phone and wallet in a fanny pack, then went out for a run. She passed Helen's house, waved to Diego as he drove past, and kept running all the way out of the sub-division. She knew the two of them would report back to Connor that she'd gone out for a run.

Once she was clear, she pulled out her phone and called for a taxi. She gave the driver the address for Grady Oil. On the way, she pulled up her phone and tried to find

Helen and Ronald on Facebook, but she couldn't remember their last name.

She scrolled through her photos until she found the picture of their wedding photo that she'd taken the other day. Running the photo through an image search, she zoomed in on Helen's face and came up with a match.

But her name wasn't Helen. Her name was Melanie George, and she was an actress with a Texas theater company. Denise sat back, staring at the profile picture. That was Helen, all right. Wow, she felt like such a fool. She would never have suspected.

Helen's last post was dated a few weeks ago.

HEY Y'ALL. *I'll be offline for a few weeks. Had an opportunity come up to do some live theater with a group of other actors. I can't really go into details, but I'll be back soon with a little extra cash in my pocket, so let the party planning begin!*

FROM THERE, it was easy enough to scroll through Helen/Melanie's pictures and friends list. There were lots of pictures of Melanie in different plays with her community theater group.

Then she spotted a familiar face. Diego. He was also an actor, named Nathan Silva. Denise clicked over to his profile. He didn't have as many pictures as Melanie did, but enough that she was able to spot Sandra, whose real name was Hannah.

They were all actors, every single one of her "neighbors." And Connor was paying each of them. How could he not be broke by now? Was he embezzling money from the company?

Her next move was critical.

The driver dropped her off in front of Grady Oil. Instead of going inside and risking the chance of running into Connor, however, she went to the coffee shop across the street.

She ordered a caramel macchiato and an apple turnover. Screw Connor and his damn bananas. She took screenshots of all of her so-called neighbors, along with their real names and acting credits.

Once that was done, she called reception at Grady Oil and asked for the HR department. They put her right through to Kelly, who sounded surprised to hear from her.

"I need to meet with you today, Kelly. I'm at the coffee shop across the street."

Kelly hesitated. "I don't think I'll be able to. I have a lot on my plate today. Could we do it another time?"

"I could. But if you value your job with Grady Oil, I suggest you make the time to meet with me."

There was a long silence on the other end. Regardless of whether she'd been in the office or not these last few months, Denise was still Kelly's boss. But maybe she needed a little more reason to drop what she was doing. "I know about a certain conversation you had in the bathroom the night of the 80th anniversary party. If you'd like me to talk to Connor about it, I'm sure he wouldn't be as lenient as I've been about keeping you on the employee payroll."

Kelly's voice quivered. "I'll be right over."

Chapter Twenty-Nine

BY THE TIME Kelly arrived at the coffee shop, Denise had finished her turnover and half of her coffee. She was fueled and ready for a confrontation. Kelly came through the door of the shop and spotted her right away. Her eyes were red and swollen. Obviously, Denise's threat had hit its mark.

Kelly sat across the table, and before Denise could even say anything, she began to apologize. "I'm so sorry. I didn't mean what I said."

"Let me guess. You were drunk, right?"

Kelly nodded, not meeting Denise's eyes.

"And the part about me possibly murdering my sister to get her husband?"

"Oh my God. Just stupid rumors I should never have repeated. Honestly, nobody really thinks that."

Denise sat back and stared until Kelly started to fidget.

"Well," she said. "I'm not here to talk about that."

The truth was, she didn't really care what Kelly thought. She just wanted to use Kelly to gather information, and if she had to threaten her to do that, so be it.

"Tell me about the hostile takeover."

Kelly looked up, apparently grateful to be off the hot seat. "I don't know much. Just that Connor says the vultures are circling."

Denise tapped her fingernails on the table. "Help me understand. How can they even consider a takeover when I own controlling interest in Grady Oil?"

Kelly looked around, as if afraid someone would hear her. "I know, but … well, there are rumors that Connor wants to sell to them."

"I don't understand how."

"Well, just between us, my cousin works for Alamo Petroleum, and he said that despite what Connor is telling his staff, he's been talking behind closed doors with them about selling Grady Oil to Alamo."

She had suspected something like that, but she felt better about the rest of her plan now that she was one-hundred-percent certain what Connor had been up to. "I haven't signed anything over to him, and I don't intend to."

"He's got that covered," Kelly said. "He told me that he's in the process of getting you declared…"

Denise tilted her head and waited.

Kelly swallowed hard. "In the process of getting you declared incompetent."

But she had foiled his plan when the doctor gave her a clean bill of health. He couldn't use Bruce to declare her incompetent, because Bruce wasn't really a doctor and didn't have the credentials to back it up. Hence, his insistence on taking her to another doctor. And insisting on watching her take her pills, to be sure she'd seem crazy at the appointment.

She stayed silent, letting Kelly squirm now that she'd confirmed that Denise had gotten it right. Finally, Kelly spoke up in a quivering voice. "Am I going to lose my job?"

Denise shook her head. "No, as long as you keep this between us." She reached out and took Kelly's hand. "I suspected some of what you've told me, but I needed confirmation. I appreciate you being honest with me.

Kelly gave a sigh of relief. "Thank you. And again, I'm sorry for the things I said."

"I have one more question. How was Laura and Connor's marriage? You worked with them more closely than anyone else in the company on a day-to-day basis. Were they have problems?"

Kelly nodded. "To be honest, things were strained. I think they were headed for divorce."

Denise wasn't surprised by that information either, although Kelly clearly expected her to be. She already had proof of that and assumed Laura had been putting on a good front for her benefit. Maybe she didn't want to admit her marriage was on the rocks. Or maybe she'd hoped the baby would change things.

"They had a difference of opinion about how to run the company," Kelly added. "You know how hardheaded Connor can be." She put her hand over her mouth, as if she'd said too much.

"Yeah," Denise agreed. "Don't worry. This conversation remains between us."

"The baby seemed to bring them together, however."

For how long, Denise wondered. How long before their differences would have torn them apart with a baby as a casualty? She wished Laura had opened up to her about Connor and whatever problems they were having. It might have made a difference to her loyalties to the man who was trying to have her committed and steal her family's business out from under her.

Denise thanked Kelly and stood. She reached out her hand, but instead of shaking it, Kelly came in for a hug.

"I really am sorry," she said. "I'll make it up to you. Anything you need."

"Thank you. You've been more than helpful."

When Kelly went back to Grady Oil, Denise called for a ride and returned to the subdivision. She got out at the entrance, then jogged the rest of the way. By the time she reached the cul-de-sac, she'd worked up a sweat. No one would suspect she hadn't been running the entire time.

She spotted Sandra watching from her house. Denise waved, but Sandra didn't respond. Denise walked up to Bruce and Cora's house, then hesitated. Which house did she wake up in? Which house would they expect her to return to? She took a chance and walked past Bruce and Cora's house. Sandra watched her the entire time. Denise marched right past her and into the last house on the cul-de-sac.

It was the right one.

Chapter Thirty

BACK HOME, Denise paced. *Fucking Connor*. Not much longer, then she could put the final phase of her plan into action. She'd make sure he paid for everything he'd done.

She went to her computer and opened the file labeled "Laura." She'd saved pictures and videos there. She pulled one up and watched it. Laura and Denise at the cabin. They were sitting around a campfire roasting marshmallows. She could almost smell the campfire and was overcome with a yearning to return to the cabin on the lake. She couldn't bring back Laura, but she could be back where their happiest memories were strongest. And she could make new memories there. Thank God she hadn't let Connor convince her to sell the cabin.

The next video was a company party. In the background, Laura and Connor appeared to be arguing. Then Laura turned and shouted, "Denise!"

The voice startled her. It sounded exactly like the recording she'd found in Connor's housecoat. He'd just taken a clip of this video to frighten her into thinking she was hearing Laura's "ghost."

Laura walked in Denise's direction, her face so dear and familiar. "Connor, get me a soda," she called out, then leaned close and whispered, "Honestly, sometimes he makes me nuts."

She had to rewind to listen to her sister's voice again. "Connor, get me a soda." Then, "Honestly, sometimes he makes me nuts." It was bittersweet, but she craved the sound. "Connor, get me a soda."

She could have listened all night, but she had to scurry to put her plan into action before Connor got home. She went to the window and saw Diego arguing with Sandra outside. He threw a suitcase into the trunk of the car, then gestured for Sandra to follow, but she refused. Finally, he gave up trying to persuade her, and she watched from the sidewalk as he roared off down the street.

Denise watched them go, then waited a few minutes before walking to Bruce and Cora's house. She entered the house, amazed again at how similar they all were, right down to the furnishings. Now she realized that it was all pre-planned. Easier to convince her she was going crazy when they moved her from house to house.

She wondered if the houses really had come furnished, or if Connor had paid for all that identical furniture too.

When she searched the entire house from top to bottom, she found Bruce's gun in the back of the hall closet of the abandoned house. She was hit with a horrific smell as she opened the door to the garage. She fumbled for the light switch, then screamed, clapping her hand over her mouth to stifle the sound. Helen was slumped over in a wheelchair, obviously dead. She'd been dead all along, just like Denise had said. They'd all been in on trying to convince her that she was just imagining it.

But Connor had murdered Helen. If she'd had any

remaining qualms about what she planned to do to him, they were now gone.

"I'm sorry this happened to you, Helen," she murmured.

But finding Helen gave her an idea for how she could make her plan even better. And much less risky for her.

She pulled out her phone and took a picture. The more evidence she collected, the better. Checking to make sure no one was around, she quickly wheeled Helen to their garage. She loosened the wire to the electric garage door so it wouldn't open.

Now to put the rest of her plan into motion.

She marched over to Helen and Ronald's house. Ronald opened the door. "Sorry, Denise. Helen is still visiting her mother."

She raised the gun and pointed it at his chest. "Don't lie to me. Helen is dead. Sitting in a wheelchair in my garage."

The color drained from Ronald's face. He stared at the gun and inched backwards.

Denise pushed him until he had backed all the way into the house again. "Let's talk."

Ronald held up his hands. "You've got the wrong guy. You need to talk to Connor. He's the one who…"

Five minutes later, a gunshot rang out.

Chapter Thirty-One

DENISE WALKED BACK to her house, the one she'd known as her house all along. She spent the time putting the final pieces of her plan into place, then sat and waited for Connor to come home.

It didn't take long. Obviously, his spies had sent out an alarm. His normally put-together suit was rumpled, and his hair looked like he'd raked his hand through it one too many times. He had the look of a man whose plans were falling apart. He had no idea things were about to get worse. Much worse.

"Hey hon, I can't get the garage to work." His pasted-on smile fell when he spotted the gun in her hand. "What? What's that?"

"A gun," she said, turning it from one side to the other while still keeping it aimed at Connor's chest. "I killed Ronald."

His eyes widened. "What the fuck?"

"I had to." She kept her voice a monotone, as if she was still drugged. "He was telling lies about you."

Connor's face paled. "What kind of lies?"

257

Denise waved the gun dramatically. "He said you were trying to make me think I was crazy. That you were going to have me committed." She managed a sob. "He said you paid him to do it."

"That's crazy," Connor said. "I wouldn't do that. Now put down the gun."

He moved to take the gun, but Denise backed up and waved it in front of his face.

He stepped back. "Careful with that. Someone could get hurt."

"Someone already got hurt." She thought of Helen who had tried to help her and paid with her life. "Ronald got hurt. He's dead."

Connor held up a hand. "Okay, let's just calm down. This is all one giant misunderstanding."

"Is it?" she asked, looking him straight in the eye.

"Of course. You know me better than that. I'd never hurt you." He opened his arms, offering her comfort in a place she'd once thought was safe and secure. But now she knew she'd been sleeping with the devil all along.

She shook her head, trying to look like the weak, confused person he expected her to be. "I don't know who to believe anymore."

"Believe me," he said. "Haven't I always taken care of you?"

She nodded.

"Now give me the gun," he said, moving slowly toward her.

She handed it over, and he breathed a sigh of relief when he took it from her shaking hand. "I think you need to get some rest," he said. "I'm going over to check on Ronald. Wait for me here."

She nodded. She'd be waiting all right.

Chapter Thirty-Two

CONNOR RUSHED OVER to Ronald and Helen's house. Ronald wasn't anywhere to be found. Fuck, fuck, fuck! He searched the entire house, but there was no sign of him.

As he was about to leave, Sandra showed up at the door. She said she'd been searching for Ronald but couldn't find him.

"He left me a strange text," she said. "Something about Denise."

Connor gave a low growl. Everything was falling apart. He had to get Denise to sign those damn papers before everything blew up.

He stepped outside and noticed Denise standing by the open garage door. He could have sworn he couldn't get it open earlier.

"Why did you go over there?" Denise asked. She pointed to the other house. "That's their house."

Fuck.

Now he was as confused as she was. He made his way to the other house with Sandra trailing behind him.

"I'm coming too," Denise called.

"Just stay there!" he shouted.

Ignoring his demand, she followed him anyway and the three of them made their way to the other house. They entered to find Ronald dead on the floor of the foyer.

Jesus. She really did shoot him.

Sandra walked over and checked for a pulse. She shook her head. "He's dead." She glanced from Connor to Denise and back. "What happened?"

Connor was about to blame Denise when she interrupted.

"He did it." She pointed to Connor. "Connor shot him."

"What?" Connor couldn't believe his ears.

Denise stared at Sandra imploringly. "He shot Ronald. I saw him."

"I didn't fucking shoot anyone!" he screamed, pounding his fist against the wall. "Denise did it."

Denise shook her head. "I was home all afternoon, and Sandra was watching the house." She turned to Sandra. "I was home, wasn't I?"

Sandra didn't answer. She pointed to Connor. "You're the one with the gun."

Connor glared at her, sending an unspoken warning. *If you want your money, you'll say the right answer.*

Sandra hesitated. She looked from Denise to Connor and back. Finally in a quiet voice, she said, "I saw Denise kill Ronald."

Good. He pointed the gun at Denise. "Nice try, Denise."

He didn't know what she was up to, but she wouldn't get away with it. He'd worked too long and hard to have his plans unravel now.

Denise didn't back down.

"How long have you been planning this charade,

Connor? Since Laura died?" She glared at him. "Did you kill her too?"

Sandra took a step back, moving away from both of them.

Connor brandished the gun at Denise and pulled out a manila envelope. "It doesn't matter. All I need you to do is sign these papers and it'll be all over with."

"I'm not signing any papers."

He pointed the gun at her, his voice a warning. "You're going to sign them *now*."

She shook her head. "No."

"Then we'll do it the hard way. I'll put a bullet in your brain, then we won't need the papers at all. I'm your beneficiary."

Denise hesitated, then took the papers to the table and signed them. "All this just to steal the company?"

"You wouldn't sell. I needed you to sign it over to me." He shook his head. "Besides, you don't want the company. You never showed the slightest interest."

"I didn't need to. You and Laura—"

"Yes. Laura lived and breathed for the company," he said. "She was *so* fucking smart."

"Smarter than you," Denise said.

"Not smart enough. She rejected offer after offer." He grabbed the papers and waved them in Denise's face. "Do you have any idea how much Grady Oil is worth?"

She shook her head.

"More than you can imagine. And you'll never see a penny."

Connor gestured for Sandra to come over and stand with him. He handed her the gun. "Keep her here until I get back."

"Then what?"

He sneered. "Then your contract will be over. You'll

get your money, and you can go back to your shitty acting job."

Sandra jerked her head in Denise's direction. "What happens to her?"

"That's none of your business."

"What about Ronald?"

"Just leave him there. I'll deal with him later. I have a deadline to meet."

Denise jumped up and grabbed the envelope from Connor. He belted her and she fell over, then scrambled back up and grabbed his shirt. He pulled away and she kicked her foot out, connecting with his groin.

"Jesus Fucking Christ!" He doubled over in pain.

Just as Denise was ready to pounce again, Sandra fired the gun at the ceiling. Denise and Connor froze.

Sandra pointed the gun at Denise. "Back the fuck off."

Denise stepped back, hands in the air.

Connor threw Sandra a grateful look. "Keep that gun aimed at her while I make a phone call."

Denise could hear his end of the conversation. "Yeah, I've got her signature. I'm ready to deal." He turned away, his voice lowered. "Fuck that. There are still two hours until midnight. Plenty of time. Meet me at Grady Oil."

Connor turned to Sandra. "Stay with her. Don't let her out of your sight. I'll take care of her after the deal is done."

With that, he turned and stormed out of the house. Denise heard his car start up and race down the street. She turned to Sandra. "You can put the gun down now."

Chapter Thirty-Three

SANDRA DROPPED her arm and let the gun fall to her side.

Denise took a deep breath. "You had me scared for a minute there. You weren't following the script."

Sandra smiled. "I'm an improv actor."

Ronald sat up. "Is the coast clear? I'm tired of being dead."

"He's gone," Denise said.

Ronald stood up. "I didn't know how bad it was going to be when I signed up. I thought it was just some silly prank." He turned to Denise. "I didn't approve of what he was doing to you, and we argued about it several times."

Denise appreciated the intent, but that didn't excuse what they'd been a part of. Once she discovered they were paid actors, she'd offered them double to switch sides. They'd both jumped at the chance.

Sandra was still suspicious. "You've promised not to prosecute, right?"

Denise nodded "You cooperated, so I'll keep my end of the deal. It's Connor I want brought to justice."

"What about Cora and Bruce?" Ronald asked.

"Since they bailed on Connor before he could do even more damage, I'll make sure they get paid as well."

"And Helen? Did Connor really kill her?"

"Yes. We really were going to get away for the weekend, but you told him that. He couldn't let her take me someplace where he couldn't reach me." It broke her heart that she was the reason Helen was dead. That was three deaths on her conscience now, Helen, as well as Laura and the baby. "I'll see that there's justice for Helen. Trust me."

She gestured to the door. "I suggest the two of you get out of here before Connor finds out you betrayed him as well.

Sandra handed over the gun. "Good luck," she said before turning to leave. Ronald followed her out and then they were gone, leaving the house and the entire neighborhood empty and silent. But this time it was a peaceful silence. Denise no longer had any fears or doubts. And soon she'd be saying goodbye to this house that was never really a home.

She walked across the street to Helen and Ronald's house. Once upstairs, she went through the pile of framed photos that Connor and Ronald had been switching back and forth. She found the original picture of Laura with the sweetest smile on her face and carried it back home, where she tucked it into her suitcase. It was one of only a few things she'd be taking with her when she left Hackberry Haven for good.

Now it was just a matter of timing. She opened the refrigerator and pulled out a strawberry shortcake. Perfect. She put it on the table, opened the silverware drawer, and grabbed a fork.

Then she calmly dialed the phone.

"911, what is your emergency?"

She whisper-shouted into the phone. "I just got home

and found my husband with his mistress. Things got violent." She went silent for a moment.

"Ma'am?"

"I'm hiding in the bathroom. I heard them screaming at each other, then things got real quiet outside the door. I think…" She let her voice tremble. "I think I heard a gunshot."

"Are there guns in the house?"

"Yes. I don't know what happened, but I heard his car pull away. I think he might have done something terrible."

"We'll send someone right over."

"But he shouldn't be driving. He's been drinking. I'm afraid he'll get in an accident."

Denise gave the operator Connor's license plate number and begged him to send someone to stop Connor before he killed someone.

That was the magic word. "Stay where you are," the operator instructed. "We'll be sending someone over shortly."

"Thank you," Denise said, in what she hoped was a timid voice. After she hung up, she went back to eating more of the cake. When she was finished, she made sure the front door was unlocked, then went upstairs and locked herself in the bathroom to wait for the police to arrive.

Chapter Thirty-Four

CONNOR WAS ALMOST to Grady Oil when he heard sirens behind him. He glanced at his speedometer. They couldn't be after him. He was well within the speed limit.

Then the lights started flashing. He pulled over just to be safe. The police car pulled over as well.

Shit. This was the last thing he needed tonight.

He rolled down the window. "Can I help you officer?"

"Let me see your license and registration."

"I wasn't speeding," Connor said through gritted teeth.

The officer glanced at his license. "Turn the vehicle off and step out of the car."

"What's this all about? I have a meeting to get to."

"Hands behind your head, and keep them there."

Connor did what he was told, still grumbling. He noticed a second policeman standing at the rear of the car. "It's an important meeting. I can't miss it."

The officer reached in the car and pulled the keys out of the ignition. He tossed them to the officer standing behind the car while still keeping his gun aimed at Connor. He heard the trunk pop open, then the second officer came around and handcuffed Connor. "You have the right to remain silent—"

"What? What the FUCK is going on?"

They ignored his question and forced Connor into the police car. He looked over and glimpsed Helen's body in the trunk of his car. *Oh shit.*

"I can explain!" Connor yelled. "My wife did it. She's been acting strange lately, forgetting things, and she had a psychotic break where she thought she was her dead sister!"

"Anything you say can and will be used against you."

"Listen," Connor said, hoping he could get this straightened out and still meet his deadline. "There are important papers in my car. I'm going to need them once we clear this up."

The officer went to the car and pulled out the manila envelope. He held it up, "This?"

"Yes," Connor said. "We can't just leave them in the car."

The officer tore open the envelope.

"Hey, that's private and confidential."

"No, it's evidence."

The officer pulled a piece of paper out of the envelope and laughed. "This is what's so important?"

He held up a grocery store receipt for strawberry shortcake.

Connor closes his eyes, resigned. He was screwed six ways from Sunday.

Chapter Thirty-Five

Six months later

DENISE DROVE up to Raquel's apartment building and tooted the horn. Raquel came out carrying Lily and an overnight bag. Denise stepped out and grabbed the bag. She put it in the back, then took Lily from Raquel who went back to get the baby's car seat.

With the baby buckled in, Raquel climbed into the passenger side. "Are you sure you don't want me to drive?"

Denise smiled. "No, I've got it. I spent too long letting fear paralyze me." She was speaking about more than just her ability to drive. She'd let Connor use her emotions against her to keep her trapped in her nightmare life with him. If he'd had his way, her nightmare would never have ended. She'd have spent decades in a psych ward, even more heavily medicated that he'd kept her.

Raquel admired her pearls.

Denise touched them again, feeling both her mother and Laura's love as she stroked them.

"They belonged to my mother," she said. "Laura and I took turns wearing them. We'd trade them back and forth on each of our birthdays."

Her brow furrowed. "I swore Laura was wearing them the day of the accident. But Connor said they were never found."

Raquel gave her a questioning look.

"The morning of my birthday, I found them on my dresser. I thought they were a gift from Connor, but he denied it. At the time, I figured it was just another ploy to make me seem confused so he could have me committed if I didn't sign Grady Oil over to him."

"God, he had it all figured out, didn't he?"

"Yeah, and it almost worked."

Denise shook her head. "Funny thing, though. Connor admitted to everything else, including killing Helen. But he swears he didn't put the pearls on my nightstand."

"It's a mystery."

Denise nodded. "Yeah, a mystery I'd rather not solve."

"Maybe they were a message from your sister," Raquel said.

Denise smiled. "I prefer to think that."

With a smile on her face, Denise drove, heading for the highway, back on the road to the cabin. "We'll be at the cabin in about an hour."

"I can't wait to see it," Raquel said. "It looks fabulous in the photos."

"It is," Denise said, glad she hadn't let Connor talk her into selling it. The cabin, along with the pearls, held all her favorite memories of Laura, memories that would someday outweigh the bad.

"So, how does it feel to be back to work?" Raquel asked.

"It actually feels good. I used to let Laura and Connor

handle the lion's share of the business. I trusted them to do everything, when I should have been taking a more active role in it. But almost losing the company made me realize how much Grady Oil meant to me. I've learned my lesson not to give over my power to anyone else."

They turned a bend in the road, then the wood and river rock cabin came into sight, with its screened-in front porch where Laura and Denise used to watch the stars at night. Nestled between tall pines, it was peaceful and calm, something Denise needed right now. She was overcome with memories of Laura and all the good times they had here. For the first time in a long time, she was able to think of her sister and smile.

She had finally found her way back home.

The End

About The Authors

Nolon King writes fast-paced psychological thrillers set in the glitzy world of entertainment's power players with a bold, insightful voice. He's not afraid to explore the darker side of human nature through stories featuring families torn apart by secrets and lies.

Nolon loves to write about big questions and moral quandaries. How far would you go to cover up an honest mistake? Would you destroy your career to protect your family? How much of your soul would you sell to get the life of your dreams? Would you cheat on your husband to keep your children safe? Would you give in to a stalker's demands to save your marriage?

Lauren Street has always loved a mystery. As a kid growing up in bible belt country she devoured every whodunit book she could get her sticky little hands on and secretly investigated all of her (seemingly) normal boring neighbors. Sometimes their pets and farm animals too. All grown up now and living in the UK with her thoroughly unsuspicious (and often unsuspecting) husband, she writes domestic psychological thrillers about families torn apart by secrets and lies. And she sometimes still peers over garden walls to check up on the neighbors.

Also By Nolon King

Replaced

Replaced

In Her Place

Cold Vengeance

Cold Vengeance

Cold Reckoning

Cold Retribution

Hidden Justice

Hidden Justice

Hidden Honor

Hidden Shame

Hidden Virtue

No Justice

No Justice

No Escape

No Hope

No Return

No Stopping

No Fear

Once Upon A Crime

Once Upon A Crime

Twice Upon A Lie

Three Times a Murder

Dead For Good

Dead For Good

Left For Dead

Dead Of Night

Wake The Dead

Dead For Life

Stand Alone Novels

Pretty Killer

12

Blown

Miserable Lies

The Target

Secrets We Keep

Close To Home

Heat To Obsession

A Simple Kill

Tell Me No Lies

Red Carpet Black

Fade To Black

Victim

Also By Lauren Street

The Bishop Smoky Mountain Thrillers

Hide Me Away

Fuel To The Flame

Closer By The Hour

A Gamble Either Way

Calling My Children Home

Too Far Gone

Replaced with Nolon King

Replaced

In Her Place